WHEN YOU LOVE A SCOTSMAN

"I have to find a place to live," Abbie said. "Maybe I could go with Reid and Robbie. The barn is still whole and they are sure to be building a shelter of some kind."

"Nay, ye will stay here with Jeremiah and Noah."

"I cannot impose . . ."

"It is not imposing." Matthew pulled her into his arms. "Ye will be staying with me."

Abigail snuggled into his embrace, savoring the heat and strength of him. He would probably think she was mad if she told him she even liked the smell of him. Clean skin and clean clothes. There was also that sense of being safe. She did not fully understand why as they were outside in an area that was overrun with marauders. They both had their guns but she knew they could easily be outnumbered. So, it was simply him; he made her feel safe.

She felt him spreading soft heated kisses over her face and sighed. They really needed to talk, and when they started this they never got around to having any serious talk. It appeared it would be her who finally put her heart out there and prayed for the best. She had at least come to the conclusion that she did not *need* a husband; she *wanted* one and this man was the one she wanted . . .

Books by Hannah Howell

The Murrays
Highland Destiny
Highland Honor
Highland Promise
Highland Vow
Highland Knight
Highland Bride
Highland Angel
Highland Groom
Highland Warrior
Highland Conqueror
Highland Champion
Highland Lover
Highland Barbarian
Highland Savage
Highland Wolf
Highland Sinner
Highland Protector
Highland Avenger
Highland Master
Highland Guard
Highland Chieftain

The Wherlockes
If He's Wicked
If He's Sinful
If He's Wild
If He's Dangerous
If He's Tempted
If He's Daring
If He's Noble

Stand-Alone Novels
Only for You
My Valiant Knight
Unconquered
Wild Roses
A Taste of Fire
A Stockingful of Joy
Highland Hearts
Reckless
Conqueror's Kiss
Beauty and the Beast
Highland Wedding
Silver Flame
Highland Fire
Highland Captive
My Lady Captor
Wild Conquest
Kentucky Bride
Compromised Hearts
Stolen Ecstasy
Highland Hero
His Bonnie Bride

Vampire Romance
Highland Vampire
The Eternal Highlander
My Immortal Highlander
Highland Thirst
Nature of the Beast
Yours for Eternity
Highland Hunger
Born to Bite

Seven Brides for Seven Scotsmen
The Scotsman Who Saved Me
When You Love a Scotsman

Published by Kensington Publishing Corporation

When You Love A Scotsman

HANNAH HOWELL

ZEBRA BOOKS
KENSINGTON PUBLISHING CORP.
http://www.kensingtonbooks.com

ZEBRA BOOKS are published by

Kensington Publishing Corp.
119 West 40th Street
New York, NY 10018

First Printing: January 2018
ISBN-13: 978-1-4201-4305-8
ISBN-10: 1-4201-4305-0

eISBN-13: 978-1-4201-4306-5
eISBN-10: 1-4201-4306-9

10 9 8 7 6 5 4 3 2 1

Printed in the United States of America

Chapter One

Ozarks—1864

Matthew MacEnroy sniffed the air and sighed. Fall was here and soon winter would come with all its misery for a soldier. The memory of how badly his brother Robbie had been injured when attacked by some men who wanted to make him join the Rebel army was no longer strong enough to make him eager to spend another year in the Union Army. He was tired of the blood, the death, the amputations, and the never-ending filth.

He glanced at the boy riding beside him and suddenly felt every hour of his thirty years and more. Boyd was still carrying the pride of turning older, to an age many considered a man, and finally leaving his childhood years. He was undoubtedly new to the army and found pride in his uniform. Matthew knew it was going to bother him deeply when the youth finally lost that glow of innocence.

The other three men who rode with them had some seasoning. Their years of fighting and lying in the mud and blood, seeing friends and kinsmen die or be horribly wounded, showed in their faces, especially in their eyes. Matthew wondered if his eyes also had that look, but he had not yet found the courage to check.

It was time he went home, he decided. He had contracted for two years and that ended in a few months. That was true of the other three men and he had no idea if they would stay or leave. He felt strongly about sustaining the Union but was not sure even that could make him stay.

"When did ye sign up, lad?" he asked Boyd.

"When the war began," the boy replied.

"Wheest, how old were ye? Ten?" He heard the three men at his back badly smothering their laughter.

Matthew bit back what he wanted to say, that the boy was a fool to leave such relative safety and comfort for the killing and filth a "true soldier" had to wade through, and just nodded.

"Sir?" James said as he rode up beside Matthew, his blue eyes watchful. "Thinking we may have unwelcome company soon."

"Then we best move a wee bit faster. There is a cabin up ahead a ways. Have passed it several times. We can hold up there."

James nodded. "If the folk in the cabin don't feel inclined to shoot us."

"Aye, true enough. Bend low in the saddle," he urged as he kicked his horse into a trot.

He did not question James's warning. The man had a knack for sensing approaching trouble. It had saved him more often than he cared to think about. Glancing back to make sure his men were with him, he saw the gray uniformed men just clearing the edge of the trees behind them.

"Ride hard, lads!" he yelled and urged his mount into a gallop.

* * *

Abigail Jenson straightened up from the weeding she had been doing, grunted softly, and rubbed at a twinge in her lower back. She hated weeding. There did not seem to be any position one could get into to accomplish the task without some part of your body aching.

She was just bending down to begin weeding a new section of the garden when she tensed and slowly straightened up. Cocking her head to the side she listened more carefully to the sound that had drawn her attention. Someone, more than one in fact, was heading toward her at an increasing speed.

Sprinting to the cabin, Abigail cursed beneath her breath. This would be the third time they had been attacked. The first had cost her her brother who was dragged off to take up arms in a war he had never wanted any part of. The second time the men had robbed them and beaten her father nearly to death when he had tried to stop them. That time she had hidden from them and still felt guilty about it, for she was certain they had done her mother harm as well. The woman had not been the same since and Abigail was certain it was not just because her father was badly injured.

Abigail rushed inside to find her mother kneeling by her father's bed, bathing his face and chest as he lay unconscious. Each time Abigail saw her father now grief choked her for she knew he would never rise again. The smell of death was on him although she was painfully aware that she could find few who would understand what she was talking about. It had been over a week since he had spoken a word or even opened his eyes. She slowed down, cautiously moved to her mother's side, and lightly touched her on the arm.

"Riders are coming. We need to hide," Abigail said, hiding her shock at the look in her mother's glazed eyes. "We must move quickly." Tightening her grip, she tried to pull her mother to her feet.

"No!" Her mother yanked her arm free. "We cannot move your father and we cannot leave him here!"

"I doubt they will do anything to him as he does not move or speak. Does not even open his eyes."

"I will not leave him. You go and hide. Go!"

"You cannot stay here! Da will not be harmed, for there is no reason for them to do so. He is no threat to anyone. We are. Please, come with me!"

"No! I will not desert your father. As I said, you go and hide if you wish to. I am staying. They can do no more harm to me. They have already done their worst." She wrung out the rag she held and gently bathed her husband's face again.

Glancing behind her, Abigail felt her heart leap. Five men were reining in in front of the cabin. She had lost her chance to flee. Racing to the fireplace, she grabbed the rifle hanging above it. Checking that it was loaded, she was just turning to aim it at one of the men when it was snatched out of her hands. All Abigail could think of was that her mother was helpless, vulnerable as she tried to shield her father. She lunged at the man and struggled to get her rifle back. There was no give in his grasp, however. Muttering a curse, she kicked him in the shins. To her surprise, he fell back and took her with him.

"Enough, lass. Ye have to stop fighting me. I am nay your enemy."

Something in his voice made her grow still. She

looked at him and suddenly thought that she would not have been able to shoot him. His face was unshaven, the dark stubble accentuating the sharp lines. His dark hair was a bit too long and a lock fell over one green eye. He had a strong, well-shaped nose and a mouth that revealed a softness she doubted he often showed. Suddenly that mouth cocked up in a small smile.

"Who are you?" she asked when she decided she had flattered him by staring for too long, but she did wonder what the accent was, for she had never heard the like before.

Matthew stepped back, letting go of what he considered a very nice armful of woman, and made a little bow. "Lieutenant MacEnroy, officer in the Union Army. We are, at this moment, fleeing some Rebs."

She looked over his uniform. "The Rebs are the ones in gray? The men now outside?"

"Aye." He turned and hurried to the door on his hands and knees.

As soon as one of the other men dragged the horses out of the barn, the lieutenant slammed the door. He briefly stood up to put the bar across it then dove under a window to the right. She jumped when he threw open the window and started firing at the men outside. The four men with him did the same and she stayed crouched on the floor and covered her ears.

Abigail looked toward her mother. The woman was still at her father's bedside, which made her a target. On her hands and knees, trying to stay low to the floor, Abigail scrambled up behind the woman and yanked hard on her skirts. When her mother sat down hard on the floor, she spun around and glared at

Abigail with such fury, Abigail let go of her skirts and backed up a little.

"You stupid girl, what are you doing?"

"The men are shooting. You were making yourself a target. You have to keep low to the floor." Abigail did all she could to keep her voice calm and steady.

"I need to protect your father!"

"You cannot protect him if you get yourself shot," Abigail snapped. "Stay down!"

The punch to the face her mother gave her caused Abigail to fall backward. She stared up at the ceiling, rubbing her cheek and fighting the very strong urge to weep. Her mother had never struck her before, not even when she had been small and troublesome. She had never spoken so harshly before either.

Her mother was not well, Abigail told herself as she slowly sat up. The woman had been broken by the loss of her son, the abuse she had suffered at the hands of the soldiers, and by what had happened to her husband. In truth, her mother had not been herself, had in fact been growing worse every day, and nothing Abigail had done had pulled the woman free of the growing darkness in her mind.

There was one thing she could do now, she thought, and scrambled to the front window. The man had set her rifle down on the floor in front of the window and she grabbed it. She would do her best to end the threat her mother chose to ignore.

"What are you doing?" demanded Lieutenant MacEnroy.

"Making certain the fools shooting up my home do not shoot my mother." Abigail took careful aim at one of the men in front of the house. "They will *not* shoot my mother."

"Tell her to get down," Matthew said.

"I did. She did not care to listen."

Matthew saw his men looking at him and shrugged. He turned back to find the girl holding the rifle as if she was very sure of what she was doing. Just as he opened his mouth to ask if she was certain she wanted to shoot a man, she fired. The man outside yelled and then fell silent. James cursed softly and turned to look at the girl. Matthew chanced a look out of the window to see that one of the ten men attacking the cabin was sprawled on the ground, his mount already disappearing into the trees. The girl had already reloaded her gun and was calmly taking aim again when he turned back to look at her.

"You killed him," he said.

"That was my intention."

"He was a moving target."

"Da always said I had a good eye."

Matthew just shook his head and returned to his own shooting. It was somewhat humiliating when she picked off another man before he had even managed to wound one. She did have a good eye and remained steady. He had to wonder what she had experienced in her life that had made her so calm about shooting at men.

One soldier pulled away and went to the side of the house. He winged another one who moved to follow. Not sure what the soldier had been trying to do, he turned to ask the woman about what other windows and doors there were, only to see her hurrying toward the back of the house. Cursing, he moved to follow.

"Do you ken where he is headed?" he asked as she opened a door and ducked into another room.

"Just a suspicion." Abigail kicked a stool in front of a small high window and got up on it so she could peer outside. "Oh no, you don't," she muttered when she saw the soldier hurriedly picking the crop and shoving it in the sack.

"What is he doing?" Matthew asked when she slowly, silently opened the window and aimed her gun.

"Stealing our crop. They have already taken my brother one time, and all our stock another time, and have murdered my father. I have had enough."

The man by the garden must have heard her because he turned and looked right at her. Abigail felt her stomach turn as she pulled the trigger and his eyes widened in shock and horror when the bullet hit him square in the chest. She swallowed a sudden rush of bile in her mouth as she watched his body fall. Quickly stepping down, she took a deep breath to steady herself and then headed back to the post she had chosen by the front window.

Matthew looked out the window she had just left and shook his head when he saw the dead soldier. This one had troubled her for he had seen how pale she had gone. As he moved to follow her he wondered why she was so shaken this time but not the others.

The moment he entered the main room he heard a cry of pain. He looked toward his men and saw Boyd on the floor, the top of his arm bleeding badly. The girl scrambled over to him, reaching Boyd before he could. By the time he reached the boy she had already cut his sleeve off and was tying what looked like a strip from her petticoat around the top of his arm.

"Bullet went right through," she told Boyd.

"Is that good?"

"Well, yes, I believe so. At least it means I do not have to go digging for it."

The young man paled. "Okay. That is good. Who are you?"

"Abigail Jenson."

Boyd closed his eyes as she turned his arm to study the exit wound. "Thank you kindly, miss."

She just nodded and scrambled over to the bed where her mother still knelt tending her father and ignoring all of them. Matthew moved closer to Boyd, politely ignoring how shiny his eyes were with tears he fought not to shed. He looked at the wound and winced. The bullet had made a messy exit. Matthew was not sure how well it would heal.

Matthew was just about to give Boyd a warning about what he may face when he was shoved out of the way. Abigail was back with strips of cloth and a small pot of something that smelled medicinal. He watched as she cleaned the wound, appearing oblivious to Boyd's badly smothered sounds of pain. She studied the exit wound with a frown he was pleased Boyd could not see, faintly shook her head, and then turned to her pile of supplies to pick up a needle and thread.

"This is going to hurt," Abigail said quietly. "Take deep breaths and let them out slowly. It sometimes helps. I will work as quickly as I can."

She also worked fast, Matthew noticed as he grabbed Boyd's hand and let the boy hang on to him. Wincing, he silently hoped Boyd would still be able to shoot. When she was done, she wiped the sweat from the boy's face and kissed his cheek. The way the boy blushed made Matthew grin.

"Could you get on his other side?" Abigail asked Matthew. "We need to tie his arm to his side."

"Why?" asked Boyd.

As she wrapped his arm, Abigail explained, "I can't say for certain, but it looks as if that bullet tore a bit of your muscle and nicked a vein. It needs a lot of healing and that means it must be kept stable. Sir"—she looked at Matthew—"I am going to slide the strip of cloth beneath him. Could you please pull it through and hand it back to me?"

Matthew nodded then did as she asked. Twice more she passed the cloth under the boy, pinning his arm tightly to his side. As she tied the bandage Matthew could easily read the dismay on Boyd's face. He now had only one usable arm and that meant his time to be a soldier was done, at best at least until the wound healed.

There was a sudden flurry of shooting, the glass in the window shattering and the sound of bullets hitting the wall, echoing in the house. Matthew ducked and, keeping low to the floor, hurried back to the window. Looking out he could count six men left, and all of them attempting to hide themselves behind rocks and trees, and half of them had dirty ragged bandages tied around some limb. Two men were slowly crawling back to their horses. Tired of the battle, he decided as he shot at a man huddled behind a tree. A loud curse told him he had winged the man.

"We gonna shoot 'em down as they try to crawl away?" asked James.

"Nay. Just dinnae let them ken we are nay going to do that."

"Is the girl going to be shooting?" asked Danny. "'Cause maybe you should tell her we ain't aiming to kill."

Matthew laughed. "True, but I think she is settled

with caring for Boyd." He was busy loading his gun when another mad flurry of shots peppered the house. "What the hell?"

"Trying to make us all hunker down so they can flee, I reckon," said Jed, daring a peek out the window. "They are all trying to back away."

"Good. Shoot just enough to keep them retreating," Matthew said and immediately shot toward another man hiding behind a tree.

Matthew could see his strategy was working the few times he was able to look out the window. Once he glanced toward Abigail and saw that she had gotten Boyd sheltered on the far side of the big fireplace. He had heard her plead again with her mother to get down, but the woman continued to ignore her despite the number of bullets that slammed into the wall near the sick man's bed. The woman appeared to be oblivious to the battle going on around her.

Taking another turn at shooting out the windows, Matthew could see that the men were close to leaving. The two who were crawling toward their horses were by the animals now and just waiting for a chance to mount and run. The other four were closer to their horses. He knew many another officer would order the horses shot but Matthew had never been able to give such an order. He also suspected it was more a love for the animals than moral uncertainty about shooting wounded men.

Another round of gunfire hit the house and he ducked down. He looked back at Abigail and Boyd again, relieved to find them unharmed. She had removed the tourniquet on his arm and was intently watching for an increase in bleeding. He then looked toward the mother and tensed. Her dress was dark but he was certain he could see blood.

The shooting eased and he went back to returning fire, careful not to aim to kill. It embarrassed him because he suspected the men running thought them all poor shots. Smiling grimly, he decided it might not be a bad rumor to start for it might aid them in future confrontations.

He was taking time to reload when he heard a cry. He looked toward Abigail and Boyd, but Abigail was staring at her mother in horror. Matthew looked back at the woman and sighed. There was no mistaking that the last flurry of shots had found their target. The woman should be dead but she was crawling on top of the man. Then Abigail was there and Matthew shook his head. He felt for the girl but there was nothing he could do. He returned to the work of making sure the Rebs hurried their retreat.

Abigail hurried to her mother's side and knew, with one look, that there was nothing she could do. The bullet had gone into her back and exploded out of her chest only to continue on into her father's stomach. For days she had known her father was dying, but that bullet had abruptly ended his long struggle against the inevitable. Fighting tears, she tried to coax her mother into allowing her to tend to her wounds but the woman fought her, trying to curl up around her father. Abigail finally let her and struggled against the urge to weep as the bed became soaked in blood.

Her mother took her father's hand in hers and settled her head on his chest. Abigail suspected there were women who would find it touchingly romantic, but she only found it heartbreakingly sad. In the last few weeks it had become clear to her that her father was all important to her mother, her son a close second. This last act only confirmed it. She took the quilt folded at the foot of the bed and covered them both. She then ducked down and scurried back to Boyd's side.

"I am sorry, Abigail," Boyd said, his voice weak and hoarse.

"My father was already as good as dead and I think my mother was ready to follow him."

"Are you sure your father was already dying?"

"I smelled it last week. He hung on far longer than I thought he would."

"You smelled it?" Boyd tried to sit up straighter and winced.

She gave him a hand in getting more comfortable. "Yes. There is a smell to the dying. No one believes me, but there is." She sat down next to him. "I tried to tell my mother, to prepare her, but she would not listen. She changed after the attack. I think it broke her. Maybe if my father had not been so badly injured she would have recovered, but . . ." She shrugged. "I was hiding and I should have come out. Maybe I could have been helpful."

"No. Who hurt them?"

"The Rebs."

"Ah. No, it was best that you remained hidden. They could have hurt you, too."

"Maybe. All I could think of was that I had not brought my rifle with me so how could I fight what looked to be six soldiers, maybe more."

"You could not have. Do not let it make you feel guilty."

She had been trying not to and it helped to hear someone else say it was unnecessary, but Abigail suspected the guilt would haunt her for a while yet. She worried about what her brother would think if he returned and she had to tell him what had happened. Abigail feared he would then feel guilty for not being here even though he had been given no choice about that. She prayed he would return alive and whole, for this cursed war had already cost her too much.

Chapter Two

"They are gone, sir," James said.

Matthew tore his gaze from Abigail. "Are ye sure?"

Before James could reply, there was the sound of breaking glass and they all crouched down. Matthew stared toward the door of the bedroom where the sound had come from but, despite a few added odd sounds, there was no sign of an attack being set up. He was just standing up to go and look when there was another crash of glass breaking toward the back of the house and he went back down into a crouch.

"Thought you said they had left," he muttered, glancing at James.

"Saw them all ride off. Didn't see none turn back."

"Yet some must have circled back."

"Not sure we can be certain of that without getting our heads shot off," said Dan.

"I smell smoke," said Abigail as she began to stand up.

"Stay there and stay down," Matthew ordered. "Skirts and fire dinnae mix well." He stood up and headed for the bedroom door.

Abigail sat down and muttered, "I am not one of

your damn soldiers." She looked at Boyd when he laughed weakly. "What?"

"In times like these we are all soldiers. A war forces us into the job sometimes."

"That is a very dark view of things." She frowned when he shivered. "You are growing cold. You should have said that you were cold."

She moved and grabbed the handle of a chest set at the foot of the bed holding the bodies of her parents. As she began to drag it over to where Boyd sat, one of the other men hurried over to help her. She looked at his roughly cut brown hair and blue-gray eyes and recalled that Matthew had called this man James.

"Thank you kindly, James," she said. "It was a lot heavier than I remembered." Matthew abruptly cursed in a loud startled voice and she looked at him. "What is wrong?"

"Handle is hot." He touched the door. "So is the door."

"The kitchen," she said, and dropped the quilt she had been lifting out of the chest for Boyd then stood up.

"Stay there," Matthew ordered again and strode toward the door leading to the kitchen. Even as he braced himself to touch another hot door handle, smoke began billowing out from beneath the door. "The fire is going weel in there, too."

"But why burn the house when they were retreating?" Abigail asked.

"Revenge for the dead and wounded," said James. "Might be hoping it will kill a few of us as well."

"Instead it will just leave nothing for my brother to come home to, if he can," she said.

"Where is your brother?"

"No idea. The Rebs took him. They said they needed men and he was not allowed to say no." She turned to look toward the wall between the kitchen and the front room where she stood. "I should move my parents. I think the fire has reached that wall."

Abigail had barely finished speaking when a creaking groan echoed through the room. She stared at the wall and cried out when it abruptly began to collapse, smoke, ash, and a hint of flame swelling up behind it. Still smoldering, the wood fell on her parents' bodies but when she moved to go toward it, two of the men grabbed her by the arms and held her back.

"They are burning up," she cried out as she struggled to get free of their hold.

"I dinnae think they would wish ye to join them," Matthew said as he took James's place and got a firm grip on her arm.

She finally stopped fighting, tried to ignore the smell of the smoke coming off the bed, and felt tears dripping down her cheeks. "I was going to bury them. Together. Now there will be nothing to bury."

"I suspicion there will be something left, but ye will be gone." Matthew winced, thinking he had just been too hard, but there was no reaction from her on his words.

"Why?" She hated how her voice sounded when she cried but forced herself to ask. "Where am I going?"

Knowing they had to get out, Matthew used a few quick but clear signals to tell his men to check outside for the enemy. "Ye will come with us. Gather what ye can and need. Quickly, for the smoke is growing too thick and the fire will soon come for us."

"That chest," she said and pointed to the one she had pulled away from the bed as she fought to push her grief back.

Abigail pulled her arm away from his loosened grip and moved to a table set near the door. She collected up the photograph of her mother and father, one of them before they had left the city to come here. She wished she had made them get one of her brother, Reid, but all she had left of him was in the trunk she had saved. A drawing of the cabin done shortly before he had been taken away, his mouth organ, and his fancy boots were all that she had left of her brother. Glancing back at the burning bed, she shook her head and strode out the door. It was so little of a life Reid had only just begun to live.

Boyd sat outside, away from the cabin, in an attempt to escape any live sparks and the smoke, her chest beside him. He watched the men gather up the horses as she sat down on the chest and tried very hard not to think of anything. Watching her home burn down held all her attention until Matthew stepped between her and the sight.

"We cannae take the chest on the horses," he said, and worried about the blank look on her face.

"Then we can use the cart," she said in a disturbingly flat voice. "George is still in the stable and he can pull it."

Matthew looked toward the barn. "Thought they took all your horses."

"George is a big, old plow horse. He did not want to go." She slowly stood up, moving like an old woman. "Da brought him all the way from Pennsylvania. I think the men tried, but it looked like one got bitten so they obviously decided to leave him. Didn't have the time to coax him, I guess." She started toward the barn and Matthew fell into step beside her. "He will pull the cart. It will carry Boyd, too."

"Oh, aye." He glanced back at the younger man. "He cannae ride weel with only one arm."

At the door to the barn he glanced down at a flat stone set in the ground to the right of the door. *Pendragon* was clearly painted on it, neatly but with a flourish. It was an odd thing to write on a stepping stone.

Abigail began to open the door, saw what had caught his attention, and sighed. "One of the Rebs shot my cat. It was a senseless thing to do. And mean. He was no threat." She wiped away the few tears that slipped the leash she held on her grief, wondered who she cried for, and stepped into the barn.

"Aye, it was senseless and probably just mean, but a lot of that happens in a war."

She just nodded, not in the mood to talk on men and their wars. "There is the wagon." George neighed in welcome. "And there is George."

Matthew looked at the horse and nearly smiled. He was a big animal obviously bred for strength. He had seen one from time to time when some farm boy joined them with his big farm horse, a mount that was soon changed. If the men she spoke of had tried to take George it was either to pull a wagon or a cannon or even to try and send it home to their farm. It was the type of horse old armored knights had ridden into battle.

He moved to the wagon first and Abigail followed him. He stared at the wagon. It was a good size and looked solid but it had been painted black, a shiny black decorated with a lot of painted flowers. Did Abigail really expect any self-respecting soldier to ride in or drive such a wagon? He also wondered why she had felt the need to do it as it must have taken her a lot of time.

She suddenly uttered a glad cry and scrambled into the back of the wagon. Matthew did his best not to look at her slim legs as her skirts rode up but failed. She moved toward the long metal box set behind the driver's seat. He hoped whatever had been in it was still there as he studied the horse and plotted the best way to approach it.

"Ha! They did not take any interest in this." Abigail pushed aside a few dresses and pulled out a small box. "They would have taken it if they had."

"Why? What is in it?"

Abigail hesitated only a moment in answering. She had seen nothing to tell her these men could not be trusted. If she proved wrong in that judgment she would deal with the consequences later. Right now, they were allies.

"A bit of money and the papers that give us the right to this land. We kept things in this box since the day the war began because we could not be sure when we might have to flee. That is why the deeds for the land are here so the one or ones who survived would have something to come back to. I never thought I would be the only one who might use them," she added in a soft, broken voice.

He watched her as she carefully put everything back in the box. Matthew did not think she was aware of it but she was a fine-looking young woman. Her hair was thick, a soft golden brown that looked as if it wanted to curl, held back only by the braid she had forced it into. She was small, but curved in all the right places. It was her storm gray eyes that were the most striking. Her face was pretty but it was her eyes that held a person's attention. He had already noticed how they darkened with emotion and lightened if she was amused. Her mouth was full and looked temptingly soft so he quickly looked back at the horse. It had been far too long since he had even kissed a woman, and watching her too closely was just asking for trouble.

They were deep in the middle of a vicious war. It was a bad time to be eyeing any woman with interest, he told himself. He had to get her someplace safe and leave her there, then get back to what he had signed up to do until his time was up. After that his plan was to get home and back to something that was normal, something that did not involve constantly killing or running or burying compatriots.

"Will George allow us to hook him to the wagon?"

"He will. He likes me and he is more than ready to do something, I think. He is, after all, a working animal." She walked up to the stall the horse was in, held herself steady when he nudged her, and patted his neck. "Now, my big boy, you are going to be put to use and you are to be polite to the gentlemen. You have been restless to do some work and now is your chance to show what you can do."

Although he was made uneasy by the way the horse eyed him, Matthew helped her hitch the wagon to the animal. Once in the harness the animal did seem pleased. He watched as she went back in the stall after fetching a stick of charcoal. She was writing on the wall of the stall and he was wondering why when Abigail stepped out and put the charcoal back on a rough shelf. She then got up in the seat and drove the wagon out of the barn. Matthew resisted the urge to go and look at what she had written and slowly followed because he wanted to see the faces on his men when they caught sight of the wagon.

"Ah, good, we will need that for Boyd," said James, whose eyes narrowed as he finally gave the wagon a good look. "What the devil is all over it?"

"Flowers," replied Abigail as she hopped down. "I like flowers and they are easy to draw."

"Why is it black?" asked Boyd.

"Because it now looks fresh and new and black paint was all I had. But the flowers dress it up nicely, don't you think?" She turned and walked over to Boyd to push open the lid of the chest set beside him to search for a blanket.

James slapped his hand over Danny's mouth when the man opened it to speak, turned him around, and shoved him toward the horses. "Very nicely done, miss," James said, and followed Danny.

"They hate it," Abigail said as she approached and paused to trail her hand along the side of the wagon. "I was much younger but, to be truthful, I still like it." She put the quilt she had removed from the chest by Boyd and spread it on the bottom of the wagon. "We best get him inside, don't you think?"

"Good idea."

"Just make sure his arm does not bump into anything or allow him to put any weight on it." She kept a close watch on Matthew as he helped Boyd climb into the wagon then hurried back to the box to close it and bring it back.

Abigail intended to slide it in next to Boyd. She felt it would keep him steady in the wagon bed. It was important to her that he did not do anything to or with that arm. His injury was one of the most serious she had ever worked on and she needed to know she had done it right. It was selfish; she knew her concern should all be for Boyd, but she could not help it. She wanted to know she had done right by the younger man and she would only be sure of that when he was healthy again.

She stood back and studied the wagon then sighed

and grimaced. Although she still liked it, she could see how the men might find it a bit less than a joy to ride in. They were probably concerned that someone they knew would see them. At that thought, she smiled, and climbed into the back of the wagon.

"I assume one of you fellows knows how to drive a wagon," she said and then busied herself fixing the quilts so that she and Boyd could ride comfortably.

"I can," James said with a reluctance he could not hide and jumped onto the seat.

Matthew and the others mounted their horses after tying James's up behind the wagon. When James started the wagon moving, Abigail settled back against the box, which she had covered with a blanket. She had no idea of where they were taking her and wondered if she should be concerned. The more she fretted over it the more concerned she became. Matthew moved to ride by her side of the wagon.

"Where are you taking me?" she finally asked.

"Bit late to ask, isnae it?" said Matthew and grinned when he heard her growl. "Back to the town we came from. There is someplace ye can stay there. There are a number of women there, ones, weel, who lost their place because of the war. Ye will do just fine there."

"Whether I want to go or not," she muttered softly.

Boyd chuckled. "It is a good place, a nice place. The women are nice."

"Well, they probably are to you."

"What does that mean? Why would you think they would be nice to me?"

"Because ye are a bonnie lad," said Matthew, and laughed when he glanced back and caught Boyd blushing.

"But now I am broken so it will be different, I think."

He glanced at Abigail when she laughed. "What do you find funny?"

"Just trust me to know, the hurt arm will simply be used as an excuse to help you with everything. It is not your arm they think of as bonnie."

The men laughed and Boyd gave them all a cross look before saying, "It is a good place, Abbie. There are about seven women there of all ages and a few children. You will not be alone, and from what little I know of them, they all seemed quite nice, friendly, and kind. Well, all except Mrs. Beaton who seems to rule the place."

"Mrs. Beaton used to be the wealthy leader of society in the town," said Matthew.

"Ah, I see. Is it her house?"

"It is. It used to be headquarters but once we had collected up several widows and a couple of children it was decided it would serve better as the house for the women and all. Fortunately she offered before someone had to demand it. We keep her supplied with what food we can."

Abigail nodded, beginning to get a picture of the place. "So it is big enough for her to have her family and a lot of guests."

"Her family was just her husband and he died so, yes, it is big enough."

"Must be near as big as your place, sir," said James.

"My place is not just mine. Whole family shares it. My brothers are thinking of adding on to it."

"How many brothers do you have?" asked Abigail.

"Six."

"Good Lord," Abigail said, and James laughed. "That is an impressive family."

"It is my brothers, my elder brother's wife and daughter and his wife's nephew Ned. We built a little cottage for Mrs. O'Neal and her kids, too. She is the one who helps around the house."

Abigail could not picture it but she nodded and smiled. She would have loved such a large family. Instead, she had had a very small family and now she had none. Hastily correcting herself, she thought she only had one left because she did not want to send Reid any hint of an ill fate. She inwardly shook her head at her own superstitions and became determined not to feel sorry for herself. For most of her life her family had been small but happy and that was the memory she would hold fast to.

"What were ye writing on the stall?" he finally asked.

"A message for my brother if he returns here."

She looked at the scenery passing her by and realized she had rarely left the cabin once they had moved in. Her mother had not liked it when she and Reid had wandered far. When their father took them for a walk he had always had a specific place and it was most often through the orchard to the creek. She frowned. Her parents had not been very adventurous despite their move to this new place. Then the troubles in the hills had begun, the harsh determination of some to make people pick a side in the coming war, and they had felt their caution had thus been thoroughly justified.

"You have a fine apple orchard, Miss Abigail," said Boyd.

"Thank you. It produced well, too. Father would take the apples to market and make a decent living. Mother kept hoping he would return to being a doctor, but he had lost the heart for such work."

"Your father was a doctor? Why did he never hang his shingle out here?"

"Well, Da had too much heart. He could not abide

causing pain to anyone or anything, and when all his fine knowledge and skill failed, he grieved. But the biggest reason was the wrong person died under his surgeon's knife."

"What do you mean?"

"He had to operate on a rich young woman, one from a very high social station. Once he opened her up he realized what ailed her was nothing he could ever fix so he sewed her up again. He always knew she was going to die. What he did not understand was why her family blamed him. But they did and their talk eventually lost him his place and he decided to just leave them all behind."

"What did she have?"

"Da called it a malignancy. He could never explain it well for me but he did say that it grows and it kills you. I gather it can grow anywhere in the body, even in blood and bone. Doctors can recognize it but cannot fix it. He suspects one day they may figure it out but not now." She shrugged. "I decided it is probably what kills people and leaves everyone surprised."

Boyd nodded and Abigail returned to looking at the scenery, leaning her head back and letting the sun warm her face. Soon, her eyes closed and she found herself thinking of her family, praying for her brother. She sighed and just let her thoughts roam through the memories.

Matthew peeked in the back and saw that both Abigail and Boyd were asleep. It was probably for the best as it would take a while to get back to their camp but a step or two outside of Missouri. He did not know how she had lasted as long as she had because there were a lot of men traveling through these hills with little concern about who lived here. There were small skirmishes all the time and few were noted. He would be surprised if he found more than half of the people who had called these hills home still lingering in the hills.

He sighed at his part in that even though he had only fought to defend. It was evident he was not a warrior, which had to be an embarrassment to his ancestors. What he ached for besides peace was home. He wanted to be in his workshop making something with wood that could be useful and beautiful. Shaking his head, he shoved those thoughts aside. They were driving a decorated wagon through woods that often served as hiding places for bands of Rebel marauders or soldiers and he could not let his mind wander.

Dan and Jed rode as if waiting for a battle. James drove with his rifle on the seat beside him. Matthew kept his weapon close but prayed they would meet no trouble. He just wanted to get Abigail and the wounded Boyd someplace safe.

"Think Miss Abigail will like the ladies' house?" asked James.

"Why wouldn't she? It is safer than where she was," said Matthew.

"Don't know except I get the feeling none of the ladies are particularly happy. Meet one from time to time and, no, don't get the feeling they are happy."

"Weel, they have all lost a lot and are probably just as weary of this war as we are."

"True. Have you met Mrs. Beaton?"

"Nay, why?"

James shrugged. "I have and she is a sour, rigid woman who has some specific ideas of how things should be done and how people should act. Reminds me of a woman back home who many of the other women disliked. A rich woman who knew little about how regular folks lived and clearly had no interest in finding out. Could be all that there is and she would be a trying person to live with."

"They dinnae have any other choice. It was Mrs. Beaton who opened her house to the women when she finally got it back. Very charitable of her." When James laughed, Matthew looked at him in question.

"Just thinking that might be what is the problem. The charity of it, especially if one is reminded too often of that very kindness. And I am thinking Mrs. Beaton is a woman who will mention it as often as she can."

Matthew chuckled. "True enough. Weel, as said, Abigail has no choice and I am sorry if it ends up grating on her heart but she cannae stay where she was."

"Nope. That lack of choice is always hard to swallow, too."

Nodding, Matthew hoped it would not be too hard on Abigail. He had a strong need to make sure she was somewhere safe, so there was no choice for him. He just promised himself he would keep a watch on her.

The rest of the way back to the little town they were headquartered in was peaceful. It was growing dark and the evening shadows grew. Pulling up in front of the house, Matthew got down from the wagon and went to the back only to find that the stop in motion was enough to rouse Abigail. Boyd slept on and she immediately checked his forehead for signs of fever.

"Ye can stay here," Matthew said as he helped her down. "It will be safe for you."

"Where?" Abigail looked around at the houses on both sides of the street.

"That house," he said, and pointed to a large white house on her right. "Do ye nay recall? We told ye there are other women there and a few children as weel. All of them have lost their homes and families. We call it the Woman's House."

Abigail stared at the big three-story house and idly wondered why such a huge fancy building had even been built here. "How sad. I suppose we will at least have something in common."

He nodded and walked her to the door as the men brought her chests. He knocked and Mrs. Beaton herself answered. At the door, he introduced her to Mrs. Beaton who directed the men to put the chests in the upstairs hall and then he left her there. He needed to get Boyd to the place where the infirmary had been set up so he shook aside his inexplicable guilt and hopped back up into the wagon seat.

When they carried Boyd into the infirmary the doctor quickly showed them to a bed. The man looked over Boyd's wound then tied the restraint for his wounded arm back on. He straightened up and frowned.

"Who tended to this wound?"

"A woman we just brought in," answered Matthew. "Her da was once a doctor and she appeared to ken what she was about."

"Oh yes, she knew. That is what surprised me. I expected to find a still untended wound under the bandages. She did much the same as I would have done. Where is she?"

"At the Woman's House. Mrs. Beaton's?" The doctor nodded. "It was at her place where Boyd got wounded. Since she was alone when the fight ended we brought her here."

"Good. I have to think on it but I might go speak with her. Help is always needed here but I rarely find anyone with any skill. That a woman may well be the one I need is a bit shocking. The boy is fine for now but I cannot say what the fate of that arm will be. May heal and still be useless."

"That is what Abigail said." Matthew shook his head. "I can only hope ye are both wrong."

The doctor just smiled faintly when Matthew shook his head and left. It was not a look that gave Matthew any hope. It really looked as if Boyd's soldiering days were over. Some might be delighted by that, but he knew Boyd would be deeply disappointed. The boy had seen little of the war so far and still held his dreams of glory in battle.

Then he and the men took the wagon to the stables. They all stood patiently as the man running the place laughed heartily over the wagon. Matthew decided it should have been expected especially after all the looks they had gotten as they had entered the town. Leaving it in the still chuckling man's care, he joined his men as they all made their way back to the tedium interrupted with moments of terror that had become their lives.

Chapter Three

Abigail slowly walked to a chair and sat down. She looked around at the other women in the room, finding that most of them were watching her. Mrs. Beaton had not bothered introducing her; she just told her to go sit down and walked away. Unsure of what to do next, she nodded at any woman who met her eyes for a moment. Finally, one woman stood up and walked over to her. She looked to be about Abigail's age and had lovely blond hair hanging loose and curly around her shoulders. There was a cautious look in her brown eyes as she took the seat nearest to Abigail's.

"Hello. I am Julia Hawkins," the woman said.

"Abigail Jenson." She stuck out her hand and the other woman looked a little startled but shook it.

"Are you staying with us now?"

"I assume so. This is where Lieutenant MacEnroy brought me."

"How did that happen?"

As quickly as she could, Abigail explained. She could not completely stem her tears when she spoke of the fate of her parents, but quickly wiped away the few that escaped. She was going to have to find the time and the privacy to give way to her grief. When she finished her tale, the other woman looked close to weeping herself.

"There is so much of that. All the women here are widows or daughters left behind. More widows than the others. There are a few children here as well. We were in another place in town for a while but it became too small to hold us so they moved us here. This used to be the headquarters of the major but, despite what I assume was annoyance"—Julia briefly grinned—"he moved. Mrs. Beaton was at first pleased to get her house back."

"How do I, well, settle in?"

"Mrs. Beaton did not say?"

"No, she just told me to come in here and sit down. The men took my chests up the stairs."

"Ah, well, you can share my room as the woman who used to has moved on. She got news that her husband was not dead as reported, just badly wounded, and she has gone to him." She leaned closer to Abigail and spoke softly. "He lost a leg and demanded that he be listed as dead. It was a friend of his who finally came looking for his wife. He thought it was foolish of his friend to try and turn away the one who might well be the best help for him, so she left with the man. She sent back a short letter when she found her husband and said they were headed back to Ohio."

"I hope all goes well for her and her husband."

"As do I, but it has left a bed free in my room."

"Thank you. Matthew told me little when he left me here. He just mumbled something about this being the Woman's House and walked away." Abigail decided Julia had a nice laugh, clear and sweet, almost childlike.

"Come, I will introduce you to everyone and show you where you will sleep."

Abigail followed her as Julia led her over to each woman in the room and politely introduced her. Most of the women were friendly, but one could almost feel their sadness. It was the same with the children that they met once they made their way up the stairs. There was a fear clinging to each one.

"The children looked so lost," Abigail said as Julia finally showed her into the room they would share.

The room was larger than Abigail had expected and easily held the two small beds with a table between them. A thick carpet covered the floor and a big fireplace sat on the wall opposite the bed. There were two small chairs flanking a fancy round table in front of the windows at the side of the room. One look at this room was enough to tell Abigail Mrs. Beaton was, or had been, a very wealthy woman. It would be the richest room she had ever slept in. Then Julia spoke and drew her mind back to the children.

"Sad, I know," Julia said. "We have no orphanages in town for them. The town was small enough that any child orphaned was easily taken in by a local family or relatives but these children are not from around here and the people still here have enough to fret about without taking in another mouth to feed. This is the best we have. There are only four of them so I think the major is hoping we'll deal with them. We do, but not as it probably should be. Most of the women are still too caught up in their own losses to deal with a child."

"That does not help the children feel secure at all."

"True enough but, truly, there are no orphanages near to take them in."

"The women, sad or not, could do something."

Julia shook her head. "None show the inclination. It is too dangerous to travel about looking for a suitable place to put them. I sometimes think Mrs. Beaton is a bit taken with the little girl so she might take that one but the others are boys and it has been clear that she finds boys, well, alarming. And who knows if Mrs. Beaton has any plans to leave while the whole country appears to be trying to kill each other."

Abigail also shook her head. "And no one knows how long it will last, I suspect."

"Robert thinks it has to end soon. He can't see how the dead and maimed can keep piling up. He said there will be nothing left of the country soon."

"That is a morbid thought. And who is Robert?"

"My beau," Julia said quietly and blushed. "Are you always called Abigail or do you have a shorter name, a pet name?"

Realizing Julia did not want to talk about Robert, Abigail nodded. "My father always called me Abbie."

"Abbie. That is nice. Less formal. It nears time for our evening meal so we had best get downstairs. Mrs. Beaton gets irritated if we are not on time for it."

Abigail followed Julia down the stairs and into the kitchen. There was one long table with benches on each side and a chair at each end. In the far corner of the kitchen, a table with four stools around it. She frowned a little. It did not seem right to keep the children separate. Then she recalled how they had been tucked up in a room upstairs with beds and just a few toys while a teenage girl sat in a corner reading a book and ignoring them. It was no wonder they had seemed so lost to her.

She sighed and asked the woman cooking if she needed any help. The woman looked startled but then carefully suggested Abigail might ready the carrots for the stew she was cooking as she was running a little late. That struck Abigail as odd but she just smiled and began to deal with the carrots. Having a conversation was difficult but Abigail kept trying and the woman began to slowly relax. The woman said her name was Mabel Stone and she was the cook and housekeeper. Then Mrs. Beaton walked in to begin setting the table and Mabel went stiff and quiet again. Abigail kept glancing at Mabel but it was clear their very brief comradery was over

Suddenly Mabel leaned closer and very softly said, "Help in the morning is never refused." She then quietly slipped out of the kitchen.

"Table is set," said Mrs. Beaton. "I will ring for the others."

"Doesn't Mabel eat with us?"

"Who?"

"Mabel Stone, the woman who cooked all this."

"Heavens, child, why should she? She is the help."

Abigail watched as Mrs. Beaton stepped out of the kitchen, grabbed a bell off the sideboard, and rang it several times. As she listened to the people coming down the stairs and the talking began, Julia edged up beside her still drying off a pot and whispered, "Mrs. Beaton was once a woman of some stature."

"You mean rich."

"Well, yes, she was rich and had a lot of others to do the work for her."

"But I was not and, I think, many of the other women here were not, either."

"True, but they follow Mrs. Beaton."

"Why?"

Julie shrugged. "Because it is her house and she was once very rich."

"So where does Mabel go?"

"I think she sits in the garden and has her own meal. Then, when everyone is done, Mrs. Beaton rings her bell again as she leaves and Mabel comes back in to clean up."

The women came into the room, the children behind them. Mrs. Beaton waved the children toward their table as all the women took their seats at the big table, then she took a seat at the head of the table.

"I feel like we should call her 'Your Highness,'" Abigail muttered, and Julia giggled, quickly covering her mouth to smother the sound.

"Come, settle down, girls. Julia, bring over the stew. And you can bring over those lovely rolls and some butter, Abigail."

Something about how the woman sat and waited to be served irritated Abigail. She grabbed the ladle from Julia, picked up the kettle of stew, and moved to serve the children. A red-faced Julia hurried over and let each child pick a roll out of the basket she had put them in. She then let Julia set aside the basket. By the time they reached the table where the women sat, Mrs. Beaton looked very angry but said nothing. Abigail just set the basket of rolls and the butter on the table and sat down. Julia had taken time to pour the stew into a fancy dish and set that on the table before taking a seat opposite her.

Just as Abigail ate the last few spoonfuls of her stew, Mrs. Beaton slid her empty bowl toward the fancy tureen and one of the women quickly stood up to refill her bowl. It was not until that woman's bowl was full that all the others who had finished and wanted more helped themselves. Abigail was pleased when the one they called Molly moved to ask the children if any of them wanted more. Ignoring them had mostly been done because it was what Mrs. Beaton had done not because of a lack of feeling. As she buttered a roll, she decided she would poke at that feeling as much as she could while she was here.

When Mrs. Beaton was done, she simply stood up and walked out. One by one the other women did the same. Abigail was staring at the table littered with dirty dishes when Mabel slipped back inside. She was just about to get up and help clear the table when she felt a light tug on her sleeve. She turned to face a small boy with big brown eyes and very red hair.

"Can I help you?" she asked.

"I would like another roll, please," he said in a soft, wavering voice.

"Of course. There are a few left." She patted the bench at her side. "Come sit next to me."

"Thank you." He scrambled up on the bench and wriggled around a little to sit very properly. "I like bread."

"With butter?"

"A lot."

She grinned and slathered some butter on the cut roll before placing it on a small plate and setting it in front of him. "I like butter, too. How old are you and what is your name?"

"I am Noah and I am four. Almost five."

Abigail decided not to ask when he would be five as she had talked to enough children in her life to realize almost could be months and months away. "Then you definitely need to get enough food. You are a growing boy."

"Yes, I am." He looked at the fancy dish that held the stew. "Maybe I need more stew to make sure I keep growing."

"Oh, that is a good idea." Mabel set the boy's bowl in front of him and Abigail put more stew in it. "There you go. Thank you, Mabel."

Mabel smiled and grabbed a few empty dishes before returning to the sink. Abigail wanted to know what the boy's story was but did not want to poke at what might be an open wound. So she sat and watched him eat. She had the feeling the children were fed but not in a manner they were used to. Mrs. Beaton did not seem the type to cater to a whine about being hungry.

She watched Mabel put together a tray with tea and a lot of little cakes and turned to Julia. "Dessert is in the big sitting room?"

"It is. Not sure why but that is how Mrs. Beaton does it. I better go or I will get nothing and I really want some tea."

Abigail frowned as Julia hurried away, but then Mabel came up to her side. "I have a little dish with four cakes on it for the children," she said. "I always put a few aside for them and for my family. You can take it up to them. This tea and cakes time lasts for quite a while."

And then Mabel slipped away. Abigail looked at the boy who had clearly heard every word. His brown eyes were wide and sparkled with eagerness.

"So you heard that."

"I did. I have sharp ears. My mother always said so." He looked increasingly sad as he spoke the last sentence.

"I am sorry you lost your mother," she said and stroked his curly hair.

"I lost everybody. My father, brother and sister, too. And my puppy. My father had only just got the puppy for me and the men who hurt us killed it."

"They killed my cat and my parents. I do not know how my brother is because they took him away. They burned my house and so a soldier brought me here."

The boy nodded furiously and said, "So you are all alone, too."

"I am, although the soldier is my friend, I believe."

"I am your friend, too."

"Then I am truly blessed," she said, and kissed him on the cheek.

He smiled and patted her on the cheek. "I have a soldier friend, too."

"Who? I only know a few though so I might not know him."

"He is called James. He is tall and has brown hair that he said needs a cut."

"I do think I know him. Are you done?"

"All done and full," the boy said, and rubbed his belly.

She did not like to think of the times he may have left the kitchen still hungry. "Then we best get those cakes up to the others, don't you think?"

"Yes, before they get eaten. By someone else."

Abigail went to the counter and looked in the cupboards finding the small tray with the cakes. She next checked the cold box and found a small jug with some apple cider in it. Once she took four small glasses and placed them on the tray next to the jug she started up the stairs. It comforted her that Mabel thought of the children.

Perhaps, she thought, the women just needed to be encouraged. Mrs. Beaton would not like it, but she did not need to be told. Yet, the children obviously wanted some adult to turn to. She wondered what had made Noah pick her.

Whatever happened, she would do her best to make sure the children did not feel cast off, hidden away in a room. Mrs. Beaton did not have to have them always underfoot, but leaving them alone as she had was wrong. After what had happened to them, they needed some touch from adults, some softness and welcome to pull them out of their sadness. Until that sadness was eased it would be hard to get anyone to take in the children once this wretched war ended.

The moment she walked into the room all the children stared at her. Noah tugged her over to the small table in the room and Abigail handed out the cakes then poured each one a drink. She knelt at the side of the table while they ate their cakes, ready to refill their glasses if they wanted more drink. Somehow she was going to make their lives better here, bring back the smiles and giggles children should have.

"Those were very good, weren't they?" she asked when they all finished their cakes.

"They were very tasty," said Mary, the only girl and the oldest at seven.

Mary took a napkin and wiped off her hands then dabbed at her mouth. A very proper child, Abigail thought and nearly laughed. The girl was beautiful with her very pale blond hair and big blue eyes. Abbie could understand why even the stiff Mrs. Beaton would be taken with the child.

The boys were all not much older than Noah. There was Peter who had a mass of freckles all over his face, reddish brown hair and hazel eyes. He proudly stated he was six with a sidelong glance at Mary that told Abigail he was probably edging close to her age. Sam was a quiet shy boy with black hair and soft grayish blue eyes who softly stated he was five. Abigail wondered how the women could so easily stay away from them. To her they practically cried out for care and attention.

"Would you like a story before you go to sleep?" she asked, and she stood up.

"Yes, please," said Mary, and all the boys nodded. "Anne reads all the time but she does not share the story with us."

A quick look around told Abigail that the teenage girl was gone. "Perhaps it is an adult book she reads. There must be some here for younger people."

After a while they all settled on a tale about a horse. The children readied themselves for bed and crawled under the covers, then stared at her as they waited for her to start. Abigail sat on the edge of Noah's bed and began to read. She was faintly aware of several women peeking into the room as she read the story and hoped that meant a change in how the children were treated. By the time she reached the end they were asleep or so she thought until she stood up and put the book away. Turning to leave, she found Noah staring at her. She hurried over and tucked his covers up around him.

"Get to sleep, young man."

"Thank you for the story." He snuggled down in the soft bed and closed his eyes. "My father used to read me to sleep."

She kissed his forehead. "Hold fast to that memory. It is a very good one."

When she went down the stairs it was to find Mrs. Beaton waiting for her. Whatever had the woman looking so sour was not mentioned for all the woman did say was, "Lieutenant MacEnroy is here to see you. In the parlor."

Although she was not exactly sure which room was

the parlor, the slight inclination of Mrs. Beaton's head told her. Abigail strolled into the room and found Matthew seated rather stiffly in a chair. "Hello. Is my wagon someplace safe?" she asked as she went and sat opposite him.

"It is." He sighed. "The man at the livery was most amused."

"I am so glad my work pleased him."

Matthew laughed. "Amused him so weel I was afraid James was going to hit him."

Abigail smiled. "Tell James I am sorry. Oh, and ask him if he knows a boy named Noah, one of the children here."

"I believe he does. He has brought a child here. A small boy."

"Probably the man then."

"How are the children?"

"Well. They are healthy and clean with a bed to sleep in." She could tell by the look on his face that she had not sounded too pleased by that and was wondering why. "The women here have very little to do with them. I also got the feeling that I stepped wrong when I tried to. Mrs. Beaton was not pleased. I just do not understand. They are all young and it would seem women would be drawn to them at least occasionally."

"But they arenae."

"Not at all. And the children need it. They have all lost everything. Parents, brothers, sisters, homes, and Noah even lost his new puppy. They do not need to be taken in by the women, but some adults tending to them might help ease that loss. Otherwise it seems to them as if they have lost everything and then been tossed into a place where there is no more than a bed and a meal. Adults can manage, but children? No, it is hard for them to understand. Noah stayed awake so that he could thank me for reading a story to them and then softly mentioned that his father always read him to sleep."

"Damn. What did you say?"

"What can you say to a child? 'Your da is dead'? I just told him it was a good memory and he should cling to it."

He smiled and reached over to pat the hands she had clenched in her lap. "A verra good thing to say."

"It was odd because at the evening meal he came to me as soon as the other women left. He wanted a roll with lots of butter so I gave him one. The other children had left already. Then he told me he was growing and he thought a bit more stew would help him grow, too." She smiled when Matthew laughed. "I know I erred by feeding the children before the ladies but still wonder what possessed him to wait and then speak to me."

"It could be as simple as ye feeding them first. Or you might have a look that reminds him faintly of his mother. The same hair or eyes. He probably cannae tell you as it is just a gut feeling. That is often what children act on."

"I suppose. So, what has brought you here?"

"I just came to see that you had settled in weel."

"It has only been one day. I have a place to sleep and got some food so I suppose it could be called fine. I just haven't gotten to know anyone except Julia Hawkins."

"Ah, Robbie Collins's lady."

"That is what she said. I know everyone's name but not much else. More takes time."

"I ken. It was just that I got to thinking on the

comments made about Mrs. Beaton and wondered. Also took Boyd to the infirmary and the doctor was quite impressed by your work." He grinned when she blushed. "You may hear from him soon as he said he is always looking for someone with a bit of skill to help him."

"Well, I would be glad to help, but we'll see if he can overcome the dislike of women doing something that comes close to doctoring. They might be letting women into the schools to learn about it but working at it is not easy."

"Nay, I imagine doctors are very protective of their place there." Matthew stood up. "Just wanted to warn ye in case he does come round."

"Thank you," she said as she stood, only to find herself so very close to him her heart skipped. "I will be ready if he calls."

For a moment, he just stared at her and then he leaned over and kissed her. Abigail was too surprised to do anything but grab hold of his coat to steady herself. It was over quickly and when he leaned back she rapidly let go of his coat. He just smiled, lightly stroked her cheek, and walked out.

Abigail just stared at the door wondering what that had been all about. Was it just a sign of friendship or was he interested in her as a man was often interested in a woman? Since he had just left her there she had no answer. Shaking her head, she decided she would not think about it for it was sure to drive her mad.

She went into the room where the women were. Only a few were left although Abigail thought it a little early to go to bed. She located Julia sitting on a small settee and sat down next to the woman. Julia had a man she called her beau so maybe she could help.

Abigail was just not sure she wanted to share the tale of the kiss as it suddenly seemed to be a very private thing.

"So what did Lieutenant MacEnroy want?" Julia asked.

"He just thought I should know that the doctor at the infirmary was impressed with the work I did on Boyd's wounded arm and might stop by to ask if I wish to help sometime."

"You know nursing?"

"I suppose you could say I do. My father was a doctor and he was always teaching me things. After looking at the wound the doctor must have decided I could be of some help as an aide."

"Will you say yes if he comes and asks?"

"Why wouldn't I if he really thinks I can help?"

Julia looked torn between fascination and horror. "Well, there would be wounded men and all the mess that goes with it and some of the men may be, um, indecent at some time."

"And I suspect that is the sort of thing that the doctor would be shielding me from. He may not even ask so no need to worry over something that might not happen. But if he thinks I can help some of the wounded soldiers, how can I refuse?"

"I guess you can't. Oh, I must tell you that you really annoyed Mrs. Beaton by feeding the children first, especially since she could not really say anything about it."

Julia looked so pleased that Abigail decided she must see it as a good thing. Abigail was not so sure it was but had no inclination to change what she saw as neglect. She just hoped Mrs. Beaton did not find subtle ways to make her pay for what the woman must see as disobedience.

"I hope I have not made things awkward."

"Why did you decide to do that?"

"Because they were being treated almost as an afterthought, like the dog that needs feeding or the like. They have been deeply frightened and wounded. Little Noah lost his parents, a sister, a brother, and even his puppy. Somehow it just seemed wrong." She sighed, leaned back, and stared up at the ceiling, which she noticed had some very elaborate plasterwork. "I just thought it wrong, that someone should take some notice of them."

"Oh, I think they will now."

"Why not before?"

"It clearly does not strike you, but Mrs. Beaton is a very formidable presence. We have all fallen into her habits and her ways and she has little to nothing to do with the children. She occasionally has a moment or two of fawning over the little girl, but that is all. I do not believe she likes the little boys much at all. Some have made mention of the fact that the children are ignored, but no one dares say so to her or act in any way that might offend her."

"I suspect I will be offending her fine senses a lot then." She smiled faintly when Julia laughed.

Matthew stepped outside and looked back at the door of the Woman's House. Her mouth had been as soft and sweet as he had thought it would be. It was probably reckless to kiss her as he did, but he had been unable to stop thinking about her mouth and thus unable to resist the temptation to taste it when it was so close. What troubled him was that he knew now he would want another taste and more.

It was early to seek his bed, but if he was going to do some thinking whether he wanted to or not, he might as well do it while lying on his back. Under the blankets was a lot warmer than wandering outside now that winter had settled into the chilly, damp night air. He suspected his mind would wind about in circles but he could not stop it from preying on the matter of Miss Abigail Jenson.

Slapping his hat on his head and doing his coat up tightly against the cold, he started to walk back to where he had his bunk. Reminding himself that Abigail was a proper girl despite the fact that she could shoot better than most of them, deal with wounds so well her work impressed a doctor, and was plain-spoken, she was not one of the girls at the saloon. He knew that reminder would not keep him away, however. He had to stop dancing around and really think of what he might want from her. One did not play love games with a girl like Abigail unless one was serious, and he was not sure just how serious he was.

Chapter Four

Looking up from her sewing, Abigail frowned as Julia slipped into the house. The woman looked extremely untidy, as if it was storming out, but a glance out the window told Abigail the weather was calm. There was a twig caught in Julia's badly mussed hair and what appeared to be grass stains on her skirts. Considering the snow on the ground, she had to wonder where the girl had been. To her surprise, Julia snatched Abigail's cape off the hook by the door, put it on, and walked over to sit down next to her.

"What have you been up to?" Abigail asked as she continued her sewing.

"I just went out walking with Robert."

"Oh. It rather looked as if you fell down." A quick glance caught the deep flush on Julia's face.

"He was chasing me for fun, but I fell and tumbled down a little hill."

"Of course." Abigail tied off the thread and carefully studied another spot on the skirt of her gown.

"Robert wants to marry me. I said yes."

"Probably a very good idea."

"What are you doing to that gown?"

"Embroidering flowers on it. It has some spots along the hem I could not wash out so I am trying to hide them."

"Oh, well, that will be pretty when you are done." Julia frowned. "Yet this takes a lot of time, doesn't it? Would it not be just as quick to make a new dress? I wager you can even get a green as pretty as that one."

"I don't think so. Cloth is very dear and rare at the moment. This war has caused a lot of trouble with that. Winter probably adds to that. It was difficult enough to get the colored thread."

Julia frowned. "I had not realized that but then I have had no need of anything yet."

"Trust me in this, Julia. I have been to the general store and the prices there make me wonder if this is a gold mining town." She shook her head. "The owner is enriching himself, I am sure of it." She readied her needle again and began to work on another spot.

"I need to go and rest. And warm up a bit. Is it our turn to help with the evening meal?"

"No, Barbara and Kate are to do it tonight. Just hang my cape up in our room. Best not to flaunt the grass stains."

Blushing, Julia hurried away and Abigail sighed. She had a feeling her words had sounded like a condemnation to Julia. She would have to make it clear that they had not been. It was all too easy to understand Julia and Robert's reckless behavior. Falling in love with a soldier was not easy, and the constant shadow of losing him at any time never left. She could only hope that they had considered all the possible repercussions, but there was something about Julia, something she could not yet point to as tangible proof, which told her it was already too late to avoid them.

She had only been at the house for eight weeks and

she had seen more than she had ever wanted to of death, blood, and horrible wounds. What she had done for Boyd had brought attention her way. The doctor himself had come to request her help. She did not really mind even though some of the wounds had turned her stomach. Men could find a way to kill each other even in the depths of winter. The doctor was a good man, one who did not just hack off a wounded limb, and he fully appreciated the skills she had gathered while working with her father over the years. He had even confided that he now believed women should be able to study all that could make them a doctor if they wished to. Yet she found it sad and wearying to see so many young men injured or dying. Blue or gray, it did not matter. The constant waste of life was beginning to sicken her.

There was one bright side to it all and she decided she needed to fix her mind on that. She had also seen to the care of the women and children in the town. The doctor was expected to care for the soldiers so the women came to her. She knew they looked on her as a particularly skilled midwife but she did not care. It was work she was happy to do because the outcomes were mostly good ones.

Her days were busy, she was safe, she had work that kept her mind and hands occupied, and she had friends for the first time since leaving Pennsylvania. Only one thing troubled her. Where was Matthew? She had only seen him once since she had been put in this house, aside from his brief stop to check on her on the day she entered the house and give her a quick kiss. It was a brief visit about two weeks ago where they had shared coffee and little cakes and talked while all the other women in the room sat nearby pretending not to listen. He had stolen another quick kiss and she began to think they were just friendly things in his mind. She sighed and concentrated on her embroidery. Matthew would visit when and if he wanted to and she would cease to take his absence personally.

Matthew watched the Rebel camp through his spyglass. It certainly looked as if they were readying for an attack. Putting away the spyglass, he started to move back, careful to make no sound or disturb any of the bushes he was hiding in. It would take him a while to get back to where Jed waited with his horse and he really did not want to cover the distance with Rebs hot on his trail. He wondered how James was doing on his spying foray and hoped whatever the man saw or heard would match with what he had discovered. The very last thing he wished to do was return and lie on the cold ground to recheck what he had seen.

What he wanted, he decided as he stood and broke into an easy run, was to go and visit with Abbie. She fascinated him, he finally admitted to himself. She could shoot better than many a man and yet she painted flowers on a wagon. She dealt with stomach-churning injuries of soldiers, yet made certain little Noah would soon get a puppy to replace the one that had been killed with the rest of his family. She had kindly mended the tear in the sleeve of his uniform but then embroidered a snake over the signs of mending. He was still not sure how he felt about that.

His conscience told him he should go to a whore and rut until every last drop of fascination with Abigail was gone from his system. Yet he had no urge to do that. He did not know if he even wanted to pursue any woman, especially not one as properly raised as Abigail had been. The war made such a thing as courting a big risk, plus he knew he had been hardened by the war, and was not even the rough-at-the-edges gentleman he used to be. He was no longer suitable for a properly raised young woman, especially one who had lost so much to the war.

"Hey, sir! Over here!"

Matthew stopped, looked around, and finally saw Jed ride out of a thick cluster of trees leading his horse. "Ye had to hide? Someone come this way?"

"Two fellars. Rebs. Think they mean to spy on the town. Thought about just shooting them but was afeared the shots would bring us unwanted company."

"It would have done. I suspicion the Rebel camp is close enough to hear them."

"Saw a whole camp, did you?" Jed asked as Matthew mounted his horse.

"I did and it kept growing, raiders riding in and staying." He nudged his mount into a slow walk. "Also saw a small troop of men with a wagon of supplies and a small cannon."

"Damn, that ain't good."

Matthew sighed. "Nay, it isnae. I'm curious to see if James gets the same information."

"I am thinking he might find that camp he went to watch is empty now."

"Aye, and if so, it certainly points to trouble for us."

Jed just nodded and Matthew sighed. They were headed for a battle. He was sure of it. There were not enough men in that camp to launch a full attack but they could start a skirmish that could cost the army and the town dearly. He would find the time to warn Abigail.

James appeared at their side. He looked sweaty and irritated. Matthew then looked at the man's coat and frowned.

"Did Abbie fix that tear in your coat?"

"Yup." James straightened his coat and Matthew shook his head when he saw a dragon over the spot where the mending had been done. "I rather like it."

"I suppose it is better than a snake," Matthew said, and James laughed.

They started riding toward the town while discussing what they had seen. James had discovered the camp he had been sent to watch was a lot smaller than it had been. Matthew suspected the men had come to the camp he had been watching.

"The fools even dragged their cannon off," James said.

"I think I can say with some confidence that your camp has now merged with the one I was watching. The question is, what does it mean for us?"

"Trouble. Unless they are marching out to join up with the main army for some major assault," mused James. "Hell, they could just be huddling together for warmth." He grinned when Matthew laughed.

"We will have to keep a close watch as they are obviously planning something."

His companions grunted in agreement as they rode toward the place where they bunked. Matthew went to the major to report all he had seen and left the man puzzling it out. He stood outside the major's office and contemplated what he would do next. There was still a lot of the afternoon left so he decided he could do something with Abigail. Maybe a walk, he thought as he made his way to the bathhouse. It was cold but there was little wind so a brief stroll would not do her any harm.

Abigail helped Julia up the stairs and was not terribly surprised when the girl escaped her hold and raced into their room to throw up into a bucket. She did wonder when the bucket had arrived. Julia was hiding things, but Abigail had to let her know that she was not hiding it well. All the other women knew the girl was with child although only two had made any comment on it, and neither of those women had been harsh. The only one who appeared to be oblivious was Mrs. Beaton.

Wrinkling her nose at the scent of sickness, Abigail got a damp cloth and went to bathe the girl's face after she lay down on the bed. As she gently bathed the sweat from Julia's face, she noticed that when lying down it was very obvious that Julia was carrying a child. Putting away the cloth, she pulled the blanket up over the girl.

"Thank you," said Julia quietly. "The sickness will soon pass."

"I know. Julia, you are not hiding much from the other ladies here, you know."

"What do you mean?" Julia asked, but revealed she knew well what Abigail meant by blushing deeply.

"Oh, I think you know, but I will make myself clear. About the only one in the house who does not realize you are carrying a child is Mrs. Beaton."

Julia began to cry and Abigail sighed. She did not like to see her friend upset but knew there was nothing she could do to change the situation the girl was in. It was past time Julia faced some harsh truths and dealt with them as an adult. Women who got pregnant and were not married were treated like pariahs and the country tearing itself apart with this war was not a good enough reason for the judgment to treat Julia differently.

"How did they figure it out?"

"Well, you are beginning to show."

"This little bump?"

"There is that and then there is your sickness and all those long walks you take with Robert even when winter has set in. It adds up and equals what ails you now. Of course, you could just marry Robert and no one would care. How far along are you?"

Julia sniffed and pulling a handkerchief from her pocket, gently dabbed the tears from her face. "I do not know."

"When did you start getting sick?"

"Months ago. I feel like I have been sick forever but it has really only been a few months. I think I might be about three months along?"

"I suspect you are more like six months along." Abigail frowned. "I would have thought you would be, well, bigger and that the sickness would have faded away."

"From what I recall, most of the women in my family carry small. A lot goes to the hips and all. My mother used to like to say the babes nested sideways in a Hawkins woman."

Abigail tried not to, but she laughed a little. "One way to look at it. May I feel your stomach?"

"Why?"

"Just to see if I can feel anything. Occasionally a good feel of the belly can tell one a lot."

"Oh. All right." Julia lifted her gown and lay still.

"What is this wrapping around you?"

"I was trying to make the bump less noticeable."

"Well, do not do that anymore," said Abigail as she unwound the binding. "It could do something to the baby."

"Will the binding hurt the babe?"

"I do not really believe so, but I cannot think that tightening the area it needs to grow in is a good thing." Under her hand Abigail felt the bump of a small foot and watched Julia flinch. "Now I understand those odd twitches you have developed. Babe is alive and moving. Do you wish the doctor to see you?"

"No. That would be akin to putting a big sign on the door, and I am trying very hard not to let the whole town know."

Abigail pulled a chair up beside the bed and sat down, taking Julia's hand in hers. "Julia, you should tell Robert. Maybe he can find a way for you two to marry now and give his child his name. You can always have a fancier service to celebrate with his family when this cursed war is over."

Julia frowned. "I suppose that would be a solution. It would not be all I had dreamed of but, you are right, it would name my child."

"I know others have done it. Well, maybe not because of a child, but they have married a soldier during the war. Half the widows here are soldiers' widows."

"I know. I will talk to him the next time I see him."

"Good. Then all you will need to concern yourself with is caring for the child you carry."

Julia rubbed her belly. "Yes. That is for the best. I promise I will tell him. I see him soon, this afternoon actually, so it will soon be done."

Abigail pulled up the blanket to hide Julia's belly when she heard footsteps on the stairs. A moment later, Mrs. Beaton stood there. The woman just looked at Julia and frowned.

"Should I tell Mr. Collins that you cannot see him now, Julia?"

"Oh no, Mrs. Beaton. Please tell him I will be down in just a moment." Julia cautiously sat up as Mrs. Beaton left. "He has come a lot sooner than I thought he would."

"That is for the best. Quickly done and problem quickly solved," Abigail said.

"I suppose."

"You said he had already asked you to marry him and you said yes," Abbie said as she followed Julia to the door.

"Yes, he did." Julia straightened up, walking to meet Robert with her head held high.

Abigail studied the man waiting for Julia and decided he could not be much older than her. He was about a head taller than her and lean bordering on skinny. His hair was as raggedly cut and long as was James's and a dark blond. When he smiled at Julia one could easily see why the girl loved him. There was a soft glow in his blue eyes that backed up the message in his smile. When the two of them went into the little parlor, Abigail walked into the main room and sat down, planning to wait until Julia and Robert called for a minister.

"She and that boy sitting in the parlor?" asked Maude as she came and sat down next to Abigail.

"Yes. No walk today."

"Those two have *walked* one time too many, I am thinking."

It was hard, but Abigail bit back the urge to laugh at Maude's pointed statement. "They have a few serious things to discuss."

"Oh, they most certainly do. Reckless children that they are."

"Maude, you can't be much older than either of them."

"You are sweet. I am nearly forty, child. None of these boys running around here in their uniforms interest me. Got my eye on the major. Man has some time under his belt but is still a fine-looking fellow. A widower."

Maude was a strong, pleasant-looking woman with thick black hair and bright hazel-green eyes. "He sounds perfect."

"No man is perfect, love, not even that Scotsman who brought you here despite how much I love how he talks, but the major is a good man, a strong man, and that is worth a lot."

"Yes, yes, it is."

"My boy is still living although he is back East, out of the war, which I am very glad about. He was in for a short time but when he left it he went to train to be a doctor. He had worked in the infirmary and got a taste for fixing people. My girl got wed three years back just as all this nonsense was winding up. So, I am a free bird and I feel like making a new nest."

She couldn't help it; Abigail laughed and Maude joined her. They then began to talk about the lack of so many things. Soon Julia dashed into the room but came to a fast halt when she saw Maude.

"Spit it out, child. What is it you are so excited to say?" asked Maude.

"Robert is going to fetch a preacher." Julia clutched her hands together and pressed them to her breast. "I hope the man hasn't left town yet."

"The minister was leaving?"

"Coward," snarled Maude. "He says the war is too close. Seems to me it is the perfect time for a man of God to minister to his flock, but he is bolting."

"That is shameful," said Julia, truly shocked.

"He can get out of the war and he is doing it, as fast as his chicken legs will let him. I think he will find that, depending which way he heads, he might have chosen dangerously, however." Abigail shook her head.

"That is a fact. Traveling anywhere is a risky business at the moment. I think the war is soon to be mostly south of us though," said Maude. "The army is gathering on both sides down that way or our way. You know what I mean. Virginia, Georgia, and all that."

"Okay. Let it all go there. Fine with me," said Abigail.

"But my major will go." Maude sighed.

"Then we will pray that he gets sent somewhere safe."

Maude patted Abigail's hand. "Thank you, child. And I will make sure he knows where to find me after it is all over." Maude glanced at Julia. "And time for us to listen to this girl who looks about to jump out of her own skin."

"I am going to marry Robert. I need to find a nicer dress."

Abigail stood and took Julia by the hand. At times, it was hard to remember that Julia was the same age as she was. Too often the woman acted so much younger than her twenty-three years.

"Then we shall go find something."

Maude stood up. "As soon as we know the lad found the preacher we will get some food together to have in celebration."

"Thank you, Maude," Julia said, and skipped over to kiss the woman on the cheek.

By the time Julia had decided on what dress to wear, Abigail was tired. The girl who had been weak with a sick belly was a bouncing bundle of energy at the moment. They finally returned to the sitting room and found it changed. The women had festooned the room with bits of bright cloth, some spring wildflowers that had bravely come early, and bows. They had also arranged the chairs to face a small table where the preacher stood.

Robert stood up quickly and beamed at Julia. He took her by the hand and walked her toward the preacher. Julia looked so happy, Abigail felt her eyes sting with happiness for her friend. She added a prayer that nothing would happen to Robert. One just had to look at Julia's expression to know if this war took her Robert she would be crushed.

The ceremony was quick as it was obvious the preacher was anxious to leave. He stayed long enough to get money from Robert though and Abigail had to bite her tongue. The man looked at his position as just a job and had no real calling, she decided. They all gathered to wave good-bye to the couple as Robert took his new bride to the hotel. Abigail looked for Maude and found her next to the major who had come to stand with Robert. Laughing softly, Abbie went up to the bedroom.

It was going to be strange to spend a night alone but Julia would be back in a few days as Robert had to return to the war that disrupted and shattered so many lives. Abbie got a book from the shelf near the fireplace and sprawled on her bed. It was rather nice to be on her own. It had been a very long time she had enjoyed such quiet.

She was lost in the story when the bed suddenly jiggled and she looked around to find Noah sitting next to her. "What do you want?" she asked as she put a piece of paper in the book to mark her place.

"Is Julia gone now?"

"For a little while. She will be back when Robert has to go back to soldiering."

"Oh. I hope he doesn't get hurt like your friend Boyd."

"I hope so, too. It would break Julia's heart."

"Wanna play a game?"

Her quiet time was done, Abbie thought as she sat up. "What game?"

"I have jacks." He held up a small cloth bag.

"I am good at jacks."

"So am I," he said, narrowing his eyes at her. "Really, really good."

"Well, we best get on the floor then."

"Okay." He scrambled off the bed and sat down on the hardwood floor.

"How about we sit on the carpet? It is a little softer than the floor."

Abigail sat cross-legged on the carpet. Noah settled opposite and emptied his bag. It was a nice set with a wooden ball and iron pieces. She wondered how he had saved this from his past life since she doubted Mrs. Beaton had children's toys scattered around her house. It was such a small thing but she was pleased he had something from the past. Then she settled into a serious game. For only a moment did she consider allowing him to win. When he revealed he did indeed play the game well, she stopped and got serious. When he still won, he leapt to his feet and danced around waving his fists in the air.

"You are right," she said when he sat back down and grinned at her. "You are a good player."

"I saved this." He frowned. "I would rather have saved my puppy."

"Did you take care of your puppy?"

"I did. I even got him to pee outside."

"Very good."

Abigail thought about the tiny puppy she had impulsively claimed and was relieved. It might be that there would not be too much trouble about bringing him to the house. She was going to have to get up the courage to talk to Mrs. Beaton about it for the animal would soon be ready to leave its mother. The woman holding the pup for her would be anxious for her to take it. It was going to be a battle to get Mrs. Beaton to agree but Abigail decided the boy's happiness was worth it.

"Wanna play again or go back reading your big book?"

"I can play again. Have to gain back my honor, don't I?"

He giggled and set out the pieces again. Abigail resigned herself to an afternoon of playing jacks with a boy of four. She guessed that there would be another game and another until he accepted her claim that she was done.

By the time he accepted her claim that she was done, Abigail had only won two of six games. The boy did have an admirable skill and it was a little odd for such a small boy. His coordination was good. The way he could concentrate on the game was also impressive. She stood up and rubbed his hair when he stood up beside her.

The boy finally went back to his own room and Abigail returned to her reading. She would have to remember to read to the children tonight, she decided. It was a good thing to do, for their minds and, she suspected, to ease their fears and sadness with something normal. She had noticed several of the women took some time now and then to talk or play with the children and Abigail could see the difference in them. There was a little less sadness in their eyes.

The problem was, too many of the women still clung to their own sadness. It made it difficult for them to deal with the children's as well. She could understand for it was not just the loss of their husbands. It was the loss of the whole life they had: their homes and the possibility of children. As hard as Abigail thought, she could not come up with a way to ease all that.

Picking up her book she started to read and quickly lost herself in the story again.

Chapter Five

Matthew took his hat off, finger-combed his hair, and waited patiently for Mrs. Beaton to fetch Abigail. After a long meeting with the other officers and planning for a possible assault he had decided he wanted to see her. He had wasted the bath he had taken the other day when the major had called for him and he did not want to waste the one he had taken today. He had a need to see and speak with her that he decided he could no longer ignore. What he did not understand was why he felt so nervous.

Looking around the parlor, he finally moved to one of the empty chairs and sat down. He hoped Mrs. Beaton would not take long to bring in Abigail. Matthew had the sinking feeling that it would not take long for his nervousness to turn into cowardice and he would run.

Abigail helped Julia back to bed then hurried to empty the basin the girl had been sick in. Either her few days away with her new husband had been too rowdy or it was the pregnancy. She decided she would ask the doctor why Julia was still having sickness when she was so far along in her pregnancy. At least the girl was now married, but there was still a chance people who knew she had carried the child before she wed could cut her.

"Is Julia still getting sick?"

Looking at the woman standing in the doorway, Abigail felt sure the woman was already suspicious about what really ailed Julia. "Illness rarely disappears in a day or two."

"Well, do something for her before she spreads the disease."

"I am doing all I can. Feeling better, Julia?" Abigail met Julia's gaze and prayed her friend could read her demand for a positive answer.

"It passes. You always know what to do."

"Thank you. Now stay here and rest until Robert comes for you. You may have some water and a few bites of this sandwich if you wish." She stood up and stroked Julia's hair from her face. "Just rest. It is what you need. I will see you later."

Mrs. Beaton crossed her arms. "You have a gentleman waiting to see you, Abigail."

"I do? Is it Boyd?"

"No. It is Lieutenant MacEnroy."

"Matthew is here?"

"*Lieutenant* MacEnroy is waiting downstairs to speak with you."

"I will be fine, Abbie," said Julia. "Go see what he wants."

Abigail took a moment to fix her hair then brush down her skirts before following Mrs. Beaton out of the room. She was surprised at the tumultuous mixture of anticipation and nervousness she felt. The man might have a simple question he needed answered.

Going down the hall and then the stairs with Mrs. Beaton made the knot in Abigail's stomach grow even tighter. Did the woman always move so slowly? Abigail lectured herself about patience, then tried to convince herself that she did not care if Matthew had come just to ask a question or because he actually wanted see her.

When they reached the parlor Abigail tensed as she saw Matthew stand up. She noticed he looked nervous and, for some strange reason, that made her feel calm. As she left Mrs. Beaton's side, Abigail smiled at him.

"Hello, Abbie," he said quietly.

"Good to see you, Lieutenant. Would you like some coffee? Maybe a little cake?"

"Both would be most welcome." He glanced toward Mrs. Beaton who appeared to be standing guard at the door. "If it would be no trouble."

"None at all." Abigail looked at Mrs. Beaton. "I can do it, Mrs. Beaton. There is no need for you to linger. I am sure you must have a great deal you would rather do. Perhaps visit the children?" She bit the inside of her cheek to keep from laughing when the woman briefly looked horrified, then nodded and left.

Smiling faintly, Abigail looked back at Matthew. He was watching her warily, a hint of confusion in his eyes. "Why did she look as if ye were about to hand her a dead rat when ye spoke of her going to see the children?"

"To her it is apparently much the same. I fear Mrs. Beaton does not like children. She considers them disruptive and destructive. They are kept in a room upstairs. I will be right back with the coffee and cake."

Matthew watched her leave. She had a strong, brisk way of walking with no hint of coquettishness. Then he looked at the doorway where Mrs. Beaton had stood. He had had no idea that the children were being kept regulated to a room upstairs. They had been put here because the major had believed the women would care for them. Being treated like unwanted guests could not be good for them. They had all lost their families and homes, were frightened and alone. It had never occurred to him or the other men that the women would not care for them. That had probably been foolish of them, and someone should have come around now and then to check on them. Matthew made a promise that he would keep a much closer watch now.

He settled back into the chair and thought about all he and James had discovered yesterday. There was an attack being planned. The only thing they could not be sure of was where and when it would happen. Plans were being made to further secure the town and the people in it. He realized he would need a better place for the women than this house with all its windows and doors, and began to think on an answer to that problem. He was just deciding the jailhouse would serve well when he heard the clink of china, looked up, and saw Abigail returning with a tray.

Abigail held the heavy tray as steady as she could. Mrs. Beaton's coffeepot was heavy and she suspected it was made of actual silver. When Matthew walked toward her she just smiled as he took the tray from her. She subtly rubbed her arms when he turned to walk over to the small settee. Seeing that he obviously thought they would sit together, she took a deep breath and went over to sit at one end of the settee.

She tried not to flinch when he sat close to her. A soldier would see a flinch as a sign of fear, and that was certainly not what she felt. There was a tickle of nerves and it was curiously mixed with anticipation. She wished she had had more dealings with men for she suspected there was a good explanation for what she felt.

She poured them each some coffee and served pieces of the cake. She idly noticed that Mrs. Beaton had left the door wide open with the doors to the main sitting room also wide open. She could see straight through to the other women. Maude even sent her a jaunty wave. Privacy was apparently not allowed. Watching Matthew from the corner of her eyes, she hid a smile behind the drinking of her coffee as he ate his cake. It was clear that even the officers did not get such treats often. He was eating that bit of cake as if he had been starved for days.

Matthew put his empty plate down and drank some coffee before looking at Abigail. "Is living here working well for ye?"

"I suppose. It is not perfect, that is certain, but most of the ladies are nice and the children are dears."

"Let me guess. Mrs. Beaton is not one of those 'most of the ladies.'"

Abigail sighed. "No. She still thinks and acts as if she is the lady of the manor. It appears I upset the proper order of things much too often."

"When we finish our coffee we could go for a walk and you can tell me how disruptive ye are."

She nodded even as she laughed. Once they were done, she put everything back on the tray and took it back to the kitchen. By the time she returned, Matthew was standing in the hall holding her coat.

"Is it cold enough for this?" she asked even as she slid it on and buttoned it up.

"There is still a bite in the air when it gets late in the day."

"Ah, of course. I missed much of winter hiding in this house huddled before a fireplace."

"Lucky you. Most of the misery should be over soon."

"I hope so." She hooked her arm through his and they headed out the door.

"Most of the snow is gone. That has been hard on the soldiers, seeing as so much of our time is spent lying on the ground shooting at the other side. But I can feel the change of season."

"Aye, so can I. Glad we are not stationed in Maine or some state like that." He smiled when she laughed. "Here we see the warming faster."

It was a pretty small town, Abigail decided. Even with the trees stripped by the cold, it was nice. It made her sad to think of all that was happening around it. The field behind the general store was filling up with the dead, chosen as the burial spot when the Union arrived and started holding it for the Union. The cemetery held both sides, gray and blue. The whole thing seemed like such a senseless tragedy to her.

Deciding an evening spent arm in arm with a handsome man was not a time to consider such serious thoughts. She glanced at Matthew and noticed he kept a close watch for any threat. Even a walk was dangerous, she thought, and shook her head.

"So where are we going?"

"No idea," said Matthew, and he grinned at her. "Not many places to walk in this town and probably not verra safe outside it. So it is up one side of the street and down the other."

"How adventurous of us."

"Verra. Or"—his smile grew wider—"we could duck down an alley."

Before she could answer that, he took a sharp

turn to the right and walked between two deserted buildings. Very little of the fading day's light entered here and she held his arm with both hands. It was a pleasant alley compared to the ones she had been down occasionally in Pennsylvania. It appeared to have grass instead of scattered trash and dirt.

"Why are we down here?" she asked.

"Privacy."

"So you keep saying, but I saw no one on the street."

"They could be peering out the windows. Everyone likes to ken who is walking around outside, especially in the evening."

Abigail nodded, easily able to understand that. She suspected it was not just the war that made a small town always curious about who was where and what they were doing. Now it could be a matter of life and death, however. She suspected not even the soldiers in blue were fully trusted. Many people sympathized with the South; they just did not feel inclined to fight about it. They also had enough sense to keep their sympathies quiet.

Matthew wrapped his arms around her and walked her backwards until her back was up against the wall. She looked at him and he held her stare for a moment as if looking for a refusal then smiled when he found none.

His mouth covered hers before Abigail could make up her mind about accepting or refusing. The moment his tongue entered her mouth she knew she was all for accepting. For a while they just kept kissing, breaking for air now and then as he spread hot kisses over her throat.

Still reeling from his kiss, Abigail said nothing as he tugged her around the corner and into the deserted house she had been leaning against. "Why are we in here?"

"Privacy. We rarely have any." He led her into what must have been the parlor. "This family ran from here a day after we marched in. Knew the Rebs would follow and there would be a fight, I suppose. They headed east so think one of them had family there."

"They are lucky it hasn't been burned down."

"It's empty. Fire is usually set to drive the people shooting at you out of the house."

"Ah, of course."

"Now, I have set up a wee feast for us here. A picnic, if ye would rather call it that."

"In this house?"

"Aye. It is cold outside." He moved to light a lantern standing on a table near the door.

Abigail let him take her by the hand and lead her into the room where a table was set against the far wall. As she took the seat he held out for her she saw the two place settings and two wineglasses. There was bread, butter, cheese, and some slices of cold chicken. The big surprise was the bottle of wine he picked up and started to open.

It was mostly soldier fare, which made Abigail smile. She did wonder where he had gotten the chicken as she doubted there was a live one left for miles around. Soldiers scrounging were as bad as locusts. The bottle of wine and the glasses puzzled her even more. Alcohol, except for the occasional home brew, had been gone from the town long ago.

"Where did you find the wine and glasses?"

"The glasses were here so I have to be sure to put them back. Mabel gave me the chicken and cheese, and the bread is from the woman who bakes for the officers when we can get her the supplies."

"Do you get the supplies often?"

"Nay. Too many of the men who drive the wagon from where they get it loaded are killed and then the wagon is stolen with all the supplies. Someone was letting the Rebs ken when and where the wagon was. I think we stopped that, but we also send men out to guard the wagon on its way here. It is a dangerous assignment."

"I can imagine it is for the Rebs have to be as hungry as you and your men."

"More so. Their supplies are harder to get."

For a while they ate and talked idly about the war. Mostly they discussed the differences between the armies. She felt sad for all the widows being made and all the parents who would never see their sons again. It all seemed such a waste to her and it was nearly destroying life in the hills.

She sipped at her wine and decided it was tasty then drank it all down. As she set the glass down she noticed Matthew grinning at her. He refilled her glass but only partway.

"What are you finding so amusing?" she asked as she put some chicken on her bread and took a bite.

"Have ye ever had any wine?"

"I do not believe so. Had a bit of whiskey once and went to sleep for a few hours." She smiled faintly at the memory. "Da kept his whiskey locked up after that."

Matthew rubbed his hand over his mouth as he fought not to laugh. "Then I think ye should be careful with the wine. Always best to go slow, take time to learn what and how much ye can drink and still remain sensible."

"Oh." She cautiously sipped the wine. "It does not taste as mighty as the whiskey did."

"Nay, but enough of it can be."

"That seems a shame." She had another bite of her food. "How did you find out about it all?"

"By getting mightily drunk on several occasions. Nay verra proud moments for me. My brothers take great pleasure in reminding me of each and every one."

Abigail laughed then suddenly thought of her brother and her amusement fled. "My brother was just reaching that age when the Rebs came and took him."

He reached across the table and stroked her clenched hands. "I hope, for your sake, he returns from this war and finds ye."

"So do I. It is difficult at times to accept that I have lost my whole family."

"I am sorry for that, lass," he said quietly. "I was lucky to settle here with all my brothers, but my parents were killed before we reached a place to settle. My elder brother, Iain, is the one I praise for that success. I believe he carries a few scars on his heart though. We have a stockade around our house." He smiled faintly at her look of surprise. "We get travelers wanting to spend a night or two inside the walls because they think it is a fort."

He shared the last of the bread and cheese with her. Matthew finished off his wine as she told him a few stories about her brother and he told her a few about his. When she began to quietly sip her wine, he collected up what he needed to return to its place in the house and cleared off the table. Then he moved to her side, took her by the hand, and led her to a large settee draped in cloths to keep off the dust.

As she sat down, a little surprised by the lack of a cloud of dust rising up, Abigail watched Matthew. They had had a pleasant meal and she was curious about what he planned to do now. She thought it strange that she was feeling nervous now, after an enjoyable dinner. When he sat down next to her, she took another sip of wine and then turned away to set the glass on a table next to the settee. When she turned back he was right there at her side and her heart made that odd little skip again that continued to surprise her.

Matthew could think of nothing to say so he just tugged her into his arms and kissed her. She returned his kiss with an eagerness that had him hardening nearly to the point of pain. He was going to have her tonight if she allowed it. If not, he knew it would happen soon. No one could return a kiss with the eagerness she returned his unless their blood was stirred as much as his was.

Abigail was getting drunk on his kisses. She did not complain when he inched her body down until he could lie on top of her because she liked the feel of his hard body on top of her, particularly the part he settled so eagerly between her legs. She knew she ought to be shocked, and a tiny part of her mind was, but most of her was delighting in the proof of how much he hungered for her.

When he began to kiss her neck, pausing to occasionally stroke it with his tongue, she became aware of the fact that he was undoing the buttons on her bodice. A little clarity came to her thoughts and Abbie considered the fact that she should stop him. Then he brushed a kiss over the top of one breast while massaging the other. Such a wide range of feelings were stirred inside of her, she was unable to say a word and certainly not the word *stop*.

"Lieutenant? Miss Jenson?"

Abbie struggled to sit up and an already standing Matthew pulled her up by one hand. She hurried to do up her gown and was just combing her fingers through her hair when Mabel came to the doorway. She knew the woman could guess what she had been doing but forced herself not to blush as she tied her hair with the ribbon that had fallen out at some point.

"What is it, Mabel?" she asked, pleased with the calm evident in her voice.

"We can't find Noah."

"What? Where could he go?"

Mabel started twisting her hands together. "We do not know, which is why I was sent to find you. I knew you were here because the lieutenant had mentioned it when he collected up the things I had put aside for him. I am sorry I had to interrupt your time together."

Abigail waved that aside. "Don't fret over that. Just tell me when Noah vanished." When Matthew held out her coat, she quickly put it on, keeping her eyes fixed on Mabel.

"He was just in his room; he went up there after lingering in the kitchen for a while. All the lightning bugs were out behind the house and the child could not stop watching them. It was not until they moved farther down the hill that he left. He said he was tired and since he is still growing he knows he should get his sleep at night."

"Oh, dear."

"What?" asked Matthew.

"I have begun to learn that when Noah mentions how he is growing, he is after something," said Abbie, and she smiled apologetically at Matthew. "This was very nice, but I think I better go and see what the child has done."

He took her arm and Mabel's and started toward the door. "Ye have some idea of where the lad might be?"

"I think I might. I shall just have to have a look."

"I will help ye look."

She did not refuse the help for she just might need it. "Why come for me, Mabel?"

"Because the boy has taken to you. Thought you must have spent a lot of time with him so you might know what he has done."

"Oh, I have a good idea, and it could well be the end of his 'growing.'" Abigail smiled when Mabel laughed.

When they reached the house, Abbie asked Matthew to wait for her and hurried up the stairs to check the children's rooms then her own. She trudged back down and headed for the kitchen. She knew the child had gone out after the lightning bugs, obviously forgetting there were all those nasty biting bugs out at night as well. It did not make her feel very kindly toward him that he was forcing her out into them just to find him.

"He came out here, didnae he?"

"He did. He loves the lightning bugs. Loves them so much he forgot about these," she growled and slapped a mosquito that had landed on her arm.

She wandered down the hill and heard a scrambling noise in the brush. "Noah?"

"Abbie! Come see the bugs. There are so many of them."

"I know," she grumbled and accepted Matthew's hand as she continued down the hill and kept slapping at the mosquitoes trying to feast on her.

She found the child crouched in the bushes, a jar in his hand already holding several lightning bugs. The fact that he had few mosquitoes around him annoyed her. The traitorous things left him and headed for her.

"What are you doing, young man?" She could tell

by the way his small shoulders stiffened that he knew he was in trouble.

"Catching lightning bugs. My mother used to do it with me and then we would set the jar in my room and snuff the light out. It was nice."

She gently touched his hair. "It sounds it. A very nice memory to have and hold close. But you should have told one of the adults that you were doing it. They thought you were in your room and got terribly worried when they could not find you."

"Oh. I am sorry."

"Well, I think you will have to say so to them."

"Now?"

"Yes, because although you and Matthew don't seem to be having any trouble with all these silly biting things . . ."

"Skeeters," Noah said and grinned. "They are skeeters."

"Fine. I see them as the Devil's minions and they are feasting on me so we will go back inside." When the boy did not immediately move she said, "Now."

Noah got up with a heavy sigh and screwed the cap onto his jar tightly. To her annoyance, he scrambled up the hill with ease while she practically had to have Matthew drag her up. Once inside the kitchen she listened to Noah very politely apologize to Mabel as she took the time to help Abbie wash off her arms. Abbie took the damp cloth, rinsed it out, and carefully wiped her face. She did not look forward to tomorrow when all the bites she had gotten would begin to itch. As she dabbed herself dry and smoothed on some cream Mabel gave her she sent Noah up to bed promising she would be along in a moment.

"Those skeeters really liked you," said Mabel, and Matthew grinned as he nodded.

"I know. Wretched things. Well, I thank you for a very nice evening, Matthew. Now I best go have a chat with Mr. I Am A Growing Boy."

He kissed her quickly and nodded at Mabel before leaving. Abbie could not fully suppress a sigh. She felt an odd mix of relief and disappointment that they had been interrupted.

The moment she reached the children's room Noah smiled at her where he was tucked neatly up in his bed. The rest of the children were asleep, or pretending to be so she spoke quietly to Noah. Not only did she not want to disturb them if they were sleeping, but did not wish to scold Noah in a way that could lead to teasing later if they were not really asleep.

"I understand your fascination with these bugs but it was wrong to go outside without letting anyone know what you were doing." She held up her hand to stop his words when he opened his mouth. "I know you are growing but you are not grown, certainly not grown enough to go out at night all on your own and with no one knowing where you are."

"How grown do I have to be?"

"A lot more than you are now. Something else, dear. You will have to let the bugs go in the morning."

"Why?"

"Because they will die in that jar."

He gave the jar a horrified glance. "Really?"

"Yes."

"How do you know?"

She sighed. "Because the ones I caught died in the jar. They are not made to be held in a jar to light up a room."

"You used to catch lightning bugs?"

"I did. My da would go with me."

"Okay. I will set them free in the morning. 'Night, Abbie."

"And?"

"And what?"

"What else will you not do?"

"Go out without letting anyone know I am and where I am going."

"Very good." She kissed his cheek and made her way to her own room.

"Did you find him?" asked Julia as Abbie began to undress.

Startled, Abbie swung around to stare at the woman. "You startled me. I thought you were asleep."

"I was. Almost. It is difficult to get comfortable at the moment. So, find him?"

"Yes. He was out back catching lightning bugs."

"Oh, I did that a few times when I was very young."

"So did I, but I believe he is now clear on the fact that he needs to tell someone what he is doing so they don't panic when they can't find him. And that it would be a good idea not to go out alone."

"Oh, good." Julia closed her eyes. "People were afraid and worried that the major would get angry since he gave the children into our care."

Climbing into bed, Abbie fought to relax. She was growing too close to young Noah. That could cause him pain when she had to leave. She had little doubt it would cause her some. Yet she doubted she would be able to draw back now. She smiled faintly when she thought how Noah would not allow it.

At some point soon, she would have to decide what she should do about the boy. She was not wed so could not really raise him as her child even if she found a home to take him to. It was sad, but she had to face facts. A young unmarried woman would have a difficult time raising a child, not to mention how suspicious it would make many about whether he was actually adopted, or whether it was just her trying to hide her own misdeeds by pretending he was.

Deciding such thoughts would make sleep difficult she turned her mind to Matthew. There were problems there too, but he was a bit more pleasant to think about. Abbie knew where they had been headed when Mabel had interrupted them, and she now feared she would have followed him there willingly. It was something she had to think about. Matthew had not even made any mention about how he felt about her, she thought crossly.

Flipping onto her back she stared up at the ceiling and sighed. Thinking about Matthew was not much better than worrying about Noah. It was going to be a very long night. She was getting very tired of those. She badly wanted to go back to a time when worries and fears did not disturb her rest.

Chapter Six

"Damnation, this is getting ridiculous," complained James as he mounted his horse and joined Matthew in riding back to town. "Maybe we should just quietly move out. This town is not worth this."

"Cannae do that," said Matthew. "The major thinks it is better to stand firm."

"He hasn't seen what is gathering."

"True, but we have gathered a goodly number of soldiers as weel. All the scouts have returned."

"I know. Reckon the Rebs are just deciding when and how to come at us."

"Slow thinkers." Matthew grinned when James laughed.

"Or they know we are spying on them and hesitate just to make us relax our guard."

"True. That is verra possible. But for all they ken, we are getting weel prepared for a battle."

"They may be right although being well prepared isn't always a guarantee of winning."

"True again, but I think we have done weel. Still it is a puzzle that they have made no move for a month now. Might as weel get back to headquarters and leave them to it. They cannae be that indecisive. They cannae puzzle over it too much longer either. It is never good to have an army sitting about for too long."

James grunted in agreement and waved at a few men as they rode through the guard posts. Matthew also took time to greet a few. It was comforting to find the guard alert. He could not shake the feeling that they were headed for a hard fight.

His thoughts veered to Abigail and he wondered if he should warn her. That would be against orders but he was becoming more and more uncomfortable about giving her no warning. He did not like leaving her unsuspecting and unready. He would feel better if he knew she was at least keeping her weapon close to hand.

When they reached the house the major now claimed as his headquarters, Matthew and James went in to make their report. As they entered the office, Matthew studied the man behind the desk. With his head bent over some papers, it was all too evident that the man was beginning to lose his hair. Matthew hoped that was the man's only loss to the war. Major Cummings was a good man, a fine officer who was neither too harsh nor too kind. He was also an excellent strategist.

"Are the Rebs still there?" Major Cummings asked as he looked up from the paper.

"Aye, sir," Matthew replied. "They have added a few more men but the constant trail of men coming in has ended. We just cannae figure out what they plan."

"But they have enough to attack?"

"They do and they also have a cannon."

"Damn. Well, we have three so we ought to be able to counter that. How many men?"

"Hard to say, sir," said James. "Not easy to count them, but I would say they have enough."

"MacEnroy?"

"Aye, sir. There are at least several companies in the camp. I even recognized one or two men as ones who led a couple of skirmishes against us."

Major Cummings rubbed his hands over his face. "I am weary of skirmishes. Little clashes where we kill each other, farms and towns get destroyed, and too many who are not even soldiers end up dying. God alone knows what is going to be left of the people who lived in these hills."

"Too few, that's certain, sir," muttered James.

"Well, we'll keep a watch on them. They may not be interested in us but there is no way to be sure of that. One cannon doesn't imply such an engagement nor does our size or theirs. That doesn't mean they won't come looking for some supplies. Or, hell, some women. Keep the watch on and alert. I have been getting rumors that a big move is planned on the South so they may be gathering to go and fight in that. So, all we can do is keep alert."

"Aye, sir." Matthew saluted and walked out, James right behind him.

"I checked and all four of us have about a month left before we would have to sign up again and decide if we are staying in or not," said James.

"Are ye staying in?"

"I don't rightly know. Damn sick of the killing. Too much of it is senseless shooting of farmers and town folk who are just trying to survive and hold on to their land. A lot of the army is conscripts now. There are just too many times when I have to stop myself from just turning my horse east and riding on home. I damn sure don't want to be in the South at this time of year."

Matthew nodded slowly. "I feel the same. I just dinnae have to ride so far to get home. But it weighs on me what is being done in these hills."

"Is your family in danger?"

"Nay more than anyone else. My brother Iain just sent word that he is a father to another, a brother for young Ned. He mentioned a few visitors who were sent on their way. The town is gone like so many others round here, and he doubts many of the ones who fled will come back so getting supplies is a chore and often dangerous."

"As it is everywhere."

"Aye, save maybe where ye come from. I doubt Maine gets many Rebs and Night Riders. As the major hinted, appears the war is headed south."

James shook his head. "This is all going to leave a scar that'll be a long time in healing."

"I suspicion a lot of countries have one, but ye are right. At this moment, I just want to wash the stink of horse off, eat something, and then go to see if Abbie wants to go walking."

"So, you and little Abbie . . ."

Hearing the amusement in the man's voice, Matthew nudged his horse until he was a few feet ahead of James. The man hooted with laughter and Matthew fought the urge to hit him. Instead he focused on what he needed to do to get to Abbie before it got too late to go out for a walk.

Abbie sighed when Julia came in and sat down beside her. The woman did not even try to hide her pregnancy now and a few of the women openly snubbed her despite the ring on her finger. For a while Julia had avoided all of them but now she came around to share a meal and talk to Abbie.

"Robert said the officers are expecting trouble soon," Julia said quietly.

"Well, I expect we will be told what to do to remain as safe as possible."

"I hope so. The lieutenant has not said anything to you?"

"He asked if I keep my rifle close but nothing else. I asked Mrs. Beaton where she had put it and, despite her many complaints, it is now tucked in a corner in whatever room I am in."

Julia looked at the rifle set against the wall in a corner near the window. "You can shoot that?"

"I can, and Matthew must think me competent or he would not ask me to keep it close in case we face any of this trouble no one is warning us about."

Julia shook her head. "Men don't like worrying women about things. Silly because, if we are warned about things, we would keep a better watch, don't you think?"

"I do but, obviously, the officers have decided otherwise."

"I often wonder how a man gets to be an officer."

"I have no idea."

"Do you ever have, well, feelings about something about to happen? Something bad or good?"

"Not really. Nothing strange. Why?"

"I am not sure, but I have a very bad feeling about what is going to happen."

"Not sure what you can do about such feelings. Do you run? If so, how do you know which way to go? Or do you run out of the house to escape an unknown fear only to get run over by a wagon? You are probably just worried about Robert."

Julia smiled a little. "Well, yes, I am. I am expecting his child. I have the ring and the paper but I would much rather have the man, too."

"Of course you would." Abigail patted Julia on the arm. "You married a soldier, dear. I suspect worry is a hazard of that."

"Not so sure I like that," Julia muttered.

"You left yourself little choice and I think that alone says you chose right."

"Maybe." Julia yawned and hastily covered her mouth. "I have to go and lie down. I am always so tired lately."

"That is because you are carrying a child. Lots of rest is important."

"I suppose. With all the food I eat and the rest I need, I begin to feel like a pig being readied for the slaughter."

Abigail laughed. "That is not a pleasant thought. Go on, go have a rest."

Watching Julia walk off, Abbie fought down her worry over the woman. Julia was a deeply sensitive woman who loved this fellow Robert. If anything happened to the young man, she hated to think of how it would devastate the girl. Julia carried his child, but she was not sure the woman had the strength to remember how important that was.

It was a worry she could not solve or plan for so Abbie decided to put it aside. She had almost finished all her flowers on the hem, hiding the majority of the spots, and idly thought on what she could do next. Then a little shadow fell over her sewing and she looked up to stare into Noah's bright eyes, surprised to find him downstairs. None of the children came down, but Noah was obviously getting confident of his welcome, at least from her.

"Hello, Noah. What might you want?" she asked.

"Are you gonna read to us tonight?"

"I thought I would. Why? Don't you want me to?"

"Oh yes, but I was wondering if you know how we could get a new book. You've done read all the others to us and we were thinking it'd be real nice to have something new."

She frowned as he sat down next to her in the chair, gently nudging her to the side until he had the room he needed. Abbie realized she had no idea how to find a new book for the children. She then tried to think if she knew any stories so that she might just tell them one but her mind was suddenly totally empty.

"I think I will have to ask the other ladies. Hunt around a little. I have no idea where or how one could get one in this town."

"The store?"

"I thought about that, but I saw nothing in there the few times I went in. The man has enough trouble just getting in food supplies. I doubt he thinks much of getting things like a children's book. But I will ask."

"Maybe your soldier friend would know?"

"Huh. Maybe he would. I will ask him, too."

"I will tell the others you are going to go looking," he said, hopped off the chair, and raced off to go back to the children's room.

"What did you just promise the child?" asked Rose as she sat down in the chair opposite Abbie.

"I did not promise anything. They want a new book to hear at story time and I said I would look for one."

Rose laughed. "To a child that can sometimes sound like a promise. Why not just tell them a story?"

"Thought about that but suddenly could not think

of a single one. Odd, because my da was always telling me stories."

"Ah, yes, that is often the way. You will recall them but not when you need to. I am not sure where or how one could get hold of a child's storybook in this town. Most of the ones who had children and would have one fled the minute the Union marched in. I doubt they left any behind." Rose looked away and rubbed her chin. "Maybe I can find out if any of the women know a good story and we can write it down."

"Make our own book?"

"Something like that. I have some ledger books we could use or the general store had a few journals for sale. Most women do not keep them because they are expensive or they just don't see the point in writing about what is an ordinary day. You know, 'Well, I washed Henry's long johns today,'" Rose said in a slightly higher tone of voice. "Not really of interest."

"Fair enough," Abbie said and chuckled. "We will see how many have something to contribute."

"Between all of us, we must have a few. I suspect we could make up a good book."

Abbie nodded. She and Rose complained about the lack of goods due to the war for a while and then Rose wandered back to where the other women sat. Abbie tried to recall if she had put aside a favorite child's book in her chests but could not remember. It would be worth a look, she decided, and then came a rap on the door.

Mrs. Beaton got up from her knitting and went to answer the door. A moment later Abbie heard the sound of a very familiar male voice. Her heart skipped and she cursed herself for an idiot. It obviously could not tell the difference between romance and friendship.

"The lieutenant is here to see you, Miss Jenson," Mrs. Beaton said in a cool voice. "I put him in the parlor."

Like he is a vase, Abbie thought, and bit back a smile as she rose and walked to the parlor. Matthew stood by the window, staring out, with his hands clasped behind his back. He stood straight as if at attention like the soldier he was. She shut the door and he turned to face her and her mindless heart skipped a beat again.

"I dinnae believe Mrs. Beaton is verra fond of soldiers coming round to visit the ladies here," he said.

"No, she isn't, but she is smart enough to know she can do little about it, I guess. And I begin to think Mrs. Beaton is fond of very little. I also think some soldiers come round not just to see a woman but to get a touch of all they left behind, if that makes sense."

"It does. They hanker for a wee bit of the gentility they used to know. And how have ye been doing?"

"Well, I have been doing as fine as can be expected. There is one thing. Noah thinks they need a new storybook, or five. None of us knows where to get one. Rose suggested we all write out stories we recall being told and that is a very good idea but it will be a while before that is put together."

"I can ask around. Come and sit with me and then, maybe, we could go for a stroll."

She laughed as she sat down on the settee and he sat down rather close to her. "I doubt this town has seen so many people going for a stroll in however long it has been here."

"Probably not but that might be a good thing. Such sights can give some the feeling of normal life and ease their fears."

"One does not want them to ease them too much, I think. Not in the middle of such a bloody war."

She realized he had draped his arm along the back of the settee and was now playing with her hair. It was oddly soothing to have him dragging his fingers through her hair so she decided to say nothing. She relaxed her head against the back of the settee and stared up at the ceiling to find it was another elaborately plastered ceiling.

"True enough. Being always alert for trouble is what will get them through this."

"I begin to fear this war will never end."

She tensed when he kissed her face, right near the corner of her eye. Even as she started to turn to ask him what he was doing, she knew it was not a good idea. He was so close when she turned, she could see what thick eyelashes he had. Then he kissed her on the mouth.

It was a deep, hungry kiss and Abbie quickly wrapped her arms around his neck to keep steady. When he put his tongue in her mouth she nearly jumped but the feel of it stroking the inside of her mouth swept away her shock and replaced it with the urge to hold on tighter. She even tentatively returned the strokes of his tongue with hers and a low growl sounded in her ears. He slowly pulled back and she stared at him, a little afraid she probably looked like a startled frog.

"We best be careful or Mrs. Beaton will banish me from the house," he said.

Let her just try, Abigail thought as she leaned back and found she was still clutching his neck. "Sorry," she mumbled as she hastily removed her arms.

"Quite all right," he said, and grinned as he stood

up and held out his hand. "How about we take a little walk?"

"Is it cold?" she asked as she took his hand and walked with him as they left the room.

"Just a small nip in the air."

She put on her coat and let him take her by the hand to lead her outside. They meandered down the street for a while in a comfortable silence. Abbie decided she liked the fact that they did not need to fill the silence with empty talk. Then she thought of something she really wanted to know.

"I did not see Boyd in the infirmary yesterday. He is all right, isn't he?"

"Aye. I only saw him the other day and he has not worsened."

"Good. I was a little worried about that but did not dare question the doctor. Mostly afraid of what he might say. The arm still does not work."

"Nay, but the doctor had a few suggestions."

"Work it, right?"

"Aye, if only to keep it from withering from disuse. I will see him tomorrow most like and can work with him. It is his spirits I dinnae ken what to do about."

Abbie nodded. "He must be so disappointed that it has not returned to normal. It is nearly as bad as losing it completely as so many have."

"It will take time for him to see it is better to have it useless than to lose it," she said and squeaked when he suddenly stopped and pulled her into his arms. "I thought we were strolling."

"This is a very important part of strolling with a bonnie lass."

"Or so men tell themselves," she said, and threw her arms around his neck.

He pulled her hard up against him. Abbie liked the way he felt against her, all warm and hard. She had done enough nursing to know that one particular part of him was very hard indeed so she decided those kisses were not signs of mere friendship. It lifted her spirits considerably.

Abbie leaned back a little to look at him, glancing around to make sure they were still alone. A glint in a tree behind caught her attention as she glanced over his shoulder. She squinted toward it, saw some movement in the branches around where it was, and felt terror chill her body. She shoved at him and he stumbled back.

"Get down!" she yelled, grabbing his hand to pull him down to the ground with her.

They hit the ground a little harder than she had intended just as a shot was taken, the bullet passing over their heads. Matthew swore viciously and Abbie had to agree with his sentiments as he started to crawl toward a spot between the buildings they were in front of. She did her best not to slow him down and ignored the occasional sound of something tearing.

Matthew sat down with his back against the wall of the building and tugged Abbie over to sit next to him. "Ye need to get back to the house. Can ye get there by going the back way?"

Abbie nodded. "I know the way."

"Get everyone to go into the jail. It is a sturdy brick building that should protect all of ye."

"What will you do?"

"Run back to headquarters and tell the major we may be under attack."

She kissed him. "Be careful."

"Same to ye, lass. Stay low and in the shadows."

Abbie scurried to the end of the alley and then

bolted for the Beaton house. They had not walked far so she was there in minutes. Bursting into the house through the kitchen she ran for the sitting room. All the women in there stared at her when she ran into the room. She was pleased to see that Julia was there as well so she did not have to worry about dragging her out of bed.

"Abbie! What is wrong?" asked Rose. "You are a bit of a mess. Did you have trouble with the lieutenant?"

"No, of course not. We were shot at and had to duck into an alley. Now we have to run for the jail." Abbie fought to catch her breath. "We are under attack."

"Why can we not stay here? It has survived other attacks," said Mrs. Beaton.

"Matthew says the jail is safer. Too many windows here and it could be set on fire. They do that to make the people run out so they can shoot them. The jail has thick brick walls. So we better get moving. I will get the children."

Hoping the women would get themselves together, Abbie ran up the stairs. She hurried into the children's room and grabbed their coats off the hooks by the door. When she turned to face them, they were all staring at her with wide eyes.

"What's wrong?" asked Noah.

"We have to go to the jail and wait there until the soldiers say it is safe."

"The jail? But I haven't done nothing wrong," said Noah even as he climbed out of bed.

"Anything wrong," she muttered then said, "The jail is a sturdier building with brick walls and barred windows."

"The war is coming here?" asked Mary in a small, shaky voice.

"It definitely appears to be," Abbie replied as she

helped them on with their coats. "One man shot at us and Matthew said to get to the jail while he went to tell the major. He is a soldier so I figure he must know what he is about and has good reason to believe an attack is coming."

"Are you coming, too?" asked Noah as he took her hand.

"Of course I am. Now, we need to move and to get the women moving."

Abigail was pleased to see that all the women had their coats on and carried bags they had filled with whatever they felt they needed to hold fast to. She grabbed her sewing basket, sent up a quick prayer that the house would not be burned as she grabbed her rifle and some ammunition, and ushered everyone out the back door. The sound of guns firing followed them as they scurried down behind the houses until they reached the jail. She went around to the front, saw no sign of soldiers, and waved everyone inside the building.

Shutting and barring the door she finally sat down and wondered idly just when she had been elected to be the caretaker of everyone. The sounds of battle were far from comforting but she leaned against the wall and closed her eyes. Panic and the need to rush could be exhausting, she decided. When she felt a small body sit next to her and lean on her, she halfway opened one eye, forced a smile for Noah, and put her arm around him. It was going to be yet another long night, she decided when she heard the boom of cannon fire. Maybe she needed to start sleeping during the day.

* * *

Matthew aimed his rifle and took down another soldier. James lay at his side in the brush and did the same. It was not a particularly large attack. More of a skirmish, an annoyance, as if the Rebs sent out the restless soldiers just to get them out of camp. It was possible it was actually some of the marauders who had caused so much trouble. The ones who could not resist the temptation of so many "blue bellies" so near. They often wore Confederate uniforms.

This time he had a personal reason to fight anyone headed to the town to do harm. Abbie had gotten everyone to the jail. He had seen the light in the window as he had run out with the others to try and stop every one of the attackers at the edge of the town. He was not sure how much he cared about the girl, but he certainly did not want to allow anyone a chance to do her any harm.

Just as he decided he and James could move he saw several Rebs gallop toward the town off to the right. "Damn, some of the buggers got by us."

"Best go and see what they are after," James said as he crawled on his belly down the slope of the small hill they were on.

Matthew followed him. At the base of the hill they stood up and ran in a crouch toward the town. They stood up straight as soon as they reached a building. Looking down the street Matthew saw the barrel of a rifle poke out of the jail's front window. Abbie was alive but it was obvious there was some trouble.

"The lass is under fire."

"Go on, then. Time to be a hero." James grinned when Matthew glared at him. "Whoever it is, he is on that roof, but I think there may be more men at that end of town. I will watch your back."

Knowing there were few better for the job, Matthew began to make his careful way toward the jail. It made him angry to see how many of their own men now littered the street. A quick look told him many of them had been shot from behind as they had run to join the battle. These men wanted to kill and he was not going to allow them to add Abbie or anyone she cared about to their list.

Chapter Seven

A shot came through the window, shattering it and scattering the glass all over the floor. The women screamed and huddled against the wall. Abigail checked Noah to make certain he had not been harmed then told him to go back with the other children who were huddled down in one of the cells. She sighed, ran, and grabbed her rifle then loaded it before going back to the window and quickly brushing the glass on the floor aside. She knocked out the rest of the glass with the butt of her rifle. Looking out, she spotted a man in gray on the roof of a building across the street. He was shooting soldiers as they ran toward the battle that was raging at the end of the street, shooting many of them in the back. Abigail aimed carefully and shot him. She was a little surprised when he fell screaming into the street for she had not thought her shot was that accurate.

She reloaded her gun and when she looked back out a Union soldier was crouched over the Reb, relieving him of all weapons. He then grabbed him, put him over his shoulder, and hurried to the house being used as an infirmary. Abigail wondered what the man was thinking as he gave aid to the enemy, one who had killed a number of his fellow soldiers. She swiftly prayed that both men survived the day.

"I think I smell smoke," said Julia and hurried over to crouch down near Abigail.

"You do. Someone set the Boardman house on fire. Set the fire at the back from what I can glimpse through the windows."

Mrs. Beaton suddenly appeared at Abigail's side, knelt down, and looked out at the burning house. "That is Betsy's house. I pray her and her children can get out. There she is!"

Abigail watched as a woman rushed out carrying a baby, three other small children following her. A man came out behind them. Mrs. Beaton stuck her head out the window to call to the woman. Abigail quickly yanked her back inside and looked out in time to see a Reb come around the side of the house and shoot the man who fell onto his stomach and clutched at his leg.

The soldier stepped closer and Betsy obviously told her children to run because the three bigger ones started racing for the jailhouse. Betsy stood by her husband, baby still clutched in her arms, and appeared to be arguing with the soldier, as she moved her own body between him and her husband. Abigail had to wonder what the woman thought she could do.

Using the confusion to her advantage, Abigail again took careful aim. Betsy clearly decided arguing was getting her nowhere and had begun to hurl insults if the look on the man's face was anything to judge by. The soldier abruptly aimed his weapon at her and the angry look on his face told Abbie the woman had only succeeded in making sure she died next to her husband. Abigail shifted her aim a bit and fired, hitting the soldier in the arm he was using to aim his gun. All the ladies in the room stared at her as she reloaded.

Mrs. Beaton recovered first and yelled at Betsy to get moving. Still somehow holding on to the babe, the woman put her husband's arm around her shoulders, then put her arm around his waist and they started moving toward the jail quickly if awkwardly. They presented a very easy target and Abbie tried to keep a close watch on every possible way an enemy could come at them. Then there was another shot fired. Abbie cursed and looked around even harder to see who she had missed spotting. Betsy's husband was hit in the arm. It caused him to stumble into his wife, nearly sending them both to the ground.

Abigail cursed because now the pair was nearly helpless. Finally she saw there was another soldier in gray in the alley next to the burning house. He was in shadow but she took aim and hoped for a good shot, good enough to put the man down long enough for Betsy to get inside the jail with her wounded husband.

Taking another steadying deep breath, she fired. The man should have fallen backward if she had hit him but, instead, he fell facedown. Abigail was puzzled by that until a man in a blue uniform stepped out of the same alley and ran toward Betsy and her husband. When he stopped to put his arm around the man, she could see it was Matthew. She was wondering where he had come from when she realized there were far more important things to worry about. Matthew was now exposed to anyone who was still able to shoot.

"Mrs. Beaton, you should let them in and make

sure the children are not standing right in front of the door."

The woman glared at her but did what she had asked. Abigail shook her head and returned to watching the street to make sure no one attacked Matthew while he helped Betsy save her husband. Mrs. Beaton might have once been rich and pampered, but by the time this war was finally over, Abigail had to wonder if the woman would still be. When she heard the sound of Matthew's voice just outside the room, she relaxed.

"Someone get a couple of blankets to put on the floor," she called out, and heard the women hurry to obey what even she recognized had sounded like an order. "And try to stay out of the line of the windows." She did not move from her post until Matthew crouched by her side.

"I can watch now," he said. "The man needs help."

Abbie set her rifle down and looked toward the man he had helped inside. The women had not only brought blankets, they had found a cot in one of the cells to spread them on. It was going to make it easier to tend his wounds. His wife knelt beside him after handing her baby over to Maude, gripping the hand of his unwounded arm and whispering what were probably encouraging words. Abbie quickly studied the man's wounds and decided if she did not have to dig around for a bullet, they would not prove to be too much trouble for her. Even better the wound on his leg was not so high up that there would be any difficulty in maintaining his modesty. Bracing herself for what was to come she took a closer look that told her both bullets had passed through and she breathed a sigh of relief.

"I need his shirt off," she said and the wife quickly

complied. "Julia? My sewing basket, please, and some whiskey if there is any to be found."

A quick look told her the bullet had not only gone through the arm but appeared to have missed anything vital. "I hope you have no sentimental attachment to these pants," she said as she knelt by the cot and took scissors from her basket to cut off the pant leg above the knee then cut the long johns he wore beneath them.

"You are a very lucky man, sir," she said when she saw that the bullet had passed right through his leg as well.

"Lucky? I got shot! Twice!" he said, his voice hoarse with pain.

"True, but both bullets had the courtesy to leave cleanly. I don't have to go digging around for them, sir."

"Oh. Guess that does sound lucky. Name is Harvey, Harvey Boardman."

"This is going to sting, Harvey," she said as she held up a bottle of whiskey and idly wondered if someone had stolen most of the sheriff's supply, "but I need to make certain the wound is clean." She got ready to pour some whiskey on the wound in his arm. "Take deep breaths and let them out slowly."

"That helps?"

"Sometimes. Ready?"

As she washed out his wounds, he breathed as she had suggested but still choked on a scream. Abigail was pleased when she was done and dabbed his wounds dry. She then wiped the blanket as clean as she could. She grabbed her needle and began to stitch up the wound on his leg. First the entrance wound and then the exit one. After she tied it off she looked at her work then stared at the needle and the tiny piece of thread left.

"Oh, dear."

"What?" demanded Betsy. "What is wrong?"

"Oh, nothing with him or the wound." Abigail sighed. "I just happened to notice that I forgot to change the thread from my embroidery work to a nice black thread." She looked at the man and grinned. "I fear I just closed the wound in your leg with yellow thread. Bright yellow."

Betsy laughed and her husband smiled, although the expression quickly turned to a grimace when he inadvertently shifted his wounded arm. Abigail hurried to rethread her needle with black thread and went to work stitching up his arm wound.

When she was done, she told his wife to clean the sweat from his face as she bandaged up his wounds. By the time Betsy was done and looked up, the three children had moved closer to stand by their mother. Their father tried gamely to smile at them and Abigail stood up.

"He should rest now." She looked around for Mrs. Beaton but could not find the woman so she just placed a blanket over the man. "It looks as if you will be staying here for a while."

As she left him to his family, Abigail cleaned up what she could then went back to the window to sit near Matthew. "Any trouble out there?"

"Nay. Think this skirmish is as good as done. We even blew their cannon up."

"One less thing to worry about."

He leaned over and brushed a kiss over her mouth, smiling when she blushed and looked around to see who had been watching. No one had been hurt aside from Betsy's husband so she began to relax. Julia was asleep in one of the cells and the children were watching Betsy's children after drawing them into the cell they were sharing. Matthew was astonished at how calm everyone seemed to be.

"Soon I will have to go and see how James is doing. He was watching my back," he said, drawing Abbie's attention his way again.

"I pray nothing happened to him. Do you think this attack will continue?"

"Nay. As I said, I am fair certain it is almost done. Some of the Rebs in a camp we were watching clearly decided they could not tolerate us so near without doing something. I was even thinking it might not be the men from that camp but some of the marauders who plague these hills."

"But they wore gray."

"Many of them do. They probably are considered part of the Rebel army but they usually do just as they want and are far more brutal and uncaring about what one calls the innocents."

"Well, one of them is in the infirmary so you may get an answer to that."

"Since these men got inside the town limits I believe I should go check on the doctor."

"It might be wise. Even if the doctor remains blind to the uniform someone wears, I suspect such men as you think these are would not care about that. I glanced toward the infirmary when I was coming here and saw no sign of trouble, but it is only lightly guarded."

"Stay here until I send word that it is safe to go back to the house."

"I will."

Matthew kissed her again and chuckled at her blush. He then stood up and after making sure the back door was secured well, went out and headed to the infirmary. He found Boyd standing and holding a basin of water for the doctor. Then he glanced at the man the doctor was working on and tensed. It was young Robert whose new wife was resting peacefully in a jail cell. Edging closer he sighed because the man had several wounds and, by the looks of the rags tossed to the floor, had already lost a lot of blood.

"It is bad," Boyd said quietly. "The doctor can't seem to stop the bleeding from the gut wound."

"Think I should get Julia?"

"If it is safe to do so," said the doctor as he stood up, "then get her. The man doesn't have much time," he added softly. "He was posted in a tree and was shot out of it. The landing was hard and there is a lot of internal bleeding I can't seem to ease."

"Aw, hell. I can get her." Matthew left and his steps slowed rapidly as he neared the jail, but he took a deep breath to steady himself and rapped on the door.

Abbie opened it and frowned up at him. "Is it clear for us to leave?"

"I think so but that is not why I am here. Where is Julia?" He watched Abbie's eyes widen and knew she had just realized why he was back so soon.

"Robert," she whispered.

"I fear so. Can you get her?"

Abbie went and roused Julia then led her back to Matthew. A soft moan escaped the woman as Matthew told her about Robert and how he would want to see her. When Julia grabbed her hand, Abbie was startled.

"Come with me," Julia said, a note of pleading in her voice.

Abbie nodded and with Matthew's agreement told the others to go back to the Beaton house. Several of the women moved to help carry the cot with Harvey Boardman on it. Abbie walked with Julia to the infirmary and suddenly Julia stopped. The woman was so pale, Abbie feared she would pass out on the street. Matthew went inside and reappeared at the door a few moments later. Abbie suspected they had tidied up the scene as much as they could.

"Come on in, Julia. Robert will want to see you. He has been calling your name," Matthew added softly.

It was enough of an inducement and Julia followed him over to Robert's cot. Julia let go of Abbie and rushed to the man's side, kneeling down so she could whisper in his ear and kiss his pale cheek. Seeing Boyd standing there, Abbie moved next to him. A sad-eyed Boyd met her questioning look and shook his head. He did not have to say a word; the look on his face said it all. Abbie fought back the urge to cry because she knew Julia needed her to be strong.

"Ah, Julia, we would have been good and our child would have been happy," Robert said in a very weak voice.

"It will be. You just have to hang on." Julia clung to his hand while tears streamed down her face.

"Want to. Can't. All broken inside. Take the babe to my family. They will help you."

"No, Robbie, no. You will come with me."

There was a high note of burgeoning hysteria in Julia's voice and Abbie stepped closer. She noticed the doctor did as well. Julia just wept and held Robert's hand to her wet cheek. It was heartbreaking but Abbie knew the girl would need strong people to be at her side once Robert slipped away. And he would, Abbie thought sadly, because he already had the smell of death on him.

"Let my kin know when the babe comes. Promise me. Let them know," Robert said with a sudden show of strength.

"I will. I promise. But you can help me do it."

"No, darlin', I don't want nuthin' as much as I want to stay with you, but I can't. My luck has run out."

"Please don't leave me. Please."

"Give me a kiss, love."

Still weeping, Julia bent near and kissed him. She was just straightening up when the man lost his grip on life. Abbie jumped when Julia screamed but quickly grabbed her when she reached for Robert's body. Matthew stepped up and took over for Abbie, holding Julia firmly even as the woman started to slump down. When Julia was finally out cold he swung her up into his arms and looked at Abbie.

The doctor stepped up before she could and did a quick examination before turning to Abbie. "She has had a severe shock. They can often bring on labor in a woman close to her time so she will need to be watched. It could happen soon or take a few days depending on how well she recovers."

"I understand. I also fear she is not one who will overcome the shock easily," Abbie replied and accepted the small bottle the doctor gave her. "What is this for?"

"If she is too overwrought, it will calm her. Try to give her as little as possible since she is with child. You just want to try and keep her calm."

Abbie nodded. "Maybe she will be a quiet griever."

The doctor nodded and patted her on the shoulder. "It is very sad. He was very happy about his child, even talked to me about how one can best care for a babe. I think he would have been a good father."

Abbie suspected the same. She also had the feeling he would have been a pretty good husband, too. It was all just so sad, even Abbie felt choked up and knew she would have a good cry about it all later. She led Matthew out of the infirmary.

"It is sad," Matthew said.

"So sad. I wish I had another word for it. It seems like it deserves a much better word. She is not going to take this well. Julia is not a strong woman. She is one who is easily hurt. I think she had a lot of dreams wrapped around Robert and their marriage. Funny thing is she asked me earlier this week if I believed in people who can sense something bad or good happening to them."

"What did ye say?"

"I did not say yes or no, just pointed out a few ways it did not make sense to put much weight on a feeling. Now I am wondering if she was having a bad feeling about her future."

"Who has not had one in this war?"

"True."

She entered the Beaton house, pleased to see everyone had returned. The women all rushed over when Matthew stepped in holding Julia. "What happened to her?" asked Rose.

"Robert died," said Abbie.

"Oh no," said Rose, and all the others clapped a hand over their mouths as they gasped in shock.

"She at least got to speak to him before he passed," said Abbie, who then looked at Matthew. "Do you think you can get ahold of his information on his family? He was quite desperate for her to get in touch with them."

"If it is there, I will find it. Now, where is her bed?"

Abbie led him up the stairs. When he set Julia down, she took off the woman's shoes and tucked her in. It was her hope that Julia would sleep for a long time. It was what she needed and it could be enough to take away some of the shock. She doubted it could ease her pain. That would take a very long time.

Matthew took her by the hand and tugged her out of the room. He had the feeling she would be stuck in there a lot over the next few days. Julia did not strike him as a strong woman, and Abigail's words had confirmed that. The woman would carry her grief deeply and for a very long time, requiring a lot of sympathy and care. He would make sure he came by and dragged Abigail away from time to time.

"He will be buried as soon as can be. Do you think she will want to know?"

"Maybe. Just let me know and I will decide then. I have no idea how soon she will be able to handle anything. It is a decision I can only make at the last moment."

"All right." He brushed a kiss over her mouth. "Don't forget to get some rest."

"I won't."

She watched him go down the stairs, sighed, and then went into the room she shared with Julia. The woman was still sound asleep but she had turned onto her side so there was a chance she had already slipped into a natural sleep. Abbie threw herself down on her bed and then realized she still had her coat on. Forcing herself back up, she took it off, hung it up, and then changed into her nightgown. Once set, she checked again on Julia before climbing under the blankets and closing her eyes.

For a few moments, she gave in to the sadness she felt for two young people who had lost their chance at a full and possibly happy future. All because the two sides of the country could not agree. They were slaughtering their young with this war, she thought, and used a handkerchief to dab away the tears on her cheeks. Women were losing their beaus and husbands, the ones they had and the ones they might have had. Mothers were weeping over their sons and so many children had no fathers now. She closed her eyes, forcing herself to stop thinking of what was lost today, and trying to go to sleep. Just as she felt it slipping over her, pulling her mind and body down, she heard Julia.

Turning over, Abbie looked at Julia who was thrashing around in her bed. She got up wondering what could be done to soothe her when Julia sat up and screamed. Even as she hurried to the bed to grab the woman, she heard all the other women racing up the stairs to come to stand in the doorway.

"No, no, no, no!" Julia cried, and Abbie took her into her arms. "My beautiful Robbie. No, no, no, no. I want him back, Abbie. I want him back."

Stroking her hair, Abbie said, "I know you do, Julia. I am so very sorry."

"It is not fair," she whined then sobbed. "We would have been such a good family."

Abbie glanced at the women in the doorway and found no help because they were all crying silently and searching for their handkerchiefs. "I know and, yes, you're right. It is not fair but I fear, quite often, life is not fair. Robert should not be dead. Boyd should not be maimed in one arm. That man in the bed next to him should not have to be facing life with his legs gone at the knee. Children should not have to stand at their father's grave and wives should not have to bury their husbands. Parents should not have to weep over the grave of a son who never had the chance to give them grandchildren. All I can say is I am sorry. More sorry than I can ever say. It is the horrible cost of war, Julia."

"I know that." She sniffed and then continued crying. "I know it in my head. But my heart, Abbie! My heart keeps crying that it is not fair," she said, her words ending in a wail. "I would have made him so happy."

"Yes, you would have. Even the doctor thought so."

Julia pushed Abbie away and lay back down. She then noticed all the women standing in the doorway. "Oh. Hello. Sorry I am such a mess." She used the sheet to wipe at her eyes and all the ladies crowded around the bed, but it did little good because the tears kept flowing.

"No, dearie," said Maude as she patted Julia's arm. "Don't apologize. We just want you to know you are not alone."

"Thank you."

As the women comforted and soothed, a few even offering the truth of their husband's death, Julia calmed a little but Abbie was not fooled. She knew she was in for a few exhausting days. Julia saw her loss as unfair and Abbie was sure that was going to cause her to cling to her upset for quite a while. She did not expect the girl to get over her loss quickly under any circumstances—she certainly had not—but she did hope Julia did not hang on to this kind of grieving for too long. It could damage the child or worse, cause it to come before its time.

By the time the women left, Julia's eyes were closing. Abbie sat beside her until she fell asleep and then crawled into her own bed. She fell asleep quickly but suddenly she was yanked awake by deep wracking sobs. She glanced at the squat clock on the bedside table and saw that she had slept barely three hours. Getting up again, she glanced at the bottle the doctor had given her. Not yet, she thought, as she sat on Julia's bed and began to rub her friend's back. It was going to be a very long night though. Just once, she thought, she would like to have a peaceful night's sleep.

Abbie woke to Noah leaning over her and groaned. Then she recalled why she was so tired and looked over to find Julia fast asleep. She wished she could do the same but looked at Noah who grinned at her.

"What do you want?"

"Just wondering if you are going to sleep all morning."

"That would be nice." She rolled over, turning her back on him, but he tapped her on the shoulder.

She rolled back to look at him. "What?"

"You told me I had to tell someone if I was going somewhere, and I am."

"Where?"

"I am going to the store."

"Alone? Do you understand the money part of it all and do you have any?"

"I have a little. I want to see if the store man can get us some books."

"Can you wait to do that for just a little while? I will get up soon and we can go together."

"Okay."

The moment he left she rolled over and closed her eyes. For a few minutes she enjoyed it, but then a nagging thought kept her from falling asleep. Noah was a child. A child would not understand that a little while could be a few hours. He would probably be back in a few minutes. Sighing, she got out of bed and rubbed her hands over her face. She promised herself a nice long nap in the afternoon.

Getting dressed, she washed her face and tied back her hair. After donning her shoes and gathering up little money she had, she trudged down the stairs. She found Noah in the kitchen eating a lovely cooked breakfast. Mabel served her a big cup of coffee the moment she sat down at the table then proceeded to cook her a breakfast. After some coffee, Abbie woke up enough to wonder where the woman got the food.

"Have some supplies come in?" she asked.

"They did. Two full wagons, so your lieutenant brought us over some."

"That was good of him. I hope they could spare it."

"I didn't ask, which was a bit rude of me, but I was not about to do anything to make him take it back."

"Probably wise."

"I did make him a nice breakfast from it though."

Abbie smiled and then proceeded to eat the plateful Mabel set in front of her. She was just wondering if Matthew would come back, when he appeared at the back door and rapped on it. Mabel gave him a gesture to come in and he did, then took a seat opposite her. He looked well rested she thought a little sourly and then felt guilty for the thought.

"Ye are up far earlier than I expected." He looked at her face. "Earlier than ye wanted to, I suspect."

"Was that a polite way of telling me I look exhausted?"

He smiled. "My poor attempt at it, aye. Julia?"

"Yes, Julia. She is taking it very hard. It wakes her up in the night."

"And then wakes ye." He glanced at Noah who was concentrating on his food. "But I suspicion it was not Julia's grief that woke ye up this morning."

"I didn't wake her up. I was just looking at her to see if she would wake up and then she opened her eyes."

Abbie could tell that the way Matthew had a hasty drink of the coffee Mabel set in front of him that he was fighting to hide a grin. "Noah wants to go to the store to see if he can get Mr. Darby to get some children's books in."

"Ah. Read all the ones ye have, eh?"

"Yes," said Noah.

"Weel, I can have a look through town and see what I can find if you want."

"That would be helpful, but I don't think we ought to just steal from anyone who left them behind."

"Nay, it isn't stealing, it is borrowing. We will put them back when they are done."

She rolled her eyes and pushed her empty plate aside. Seeing that Noah was done she added his empty plate to hers and carried them to the sink. Then she sat back down to finish her coffee. When she finished her coffee she looked at Noah.

"We can go now."

The boy jumped out of his seat and waited with obvious impatience for her to join him, but Abbie looked at Matthew. "Perhaps I will see you later."

"I think that is a real possibility."

Walking off with Noah to get their coats, Abbie decided that Matthew was a bit fresh in the morning. She caught the boy by the hand and they walked off to the store. It did not surprise her to find no books there, but the man kindly lent her two that he and his wife had kept around for their grandchildren when they came to visit. Then she walked back to the house and, once inside, looked at Noah.

"I am going back to bed for a while."

"Why?"

"Because Julia is very upset and kept waking me up all night long and I got very little sleep."

"Oh, but will you be awake later to read us a story?"

"I will do that when it is time for you to go to bed."

"Okay."

She shook her head as she watched him run up the stairs and into the children's room. Then she slowly made her way back to her own room, found Julia still sleeping and, after hanging up her coat, she got ready to go to bed. She prayed no one had any emergency or upset because she intended to sleep for a few hours, and if someone woke her before then, she suspected she would not be pleasant. She crawled into bed and snuggled down beneath the covers, tensing when Julia whimpered. When no other sound came after a few moments she closed her eyes and went to sleep.

Chapter Eight

"It still cannot be moved much."

Matthew grimaced. "It has just finished healing, Boyd. The scar is still raw. Ye need to give it time."

Boyd slumped in the chair he sat in. "There is no strength in it at all."

"It needs to be worked with. That is what the doctor said. The strength will come if ye work it enough and in the right way."

"What is the right way?"

"Ye should be asking the doctor about that. He will ken what it needs."

Boyd sighed and rubbed a hand over his forehead. "Do you think Abigail might have an idea?"

"Lass kens a lot that surprises me so she might do. Ye want me to bring her round? Or we can go to see her in a few hours. She is helping the doctor right now."

"Ah, he did say she was good. He even said she could be a doctor as she has the instinct if people let her. Did you know she talks to every Reb brought into the infirmary or captured? She asks after her brother."

"She told me. She hasnae gotten the answers she seeks yet."

"Do you think she ever will?" Boyd asked.

"I dinnae ken how she can find out anything. Armies are too big and spread all over the country. There were a lot of men coerced into the army or dragged in. Too many, I think, for anyone to recall one fellow. No one is going to recall one young man out of hundreds."

"No, most likely not."

"She'll find him when he wanders back home."

"*If* he wanders back home."

"Nay, we will think *when*. Dinnae want to tempt fate."

"Certainly don't," Boyd muttered, staring at his limp arm.

"Laddie, ye still have the limb. Many a field doctor would have lopped it off."

"Why?" Boyd reached for his wounded arm, absently rubbing at it.

"Infection, the way some limbs can wither if unused, and who kens what else. Ye still have the arm. Let that be enough for now. And I think ye havenae given up all hope yet. Ye are rubbing it just like the doc and Abbie said ye should. Really, give it time." Matthew moved his seat closer. "Now, how about we try some of the lifting that they did suggest."

"Don't understand why one should work a dead arm," Boyd complained as Matthew wrapped a sandbag around his arm just below his elbow and tied it on.

"Keeps it from withering, I suspicion. Let's see if we can lift the arm up."

Matthew only got it lifted up once and Boyd moaned,

sweat breaking out on his brow. "Not ready for that then." He started just gently lifting Boyd's forearm up until the boy regained his composure. "Keep it simple. The upper arm obviously needs more time to heal."

"Do you think that is why I can't move it?"

"Could be. Too soon to ken that, but this is good, too."

After a half hour Matthew took the weight off. He looked at Boyd. The younger man look exhausted and it puzzled him. If there was no feeling in the arm, why would it being moved tire him out? Then he reminded himself the wound had been a bad one.

"Are ye staying here at the infirmary or coming back to where we're bunking?"

"I think I am staying here a little longer."

"Probably best until lifting that arm doesnae make ye nearly go down. Weel, I will wander by tomorrow. For now I am going to see Abigail. She must be back at the Beaton house by now."

"How is she doing? Getting along fine at that house?"

"Aye, but I have the feeling young Abigail is one who can make her way anywhere." Matthew smiled when Boyd laughed. "Perhaps this time she and I will go walking to get away from all the women and will not get shot at."

As he left the infirmary, Matthew hoped the young man's arm would heal. It would almost be better to have lost the arm than to go on with it hanging uselessly at one's side. He suspected Boyd might not agree. Despite how despondent he got over the problem, it was obvious that Boyd still clung to the hope that it would get better, which was a possibility. Matthew would do his best to say nothing that might crush that hope.

He had had enough of the war. It was undoubtedly selfish and unpatriotic but he was worn to the bone. He missed his home and family until it was a continuing ache in his very bones. He decided what he needed was to see Abigail, then groaned. When his body tightened at the mere thought of her, it was past time for him to do some hard thinking about the woman and their future.

He rapped on the Beaton house door and Mrs. Beaton answered. If he did not already know the woman he would have been cowed by the scowl on her face. Instead he asked for Abigail and was told to wait in the parlor. He hoped it would not take too long to get her and went to sit on the settee.

"The lieutenant is here again."

Abbie gave a start and looked up from the book she was reading. "Where is he?"

"In the parlor. Waiting. Looks like Julia is resting so you do not have to keep watch for a while."

Glancing at her friend, Abbie had to agree. Julia was finally having a good rest. She'd given her a tiny drop of the medicine and it was doing the job. Abbie hoped it was not going to hurt the child in any way. She checked her hair, tightened the ribbon on it, then brushed her skirts down and followed Mrs. Beaton down the stairs.

Matthew stood up as she came into the room and smiled at her. Abbie sighed quietly because that was always a fine thing to see. "Afternoon, Matthew."

He stepped close and kissed her hand. "I was wondering if ye would care to go for a walk."

Glancing at the sun beaming through the window,

Abbie nodded. "Yes, I think that would suit me very well."

He took her by the arm and led her out into the hall, idly wondering why Mrs. Beaton was lurking around. After helping Abbie into her coat, he smiled at Mrs. Beaton and led Abbie out the door. He heard the door shut behind them with a sharp click and wondered why the woman was in such a sour mood.

"Is something wrong with Mrs. Beaton?" he asked.

"No. She is just in a bit of a snit about Julia having a child."

"Weel, not much can be done to change that."

"I know. I am just hoping she gets over it. After all, Julia is married."

Enjoying the quiet of the day, Abbie barely noticed when he abruptly turned into an alley between two deserted houses. "Why are we in here again?"

"Privacy," he said as he walked her back until she was pinned between him and a wall. "We so rarely have any."

Before she could respond to that truth, he was kissing her. It was not long before her tongue joined his in the play and she tightened her hold on him, loving the feel of his warm, hard body against hers. The way he rubbed his hands up and down her back, skimming her sides, fired her blood. When he ended the kiss even she recognized the sound she made as one of protest.

He took her hand while she was still reeling from his kiss and led her into the house she had just leaned against. "I should have recognized that move, sir."

"I shall have to come up with a new one. Cannae tolerate being predictable."

She bit back a laugh. "They are lucky this house has not been burnt down."

"It is empty. Fire is usually set to drive people out."

"Ah, of course. There probably will not be much left in the area to come back to, however."

"No, and that is a shame, but I suspect it will return in some form before too long. "Now"—he led her into what she suspected had been the parlor—"I have set up a small feast for us in here. A picnic ye might call it."

"You are getting a lot of use out of this house."

"Aye." He moved to light a lantern he brought in from the hall where it had sat on the table near the door.

Abigail saw the same table they'd had their picnic on before. There was the bread and cheese and this time it was with thinly sliced ham. Yet again there was wine and glasses to sip it in.

"Did you play cards with the major again?" she finally asked.

"I did. He did say he suspects I put the drink to better use than he does and I already opened it to pour him a glass. Used my share of the rations to get the bread made and paid a woman for the bread, cheese, and butter."

"Oh yes, I heard you had gotten a recent hearty delivery of supplies."

"It was, but the supplies are already going down. A lot of the people in town either sneak or beg some. It is not attacks by Rebs weakening our supplies now but the need of the people in town. The prize still being sought is food. It is in short supply in too many places."

"Probably has always been the same where armies are."

"Aye. It is why my brother keeps having troubles, from the gray and the blue. We have lost a number of our sheep, which angers the Jones brothers. They are our shepherds. David and Owen."

"Sheep? You sell mutton?"

"And wool, which brings us more actually." He placed a piece of ham on a slice of the bread. "I never thought I would say this, but I miss the shearing."

She laughed as she added a bit of ham to her meal, placing it carefully on the bread. "You miss the companionship of your family I suspect, so anything you did together shines brighter in your mind."

"That is probably true."

"I wish I knew where my brother was so I could return to him. Together we should fare well enough."

"If he had gone with the Blues, maybe I could have helped more."

"The Union had its draft. It is a way of roping in someone who doesn't really want to be a soldier."

"True." He stood up, walked over to where she sat, took her by the hand, and pulled her to her feet. "When the leaders decide they are going to fight they will get the men they need any way they can." He sat down and pulled her down beside him. "But"—he pulled her into his arms—"I dinnae want to talk on war or leaders."

She leaned into him. "What do you want to talk about?"

"This."

He kissed her, and as he stroked the inside of her mouth with his tongue he pushed her down onto the settee so that he could sprawl on top of her. Abbie loved the feel of his body on hers. She knew he held up most of his weight on his forearms but the weight he did allow to rest on her felt as warm as a caress. Abbie wrapped her arms around his body and held him close, savoring the hardness of him between her thighs.

He began to stroke her, his hands going up and down her sides, brushing against the sides of her breasts. That felt good, but then he undid the buttons on the bodice of her gown. She was enjoying the seductive play with his tongue, the hot kisses followed by the kisses on her throat and neck, when she suddenly became aware of the fact that he had finished opening the bodice of her gown and was covering the swells of her breasts with the damp heat of his kiss.

He returned his kisses to her mouth as he slipped his hand beneath her skirts. Abigail tensed as he touched her where no man had ever touched her, but with one stroke of his fingers she lost the unease that had gripped her. She clutched at his shoulders as he teased her body to a blaze. Then she felt him tug at her drawers and lifted her hips a little. When he tugged them off her, she blushed even as she kissed the hollow of his throat.

It was not until he tugged her bodice down, exposing her breasts that she got nervous. Or embarrassed. She was not sure which it was that had her hastily trying to cover her breasts with her hands. He smiled then caught her hands in his and pulled them away. Then he licked her nipple and she shuddered with the strength of the feeling that went through her.

As he kissed and licked at her breasts, Matthew released himself from his breeches. This was not the way he planned things, but he would take his chance now and try to make the whole matter more romantic for her later. Kissing her mouth even as he kneaded her breasts he eased himself inside her. He heard her squeak in surprise, maybe even pain, and tried to move slowly but his body had different ideas. He grabbed the back of her legs and lifted them until she curled them around his waist. Kissing her mouth, he moved and this time she moaned in a way that fired his blood.

Abbie gasped from the pinch of pain as he entered her then felt the fullness of him inside of her. She was still savoring the sensation when he began to move and kissed her. When he lifted her legs, she wrapped them tightly around his body and the sensation of him moving inside of her grew stronger. She clung to him as he moved faster and her body grew tighter. Then the heat that had been building inside of her swept over her and she cried out against his mouth. She was still shuddering from the waves of feeling as he moved faster, drove himself as deep as he could, and tensed, a low growling noise escaping him.

When he slowly left her Abbie became all too aware of what they had just done. She hastily pulled and tugged at her clothes to make sure everything was covered when he moved to the side. Her first clear thought was: What did someone say afterward? Should she politely thank him or yell at him and leave? Then he brushed a kiss over her mouth. Moving her hands, he carefully redid the buttons on her bodice.

"Abbie?" he said softly.

"What?" she asked as she searched out her drawers and tried desperately to put them on again without exposing herself.

He put his arm around her and gently kissed her on the forehead. "I cannae tell if ye are just embarrassed or upset with me."

She rested her head against his shoulder. "Neither can I." She smiled faintly when he laughed. "I just didn't know what one says afterward or if one says anything."

"I have no idea. Interesting thought. Compliments?"

"About what? None of the things that happened are things I can speak about."

"Of course."

"And how could I give compliments? You must have guessed I have never done this before."

"Um, yes, I noticed."

"Lieutenant? Miss Jenson?"

"Oh no, not again," Abbie groaned, and thumped her forehead against his chest.

"That you, Mabel?"

"Yes, miss. I was sent to tell you that Julia, well, it is time."

"Time for what?"

"The baby, miss. She is having the baby."

"Oh no! I will be right there." Abbie hastily checked her clothes and decided they were in relatively good shape, then began to dig around for the ribbon she had had tied in her hair.

"Here," Matthew said, and waved the ribbon in front of her face. "And may I suggest ye cease to act so guilty if ye dinnae want anyone asking questions."

"I was not acting guilty." She quickly tied her hair back and reached for her coat.

"Oh, aye, ye were." He stood up when she did and yanked her into his arms to give her a hard kiss. "I will speak with ye later so think on some compliments." He grinned at the sound of annoyance she made before hurrying off with Mabel.

As he picked up things and put the wineglasses away, he decided to check and see if the family had left any children's books behind. Walking up the stairs he looked around and approved of the woodwork even as he looked for a child's room. Finding one at last he searched it and found three little books; in another he found a big book that had a collection of tales. Satisfied, he carried them back downstairs and put them in his bag before continuing to clean up.

They would not come back to this place, he decided. Being found here twice was enough. If he got another chance to get Abbie alone he did not want to fear an interruption. He hoped all went well for Julia. Robert had been a good man. He deserved to have his child grow up straight and proud.

He stepped outside and scowled up at the sky. A raindrop hit him in the face and he started to run. He hoped Abbie got home before this, and a quick glance at the Beaton house as he rushed by reassured him. If Abbie was still out the light would be on. All he had to do was get himself inside. When the skies opened and the rain began to pour down he ducked into the infirmary. Maybe he would visit with Boyd again.

Chapter Nine

"Julia has gone somewhere."

Abigail looked up at Maude and frowned. "Where? I thought she had started her labor and that was why I was fetched."

"None of us knows and she spoke to no one so we have no idea."

For a moment, Abbie thought about where Julia would go. The woman had been so sunk in her grief for the last three days it was hard to think she had anyone she wanted to visit or even that she may have gone for a walk. All Julia wanted to do at the moment was lie in bed and cry and her labor beginning had not lessened that at all. It was an effort to get her up and move or to eat for the sake of the child she carried. Then Abigail suddenly knew exactly where Julia had gone, despite the cold rain pouring from the sky.

"I have an idea of where she is," Abbie said as she tossed her needlework aside and jumped up. "I thought I was having a nice break from her labor. Should have known better. Foolish girl has gone to Robert's grave."

"In this?" asked Mrs. Beaton as she stared out at the rain pouring down.

"I fear so." Abbie put on her coat and looked around. "Does anyone have a hat or an umbrella?"

"I have a hat," said Maude as she ran off.

"You cannot go out in this. You will catch your death," said Mrs. Beaton.

"I will be fine but Julia has more than her own health and well-being to worry about, and she needs to start doing that."

When Maude brought the hat, Abbie put it on and strode out to go find Julia. She trudged through the rain, cursing as her feet got soaking wet, and prayed she was right. The moment she walked toward Robert's grave she saw her. The foolish woman was draped over his grave soaking herself in the muddy water that covered it. Abbie told herself to have patience but suspected it was going to be a hard thing to grasp.

"Julia!" she cried as she ran up to the woman. "What are you doing?"

"I came to see Robert. To tell him the baby is coming."

"I can see that but it is raining and you are now covered in mud."

"I just needed to be with Robert for a moment."

"Then do it on a sunny, warm day. Julia," she said in a softer tone as she pulled the woman to her feet, "you carry his child. If you were not lying . . ."

"I just wanted them to go away so I could come here."

"If you keep doing foolish things like this, you will not only hurt yourself, you will harm the baby."

"I will?" Julia asked in a dazed voice.

"Yes, most assuredly. Now come with me and we will get you inside, dried off, and warm again."

Abbie fought to control her temper as she walked the woman back to the house. To her relief, all the other women took over Julia's care and not one mentioned the absence of the labor Julia had claimed to be suffering. Taking off her coat and Maude's hat and hanging them in the kitchen to dry, Abbie went and sat down in the front room and closed her eyes.

"Are you ill?" asked Mrs. Beaton from across the room.

"No, I am tired. I understand her sorrow but she was out there in this weather lying in the mud on Robert's grave. I just need some time to make sure I have my temper under control as angry words will do no good right now."

Mrs. Beaton sat down in the chair opposite her and said, "I do not think the girl would even notice. She does not appear to be in her right mind at the moment."

"No, I do wonder at times if Robert's death and the pregnancy have been enough to break her, in her mind. No sensible, rational person who is with child would go out in this with nothing extra on and hurl themselves on top of a muddy grave, especially one who thought she was in labor."

"I think not."

Abbie took a deep breath and let it out in a huff. "I am calmer now so I will go and tend to her."

"You need sleep, Abigail."

"I know. This cannot go on for much longer. If nothing else she will soon have a child to care for and perhaps that will pull her out of this nonsense. And my temper is still lurking or I would not call it nonsense.

It is a deep grief. I will wrestle it down though and try to get her to see clearly."

"I hope you are successful."

So did Abigail if only so she could sleep through the night. Julia also needed to sleep. She was looking very worn down and Abbie worried about the child she carried.

When she stepped into her room Julia was already tucked up in bed and almost asleep. Maude sat with her so Abbie took the time to wipe herself dry, dress for bed, and crawl under the covers. It was rude but she just wanted someone else to watch over Julia for a little while.

"Sleep, Abbie," Maude said. "I'll keep a watch on her for a while."

"Thank you, Maude," Abbie muttered even as she fell asleep.

When Abbie next opened her eyes, she was startled to find the sun shining through her window. She sat up and looked over at Julia's bed only to find it empty. Hopping out of bed, she cleaned up, dressed, and then hurried down the stairs. In the big front room she found all the women and Julia talking merrily and just stared. It was as if the rain had washed Julia's madness away, but Abbie did not fully trust that. She was just having a moment of calm.

"Ah, there you are, Abbie," said Maude and walked over to her to say softly, "She is having a good morning."

"I can see that. The best one since Robert was killed."

"I am not sure how long it will last but take advantage of it. Do as you please today."

"That would be nice."

"Good. Then start with the man in the parlor who has patiently been waiting for you to wake." Maude chuckled and walked back to rejoin the others.

Abbie walked into the parlor and caught Matthew having a little nap on the settee. She softly hurried to his side and gave in to impulse, kissing him on the cheek. A squeak of surprise escaped her when he grabbed her and pulled her down onto his lap.

"Done sleeping?"

"There was no need of you lingering here until I woke up. There must be things you need to do."

"Not really. Thought to take ye for a walk. Ye need to get away from here for a while, I am thinking. Just as ye needed to rest this morning."

"A walk would be lovely." She wriggled out of his hold and stood up. "And it would also be best if we don't let Mrs. Beaton see us like this."

"Oh, I am beginning to think Mrs. Beaton is nay as . . ." He hesitated as he struggled to find the right word.

"Prissy?"

"Aye, that is good. Prissy as she was. Ye must be having some influence on her."

"I doubt that and, in fact, it makes me sound a bit like a catchable disease."

He laughed. "Get your coat."

"Yes, sir."

Abbie found her coat in the kitchen. It was dry and still a little warm from the heat of the stove. Mabel gave her some coffee and she drank it as she put her coat on. The moment she was done, she took the cup of coffee and finished it.

"Thank you, Mabel."

"What about breakfast?"

"I will have something to eat later. Right now, I think Matthew is right and I need to get out of this house for a bit."

"Miss Julia is a trial. I understand her hurt, but she is, well, too intense and demands a lot of work."

"I know. I suspected she would be like that. She is actually rather fragile. See you later today."

Abbie met Matthew in the hall. He hooked her arm in his and walked her out the door. It was still early in the morning but she could feel that it was going to be a good day, probably warm and sunny. That lifted her spirits as well. There was a nice, fresh scent in the air from the rain having washed everything clean in the night.

"It is going to be a lovely day, I believe."

"Aye. My family is probably out and working to plant the garden. I wish I kenned what they were planting this year. Emily, my brother Iain's wife, gets fancy now and then and we end up with a few odd things planted. Weel, odd to us."

"At least he is nice enough to consider what she wants."

"Maybe, although he doesnae plant it. Just marks out a space for her and says she can put her whim in there." He grinned when she laughed.

"You miss your home."

"I do, and it gets worse every day. Never thought it possible but I miss my wretched brothers as well. And Mrs. O'Neal who cooks and cleans for us."

"So you hired someone to do all that woman's work," she teased.

"We didnae hire her. She showed up with her children after her husband was killed. She wanted to live behind our walls with her bairns. So we came to an agreement. She sees what she does as paying for the wee house we built for her and the children. It works out weel for all of us. She also raises pigs for her money. Built them a good pen near the barn."

"That is a good arrangement for all of you. She is a very lucky woman."

"Oh, nay, we are lucky. We were thinking of hiring a woman but now dinnae have to."

"No, I mean lucky in that it sounds very much as if she has become a part of your family, her and her children."

"She is, but I think I see what ye mean. Maybe that was what she was really looking for although she does admire our walls and we have seen the good use of them a few times."

"This is a rough country."

"Ye would have something in common with Emily. She also lost her whole family to men who attacked and burned the cabin they were in."

"Marauders?"

"Men hired by her kinsmen to be sure her nephew wouldnae grow up to return to England and claim his inheritance."

"Oh. They came all the way here to do that?"

"Aye. Hard to understand that kind of greed."

"If it is a lot that can push people to do all sorts of evil things to try and get a hold of it."

"Weel, these fools didnae count on Emily. She got her nephew out of there, through the woods and into a hiding place her brother-in-law had dug out. When my brother found it and peeked in he met a knife."

"She stabbed him?"

"Nay, just held it at his throat and her with a bullet wound in her leg and a bullet burn on her arm. Looks like a bonnie little doll but has a spine of steel. Good wife for Iain."

The way his fingers stroked the back of her neck made Abigail lean against him. "Sounds it. Especially in these hills. Life is not easy. Even before this war life was often a continuous struggle."

He grunted his agreement, his eyes on the land around them. They were well hidden in this place, the trees, now getting greener every day, provided good cover for them, and his last time spent spying on where the Rebs had been camped had revealed nothing. The whole lot of them appeared to have marched away.

Deciding they were safe enough where they were, he glanced down at Abigail and shook his head. She had gone to sleep. He only briefly thought of waking her up to satisfy his hunger for her. Caring for Julia was sapping her strength. He hoped the girl regained her full senses soon. As carefully as he could he lay down and held her against his side. He watched a squirrel leaping around in the branches of a tree and decided he could do with a bit of rest himself.

When he woke up the sun was beginning to set and he rubbed one hand over his face. He then looked over at Abigail who was using his arm as her pillow and smiled. At least he knew now that she did not snore, he thought, and chuckled to himself. Knowing the rest of the ladies might start wondering where they were, he gently shook her to wake her up.

Abigail swatted at the hands shaking her awake and heard a soft, deep laugh. Why was Matthew in her bedroom? As she lifted her head to tell him to get out, she realized she was sleeping in a meadow. Groaning softly, she turned onto her back and stared up at Matthew. As her mind cleared she recalled why she was there. She suspected watching over a sleeping woman was not what he had in mind for the afternoon.

"Oh!" She sat up. "I forgot all about Julia."

"I am sure she is fine or Mrs. Beaton would have sent out people to find us. And, ye havenae been asleep all that long." He reached out a hand and helped her stand up. "I dinnae see why ye are the only one who needs to keep a watch over her."

"She learned Robert had died, was right there when he did, and she is with child. A shock such as she has had could easily start her labor."

"The shock was a few days ago now."

"True, but the effect of it may well take some time to reveal itself."

They had had a nice time away from it all but the passionate moments he had contemplated would not come now. Their time away was very clearly over. He took her hand and they started back. She said nothing that showed she knew what he had planned by bringing her out here and took that as a good sign. He had still been ready for some reaction over what they had shared before being interrupted yet again in the house he had used, but no guilt and no hint of shame. That had him wondering when he could arrange another time and place away from all the others. It was far past time that he started thinking about what exactly he wanted from Abigail Jenson.

Then he thought about Julia, a young woman who carried a child but no longer had a husband because the man who had wed her had been killed. His time would come, too. A man could not keep riding into battle as he did and not face his death. When he thought of Abigail and how she might fare if left alone with his child, he knew it was definitely past time for him to think beyond his own needs and wants and consider the future.

Before they were in sight of the town, he tugged her into his arms and kissed her. Her tense surprise melted away quickly and she became soft and willing in his arms. His body responded until he was so hard he almost groaned with the need to take her. When he leaned back, breaking the kiss, he thought she had never looked more beautiful. She stared up at him, her cheeks lightly flushed and her lips slightly parted.

"Someone might see us," she said in a soft, husky voice that fired his blood.

"Nay, but we best behave or I will be tempted too sorely."

Abigail heard herself giggle and almost groaned. She never giggled, had forced herself to stop once she became an adult, except when her father had tickled her. That thought made her sad but she tried to shake the sadness away. As she had told Noah, it was a good memory and one she should cherish.

"What is wrong?" he asked, stroking her cheek to try and ease the sadness that had abruptly darkened her eyes.

"Oh, nothing really. I just had a memory of my father."

He grimaced. "Not exactly what a man wants to hear, Abbie."

Abigail smiled. "It was a very pleasant memory."

Matthew shrugged then put his arm around her shoulders and held her close to his side as they began walking again. "I hope Mrs. Beaton isnae waiting on ye."

"I doubt she will be. She never waits for any of the women although I believe she knows who is out walking with a gentleman until late. There is no scold but there can be some haughty looks of disapproval."

"How is she treating Julia now?"

"As if she doesn't exist. Julia says she has to pinch herself now and then to make certain she is actually still visible. I was afraid it would hurt her feelings but the other women are so nice to her she doesn't seem to care. Or, rather, doesn't care anymore. At first all the women were a little cool to her."

"Does it really matter?"

"No, but then there have been so many odd turns to this, I am not sure what to trust any longer."

"What odd turns?"

"Oh, let us start at the beginning, shall we? When I asked her when she thought she got with child she told me one thing only to later mention that it might have been three or four months before that. Then I wondered if she was still wrong about that because she was not really showing much only to have her tell me all about her family, the women especially, and how they never show until late." She leaned closer and whispered, "They tend to carry wide." She shook her head. "So when she started showing she was actually sure she was wrong about when she got with child, plus she had taken to wearing a binding to hide it.

"Then Robert died. She insisted on being there even though she could barely stand upright, she was weeping so hard. Now she takes it into her head at odd moments to visit his grave and then I have to go and fetch her back."

"So she is near her time already and has had a hard shock."

"It sounds so simple when you say it that way, but if her shock starts her labor, will the babe be full term? And if the babe does come and it is early what will that do to her? I do not know enough about it all to be confident enough to deal with such a thing. All the women I dealt with before were sturdy country stock."

"Then call in the doctor," he said as they stopped in front of the door.

"Maybe." She opened the door only to be dragged inside by a frantic Mrs. Beaton. Behind the woman ranged all the other women and every one of them looked frantic. She glanced up the stairs and saw the four children sitting there trying not to look scared and failing. Noah saw her and ran down, quickly followed by the others. If Matthew had not had a hold on her she suspected she would have tumbled down the steps when they all slammed into her.

When she finally got the women to be quiet, Abbie could hear the noise Julia was making. She patted Noah's head as he clung to her legs and she looked at Matthew. "Can you help the children?" she asked.

"Of course," he said, and tugged Noah away. "Go on up. See what needs to be done. If ye need anything just give a bellow."

"I never bellow," she called back as she ran up the stairs.

Abigail threw her coat over the hall railing and raced into her room. Julia was in bed clutching the covers and moaning. After getting a pan of water, Abigail got some rags. She then put several bedsheets under Julia. As she sat down near the bed, she sighed because she had the feeling it was going to be another very long night.

"It is all right, Julia," Abbie said.

"No, it isn't and it never will be. My Robert is gone."

"I am more sorry than I can say about that but right now you carry a piece of him and I am here to make certain you birth a healthy child. Put your mind to that, to the hard business of having his child."

"I will," Julia said although her tears slowed only a little. "He was so happy about the baby."

"Just remember that. When did your pains start?"

"Just a couple of hours ago. I was so uncomfortable up here so I went down to sit in one of the comfortable chairs and talk with the others. Then I was suddenly sitting in a puddle and the pains began. Will it be done soon?"

"I have no idea, Julia. Every woman is different."

"They are indeed," said Rose as she strode into the room. Rose walked over and sat in a chair on the other side of Julia's bed. "So, child, your time is here."

"It is. No one told me how much it hurts."

"Don't fight the pain and it will be easier."

"That makes no sense."

"It does, Julia," Abigail said. "If the pain is all your mind is set on, it makes it seem greater than it might be. I always tell people to take deep breaths and then let the air back out slowly."

"And that works?"

Abigail shrugged. "Most times. I like to think it is because your head is now fixed on something else, not the pain."

"I do not know how one can forget about this pain," Julia muttered then tensed, took a deep breath, and let it out slowly until she relaxed a bit.

Rose wiped Julia's face with a cool cloth. "You will forget all about it when you hold your child for the first time."

For a while Julia tried not to fight the pain and breathed as Abigail had suggested, but then she returned to moaning. "Robert should be with me," she cried and Abigail saw Rose roll her eyes.

"He is gone, Julia," Abigail said, "otherwise I am sure he would be here so that you could crush all the bones in his hand instead of mine."

"Sorry, Abbie." Julia loosened her grip on Abigail's hand. "I will try to stop."

"Do not fret over it. At worse, I shall have a few colorful bruises. But you must keep your mind on birthing your child. It is important that you concentrate on getting this baby out and nothing else."

"I know. I know."

For a while Julia did as Abbie and Rose wanted. Abbie began to hope it would go well all the way to the end. Then Julia just stopped doing everything that had worked so well for her. Abbie feared something was wrong for a moment, but then Julia moaned again.

"You were doing so well, child. Surely you could see that," Rose said to Julia.

"I could see that I was exhausting myself for nothing."

"What do you mean, 'for nothing'? You are bringing Robert's child into the world," said Abbie.

"It does not appear to want to come out now."

"He or she will be along soon," said Rose, weariness adding a little bite to her words.

Abbie could see Julia's stomach move as if gripped by another contraction but the woman showed no sign of being aware of it. She stood up, framed Julia's face in her hands, and stared into her eyes. They were glazed and Julia stared at something in the corner of the room. A faint smile curved the woman's mouth and it affected Abbie strangely. She itched to slap it away. She glanced at Rose who was watching Julia and frowning deeply.

"Yes, he will. I am going to have a boy," Julia said in a singsong voice. "Robert wants a boy."

"Oh, hellfire and damnation, the girl thinks she sees her husband."

"Well, I wish her husband would tell her to get back to business," Abbie snapped, and Rose laughed.

"Never seen anything like it and I have tended a lot of births."

"Julia!" Abbie snapped out and her friend turned those faraway eyes to her.

For a moment, Julia said nothing then closed her eyes. "I need sleep."

"Julia!"

"It is all right, Abbie. Robert says our babe will need all my strength soon but not today."

"Well, that is strange," Rose said.

"How can she just stop?" Abbie felt Julia's stomach, holding her hands there for a long time.

"But she has, hasn't she?"

"Yes, it appears she has. I just don't understand. I have helped in a lot of births but never seen it start then stop."

Rose stood up and rubbed at the base of her back. "Maybe you should speak to the doctor you sometimes help out. He has more book knowledge about such things than we do. We just have experience."

"Well, I will in the morning. I think it might be wise if I grab some sleep while I can."

As she started out of the room, Rose patted her on the back. "Definitely. This girl has stolen a lot of that from you."

That was true, Abbie thought as she felt Julia's forehead and found no hint of fever. Then she undressed and put on her nightgown. As she crawled into bed she decided she would go talk to the doctor as soon as she woke up. She hoped he would have some answers.

Chapter Ten

It took her a while before she got to speak with the doctor. She had to help him clean a wound first, one that had begun to show signs of infection. After they cleaned up he took her to the small room he used as an office. She saw the blanket-covered cot in the corner and decided it must be where he collapsed to sleep at the end of a long day. Abbie wondered if this war had given the man as much doctoring as he had the stomach to take or if he intended to continue when the war was over.

"Drink?" he asked as he poured himself some whiskey.

"A very small one as I believe I will need to stay awake for a long time."

He laughed and poured her a small amount of whiskey. "What did you want to ask me? And thanks for the help. I think we caught that infection in time."

"Good. There is too much lost to it."

"Indeed. So, your question?"

"It is time or very near time for Julia to have her

baby. She thought it was time yesterday, but despite having pains and all, it stopped, just stopped. Does that mean something is wrong?"

"No. Women can even have fraudulent labor. I have had the husband drag me out in the middle of the night, rush me to his house and then, by the time we get there, the woman is fine."

"So she is not having the baby now? Does this wait last long or is it just a quickly passing thing?"

"Sometimes it can happen long before the true time. Those times we usually try to stop it or make the women stay abed with her feet up, both actions I have never decided on the worth of. Sometimes it is a warning and the true time will come along soon after. Point is, it is not usually a sign that something is wrong."

"All right." She sipped her whiskey. "So she may well start up again before too long."

"I fear so. I thought you said you had helped in a lot of births."

"I have, but they all started and stopped as one hears they should."

"Ah, well, every woman is different. I have had women scream as if they are being ripped apart and others who sit there calm and smiling, chatting away with anyone who stops by, then suddenly she is a mother."

"A strange business," she said, shook her head, and finished the last bit of her whiskey.

"No question about it. Ah, I believe we are about to have some company."

Wondering why the doctor suddenly looked amused, she turned and saw Matthew. He walked into the office, glared at the empty whiskey glass, and then scowled at her. "What are ye doing?"

"I was talking to the doctor about Julia's baby coming. I had a few questions."

"With whiskey?" he grumbled.

"It was courtesy that made him offer and I was in need of something after spending a few hours with Julia. I got the answers I needed and the whiskey was much better than Reid ever offered me or my father's brew."

Matthew glanced back at the doctor who was hiding a big grin behind the sipping of his drink and failing to disguise his intense amusement. Muttering to himself, he led Abbie out of the infirmary. He decided it was just luck that kept him from meeting James, Dan, or Boyd as he left.

"Why are ye out wandering around? I thought Julia was having her bairn?"

"I thought she was too, and then she stopped. Everything just stopped. I was afraid something nasty had happened, that the baby would be hurt, but the doctor says it is normal enough. So I had to get away from her for a bit." She looked at Matthew. "Why were you looking for me?"

"I wasnae. I was just going to look in on Boyd and saw ye drinking with the doctor."

Abbie wondered why that sounded like an accusation but followed him as he led her away from town. "I am not sure I ought to go far now. Julia could need me again at any time."

"I am sure we will hear about it," he said as he led her into the trees.

She was looking around at the trees and realizing it was a very private spot but not the one he had taken her to before. Then Matthew pulled her into his arms and kissed her. Her surprise quickly faded and passion rose as he went down onto the ground, pulling her down with him. When his body settled over hers she snuggled up against him as close as she could. She knew what he was planning to do and she found she had an eagerness for the same.

As she tilted her head so he had an easier time in kissing her throat she felt him undoing the buttons on her bodice. It struck her as odd that his doing that was enough to make her blood heat in anticipation. When his hand settled on her breast she arched into his touch, welcoming it. The touch of the heat of his mouth there made her shiver. Then he began to kiss her again and she sank into the kiss, losing the ability to follow his every move.

Matthew did his best to keep her drunk on his kisses discovering that he was finding it nearly as heady himself. Her mouth was addictive, a sweet and hot magic in every kiss. He moved his hand under her skirts eager to feel the heat of her. A soft groan escaped her when he stroked her and he savored the sign that she was as caught up in the moment as he was.

Abbie closed her eyes, savoring the feel of his touch and his kisses without letting the world interfere. She just let the sheer pleasure of it wash over her, savoring every tremble that came as he kissed her breasts. Threading her fingers in his hair she tried to hold him there but he slipped free. A moment later he kissed her between her legs and she shook with both surprise and delight. She was just thinking she needed to push him away when he began to lick her and she lost all urge to make him stop. Her insides tightened until it was almost painful.

When he pushed her legs up, she made no protest, focused on the sensations pounding through her.

Then, abruptly, she wanted something and tried to pull him up her body. He rose over her and was inside her before she could complain and she clutched at him as he thrust into her. It took very few times before she shattered and cried out, pleasure rippling throughout her body. She wrapped her arms around him as he moved in her then stiffened and groaned out her name, then held him close when he slumped against her.

For several moments, they lay entwined, silent, and still joined, but then Matthew pulled away and rolled onto his side to fix his trousers. He looked at her and smiled. Sprawled on her back with her gown undone, Abbie looked deliciously wanton. He felt himself harden a bit at the view and almost grinned, knowing he should feel pleasantly satisfied and not hungry again. He bent and kissed her breast before fixing her clothes.

Although she suspected a proper woman should be thoroughly embarrassed, Abigail felt nothing but a lazy contentment. Whatever he had just done had left her feeling soft and relaxed in a very pleasant way. She now understood why people did this, married or not. A glance at Matthew was enough to tell her he was in an extremely pleasant mood as well.

When he bent his head to kiss her again she shook her head. "I still have to see to Julia."

"Ah, of course." He reached out to toy with her tangled hair. "It was just a kiss."

"Well, we just saw what just a kiss can lead to and I don't want to be interrupted during, um, that, by Maude's pig call."

"Maude's what?"

"She said if Julia needs me again and they don't know where I am she'll just go to the door, stick her head out, and give her pig call. She said it can be heard for miles around." She cocked her head. "I doubt it is miles, but I bet it can be heard from a pretty great distance. Also Mrs. Beaton looked horrified, but that won't stop Maude."

He sat up and rubbed his knees. "Is Julia having a lot of trouble in birthing the babe?"

"I don't know. She thought she was having it and then she wasn't." She sat up as well. "That was what I went to talk to the doctor about. It was just a false alarm but the real could follow the false real soon so . . ." She shrugged.

He nodded. "So a false alarm but also a warning sign."

"Yes, and Julia doesn't handle pain well at all. She seemed quite dismayed that it should hurt. She also claimed to be seeing Robert in the corner of the room, telling her things. I had meant to ask the doctor if delusions were any sign of problems."

"I can take ye back there if ye want."

"No. I believe it is just a touch of hysteria and the pain she had not been ready for. She also is still sunk in grief so I suppose it is not that strange that she would see him in her time of need. I think he had become the rock she clung to in the misery her life is now."

He was about to comment on that when a piercing yodel cut through the silence. "What the devil?"

"I believe that is Maude. It is quite an impressive call. No wonder she is proud of it."

Abigail stood up and brushed off her skirts. She idly noted there were a few grass stains but shrugged. If Maude was calling because Julia was in labor again, she doubted many would take note of the grass stains on her skirt.

"Well, after such a fine performance, we should hurry."

"I agree," said Abigail and sprinted away.

Laughing softly, he followed her, easily catching up to run at her side. Once they reached the house he complimented Maude on her call as Abbie and he stepped into the hall. Since nothing was planned for his afternoon, he decided he would linger and wait for some news before he wandered back to his bunk.

Abigail ran up the stairs and quickly hung up her coat. Julia was already making loud complaints about a pain. It was clear the girl had no idea of what was coming.

"So, Julia, you believe your babe is coming this time?" Abbie said as she went to stand by the bed.

"Yes. You need to get the doctor. This is much worse than it was yesterday."

"Doctors don't usually attend births unless something is going wrong."

"Then who else does the work?"

"Midwives."

"Why?"

"I have no idea. I believe some very rich ladies can pay to have a doctor but most women do it themselves, maybe have a few friends to help, or get a midwife."

"Oh," Julia said, and her reply turned into a long moan of pain. "Like before with just you and Rose. Are you a midwife?"

"No one has named me one but I have attended and helped in many a birth with midwives and with doctors and they were all satisfied."

"They are not the ones having the baby."

"True enough. I was just telling you how much assistance I have done and learning I have gained."

"All right. But you will get the doctor if something

happens you do not know or something goes wrong, right?"

"Yes, but nothing is going to go wrong."

"Why does it hurt so much? It didn't hurt like this the last time," she whined.

"Maybe because that was a false alarm. Now your body is trying to push the baby out and the baby doesn't feel like coming out. Last time was clearly false labor. That can feel pretty real but it isn't and that is why it stopped. I have no good answer, just that it does and always has."

"That seems grossly unfair."

"Most certainly."

"How does this not rip a woman apart?" Julia asked in a swiftly rising voice that hurt her ears. "Something has to be wrong!"

"It isn't. I'm sorry you were never informed about the whole process."

"Why should I be? I was not supposed to be doing this until I was safely married."

"True, but you are married now and it is time to stop fretting on how much it hurts or how hard the work to birth is, and just get on with it." Abigail could tell by the wide eyes Julia stared at her with that some of her irritation with the woman had sounded in her voice.

Julia opened her mouth to say something that Abigail thought was probably another complaint and then screamed softly. Abbie felt her stomach and felt sure this time it was real labor. She looked across the bed at Rose who had come into the room and taken her seat.

"Real?" asked Rose.

"I certainly think so."

"Good. My cousin had false labor several times

before she got down to business, and it was a relief when she did. So we settle in for a long time."

When Julia screeched again, Abbie winced. "I hope for the sake of my hearing it is not too long."

Julia obeyed nearly everything they told her to do but her temper flared several times. Abbie was tempted to tell her what kind of messes she and Rose were having to deal with just to make Julia be quiet but decided that would be mean. She was not yet tired enough to be mean.

"I am so tired," Julia said in a soft voice after about three hours of complaining and yelling.

"It is almost over," Abbie said in as soothing a voice as she could muster. "Now comes the time when you need to start pushing."

"You certain she is that close?" asked Rose even as she stood up.

"I believe so although this hasn't taken as long as I thought it would." She suddenly looked at Julia. "Did your pains come earlier than you said?"

"Don't think so. I was sitting up here being careful and then my back hurt. I tried to ignore it but it kept right on hurting. I went to sit downstairs for a while and visit with everyone when all of a sudden I got a real pain. Rose told me that was a sign to get to bed."

Abigail sighed. "That discomfort was early labor, Julia. You have been in labor for quite a while."

With Rose standing in a position to be ready to take the baby, Abbie stood and held Julia's hand in hers. Despite her growing questions about Julia's sanity, Abbie was determined to see this birth completed. When Julia began to stare off into the corner of the room and smile, she still pushed with admirable strength when told to. Soon Rose joined in the encouragement and Abbie knew the baby would arrive soon. A healthy baby boy slid into Rose's hands. They smiled at each other when the child let out a strong wail and then Rose placed the baby on Julia's chest.

Suddenly there was clarity in Julia's eyes and Abbie was certain that Julia actually saw her child. While Rose helped Julia attempt to settle the baby at her breast, Abbie tended to the cord and cleaned up Julia and the bed. Abbie waited tensely for Julia to have another spell. From what she could see of the other woman's face, so was Rose. Then the blank eyes returned as the baby went to sleep and Julia held the child out to Abbie.

"His name is Jeremiah Robert Collins." She smiled at whatever she could see in the corner.

"A good strong name." Abbie tidied up the stem of the cord still attached to the child, tying it off before wrapping the baby in a small blanket. "He has a good head of hair for a newborn."

When Julia said nothing, Rose nodded. "Have to see how long it lasts. Babes tend to lose it at first." Rose looked at Julia who had fallen asleep. "She has lost her mind, you know."

"Actually, I think it is broken. She's lost too much. Her family, her home, and all that."

"So have we all and more."

"I know, but Julia doesn't have the strength the rest of us do. When she lost Robert too, it broke her."

"So what happens to the babe?"

"I don't know. I can only hope Julia pulls herself together. Now I have to go downstairs and relieve Matthew. He is watching the children."

"Want me to take the babe?"

"No need, but thank you. He is lying quiet and it is a small weight."

"So, what do we do?"

"Wait and see."

Abigail could tell Rose was not happy with that answer but she had no other. The child would either pull Julia out of her obsessive grief or not. They would have to wait to see what choice she made, then decide. As she had feared, the child was small and she was glad it had been born when the weather was warm and would be for a few months. She headed down the stairs to show the other women and was not surprised when Noah appeared at her side.

"Is it a boy?" he asked as he hopped down each step at her side.

"Yes, his name is Jeremiah Robert Collins."

"That's a big name for such an itty, bitty baby. And he is red."

"That will fade and, yes, he is small but he will grow. Babies grow fast in the first year or so."

"Probably so they learn to run quicker and get away from danger."

She looked at the boy and shook her head in surprise at his remark. It was a surprisingly astute observation for such a small boy. Abbie had to admit she adored the child because he talked so well, was mischievous, and he seemed attached to her, but she was beginning to think there was a very clever brain hidden behind those big eyes.

"Puppies learn that fast, too."

"They do indeed." She reminded herself that she had a puppy she had to collect soon. Abigail walked into the main room and all the women got up and ran over to her. She let Maude take the baby and then went to sit on the settee. She was tired but knew she had to hold on until she was certain it was safe to leave the baby in Julia's care. She also had to relieve

Matthew, she remembered, and slowly pushed to her feet.

Noah edged next to her. "Why are they all making those funny noises at the baby?"

"Because he is a sign of hope. He shows that there is a future when this war can make us often forget that."

He frowned and Abbie knew he was turning that over in his clever little brain. "Babies are always a sign of hope but, I think, more so in times like now."

"Why isn't he with his mother?"

"Because Julia is very tired right now. Having a baby is very hard work."

He nodded and looked over at the child who was being passed around. When no further questions came, Abbie decided it was time to go and relieve Matthew. He had been kind to take watch over the children, but she suspected his patience might be waning after so long. She walked over to the parlor.

Abbie took one step into the room and stopped. Matthew sat on the settee laughing while Mary promenaded around in his hat. A boy sat on each side of him, also laughing. He appeared to be quite content where he was.

"Ah, Abbie," he said as he turned toward her and smiled. "Is Julia a mother now?"

"Yes." She started toward him as she ran her hand through her hair. "It went well, as far as I can tell." Peter moved so Abbie sat down next to Matthew.

"Tired?"

"To the bone." She noticed the children talking to each other and then they started toward the door. "Where are you going?"

"To see the baby," replied Peter.

"Don't get underfoot."

"We'll be careful," said Sam. "Are you going to read us a story in a while?"

Even though she just wanted to go and crawl into bed, Abbie said, "Yes, so go to your room and be ready after you see the baby."

When they left, she sighed and leaned against the settee back. "I guess I must read a story soon."

"Can someone else not do it? You need to get some rest."

"If they can, they will offer as I leave to go up the stairs, but I suspect it will be me. Maude is out with your major and Rose is just as tired as I am and probably already in bed."

He put his arm around her and let her rest against his chest. "Is Julia truly well?"

"The birth was fine but I think she is still well, unwell in her mind."

"Ah, so you are still keeping a watch over her."

"I am, but not as closely as before." She started to close her eyes and sat up quickly. "No, that was too comfortable and I will fall asleep. I think I will go collect the baby, read the story, and find my bed. I am hoping Julia has a restful night." She kissed him on the cheek. "Thank you for keeping the young ones busy."

He stood up and helped her to her feet. "I did not do too well in keeping Noah corralled."

"I doubt anyone could successfully manage that."

He bent to kiss her and idly wondered if she knew how completely exhausted she looked. "I will come around sometime tomorrow."

"I will see you then," she mumbled as she left the room and headed to the sitting room.

Matthew picked up his hat from where Mary had tossed it and left. If she was not rested when he came tomorrow, he would see to it that she got away from this house and to somewhere she could actually get a good sleep. He grinned. It was an odd thing for him to want to get her alone for.

Abbie put the sleeping baby into the small crib Betsy had loaned them before they had come to stay with Mrs. Beaton for a while and then went to the children's room. She did her best to read them a story and was relieved when they all looked more than ready to go to sleep as she got up to leave. She only went a few steps when her skirt pulled at her and she turned back to find that Noah had grabbed hold of it.

"What is it, Noah?" she asked softly as she went to his bedside.

"Are you going to keep a watch on the baby?"

"Yes, until his mother can do so."

"Good." He let go of her skirt and closed his eyes. "He needs to be watched because I don't want him to be shot like my baby sister was."

Abbie sighed, reached out to brush the hair from his forehead, then went to find her own bed. She did not even want to know how his baby sister had died. She had had enough of sad stories. Despite her effort to put it all from her mind, she did feel a surge of pity for Noah. The boy had seen too much, lost too much.

So had Julia, she decided as she checked the woman to be certain she still slept deeply. The woman had not had a particularly difficult birth, but it had been enough to put her to sleep for what Abigail prayed would be a full, long night. She undressed and crawled into bed after tying a small bell she had found to the door. Just in case, she told herself as she lay down and closed her eyes.

* * *

Abbie opened her eyes and wondered what had woken her. Sitting up abruptly she looked toward the open door of the bedroom, and realized the bell she had tied to the door must have chimed. A curse escaped her as she got up and started dressing. She glanced at the crib and her heart sank. The foolish woman had taken her child with her.

As quietly as she could, yet keep up a decent speed, Abbie left the house. She went straight to the graveyard behind the house. It did not surprise her to find Julia sitting by Robert's grave, talking to him, but it did anger her that she had the child out in the cool damp of the evening. Walking over to the woman, Abbie took the baby from her and wrapped it more tightly in its blanket before holding it close.

"I was just showing him our son," Julia said and reached for the child, only to have Abbie step out of her reach. "A father needs to know his babe."

"Julia, there is nothing wrong with you coming to speak to him although it might have been better for you to dress warmly first. But to bring a newborn, a small newborn, out into the damp of night was foolish."

Jumping up, Julia stared down at the child in Abbie's arms. "Is he too small? Is there something wrong with him?"

"He is small. I think he may have been a little early. But I have found nothing wrong with him. Let's go back into the warm house." She did not even wait to see if Julia followed but began to make her way back to the house.

Julia stood by Robert's grave for a minute, said farewell, and quickly followed. By the time they got inside and up to the bedroom, she started to complain.

Abbie ignored her until she had the baby settled back in the crib then turned to Julia.

"Get in bed, Julia," Abbie said.

"I don't understand why you are being so unkind," Julia said as she crawled into bed. "I just wanted Robert to see his son."

"Neither you nor the child should be seeing anyone in the dark and cold."

"It was not that cold."

"Cold enough to give a small baby a chill and a mother who wasn't dressed warmly as well. You and the baby must stay warm and get a lot of rest for now."

"I feel fine."

"Good. Let's hope it stays that way."

Abbie walked back to her bed and snuggled down into the covers. It had definitely been chilly out there and she could not believe Julia had not noticed. She was going to have to keep a very close watch on both of them now.

Chapter Eleven

"Abigail, you have company."

Abigail slowly opened her eyes and looked at Mrs. Beaton. "Who?" she asked as she struggled to sit up.

"The lieutenant of course. He is waiting in the parlor."

"All right. I will be down in a few minutes."

"You are not sick now, are you? Although, come to think of it, Julia never was sick, was she?"

"Not at all. I'm not, either. I was just having a good, deep sleep. Need to freshen up a bit."

"I will tell him it will be a few moments then."

Abigail staggered over to the washstand and splashed the cool water on her face. It took a few doses of that to make her feel more awake. Drying her face, she then cleaned her teeth. What she really needed was a good night's sleep.

After a quick brushing of her hair, she tied it back with a ribbon and smoothed down her skirts then began to make her way down the stairs. She walked into the parlor and saw Betsy sitting in the far corner of the room with her children. Mrs. Beaton was getting sneaky about chaperones, she decided, then smiled at Matthew.

"They were in here when Mrs. Beaton sent me in," he said quietly as he bent to gently kiss her cheek.

"Chaperones. The woman is very good at sneaking one or more in. Very devious."

He laughed softly. "Shall we go for a stroll then, Abbie?"

"That would be very pleasant, Lieutenant MacEnroy. I will just get my coat."

Matthew gave Betsy a quick smile while he watched Abbie in the hallway put on her coat and the woman grinned and winked at him. "Nice to see ye again, ma'am. How is your husband?"

"He is doing just fine, sir. The wounds are healing beautifully."

"Abbie is verra good at tending wounds."

"She certainly is."

Abbie was just buttoning her coat up and talking softly with Rose when he stepped out into the hall. He moved to stand beside her and wondered about the reason behind the deep serious looks both women wore. Something was still not right at the Beaton house.

"Oh, it looks to be a lovely day. This coat may be more than I need," said Abbie as they went down the front steps.

"I believe I would not be put to the test too hard if I had to carry it for you." He smiled when she laughed.

"It is good to get out of there for a little while."

He took her arm and they started walking. "Is Julia still causing problems?"

"I fear so. It would be too easy to get angry with her except I know it is because she is not really well. I had hoped the baby would pull her free of what ailed her, but it does not seem to have accomplished that. Last night she took that newborn baby out to his father's grave. She didn't even get dressed or wrap the child in extra blankets. Just stepped out of bed, picked up the child, and went. If I had not tied a bell to the door, I fear we may have found both dead on his grave."

"It might just take her a wee time to shake free of the grief."

"That is what I am hoping. Just some time and then the child will reach her and she will slowly stop seeing Robert everywhere and talking to him and see his son instead."

"She sees and talks to Robert?"

"I fear so." Abbie sighed. "It is why I have Rose keeping a watch over her while I am out."

Seeing no one else out, he put his arm around her shoulders and tugged her up against his side. "It will pass. Grief is an odd thing. Some soldiers get through it just fine and it can actually break some but, I think, most are someplace in the middle of that."

"If she would just inch into the middle it would help. Where are we going? This is a new direction for us."

"We are going to the riverside. One of the men put up a rough bench so he could sit and watch it. Said it soothed him. I thought it might help ye."

"Oh. It just might although I had not thought myself too uneasy." She thought about it for a minute. "I might be though. I worry about the child."

"Only right. A bairn that small cannae do anything to help himself."

As they walked down a small slope away from the road, she saw the river and smiled. It was not a soothing sight at the moment since it was swollen from melting snow and all the rain they had had lately, but the sound of the water rushing over the stony riverbed was calming in an odd way. She sat on the bench after checking on the roughness of the seat and then looked out and sighed. Even if she found no ease in the rushing water, the forest on the opposite bank was pleasant to watch.

"It is a bit fast and loud today," Matthew said as he sat beside her.

"Yet strangely fascinating, but the trees opposite are very soothing. Peaceful and green, with the promise of better weather."

Matthew smiled faintly. He had been concerned when he saw the state of the river for relaxing was not something one could do near such a torrent. Yet she found something to slowly wash away the tension he had sensed in her. He put his arm around her and pulled her closer, pleased when she rested her head on his shoulder.

Glancing behind him he saw that the back of the bench had been made smooth so he leaned back taking her with him. He had not had any plan for being with her today except to get her away from the demands of Julia, but he was beginning to get a few ideas. He grinned and kissed her cheek.

"Are you certain it is safe out here?" she asked, looking around.

"We have found no sign of the Rebs or the marauders in days," he answered, and turned to pull her into his arms then kissed her.

Abbie relaxed into his kiss, returning it with all the desire she felt for the man. It was dangerous, a voice whispered in her mind, reminding her of the situation Julia was now in, but Abbie ignored it. There were times when one just had to roll the dice and pray for the best outcome.

Matthew pulled her onto his lap, positioning her so that she straddled him. When she rubbed against him, he growled out his approval. Kissing her throat, he slid his hand beneath her skirts so he could stroke her. When she gasped softly he kissed her again. Her arms tightened around his neck and he felt her damp heat against his fingers.

Fighting to control his rapidly mounting need he undid her bodice and kissed the gentle swell of her breasts. He gave a little start of surprise when he felt her slender fingers undo his coat and shirt. She ran her fingers over his chest and he was surprised by how much that tentative, innocent touch fired his blood.

When Abigail kissed him, he freed himself from his pants and clasped her by the hips. For a moment the feel of her heat against his skin was enough, but that satisfaction quickly grew into a greedy hunger. He lifted her up a little and settled her over him then, keeping in mind that she was still a novice, slowly joined their bodies.

Shocked, Abbie buried her face in the side of his neck as he moved her body on his. That feeling soon gave way to pleasure and she quickly caught on to what he wanted from her, moving on him without guidance. Her breasts rubbed against the hair on his chest even as he moved his fingers to a spot near where their bodies were joined. That puzzled her until she felt the pleasure inside her begin to rapidly build.

Increasingly desperate to ease or end the need he was stirring within her, she began to move faster as if she was racing toward a finish line to win some grand prize. A heartbeat later, she did. She buried her face in the curve where his neck met his shoulder and cried out as her body shuddered. Matthew sat up straight and moved her body on his until he tensed and groaned from the strength of his release.

They were both panting as if they had just run a hard race, thought Abigail. She then wondered how one delicately got out of this position. Just as she was beginning to think there was no way, he lifted her up and set her down at his side. She busied herself with smoothing out her skirts as he tidied himself up. She wondered idly how something done so quickly and stealthily could give such satisfaction but it did. Someday, she thought, they would have to try and perform the act with more leisure.

Staring at the river as she wondered what to say, Abigail spotted something floating by on the water. It got caught on a branch that had broken off one of the trees lining the bank. Curious, she got up and hurried to grab it before the flow of the water ripped it free. It was a cap, a gray cap, and her heart began to pound with alarm. It was something only a Reb or a marauder would wear, which meant trouble was near.

"What have ye got?" asked Matthew as he stood up and stretched.

"Trouble, I am thinking," she said as she hurried to his side and showed him the cap.

"Damn." He hurried to the bank and, hanging on tightly to a low branch, went out as far as he dared to look up the river.

When staring up the river revealed nothing for several moments, he began to think the cap had come from some dead man killed near the river. Just as he was about to go back onto the bank, he heard the faint sound of oars being used and looked again. The instant he caught sight of the boat he hurried back to Abigail.

"Rebs or marauders," he said as he grabbed Abigail

by the hand and started back to town as fast as he could.

"You think they are going to come ashore here?" she asked as she did her best to keep pace with him.

"Only good place for docking there is for quite a stretch. Also think we are the last of the Union soldiers in the area and would be a perfect target. Waiting for a couple of men to be healed enough to move."

As they reached the road into town, he hesitated for a moment and listened. The men obviously did not expect anyone to be down at the riverside because they were talking to each other freely and above a whisper. Since supplies were no longer coming in that way and the dock had been destroyed, he supposed it was a reasonable assumption for them to make.

"Go warn the women," he told Abigail.

"Do you want us to go to the jail again?" she asked.

"If ye can. It is the sturdiest place to shelter in. Go! I need to warn the men."

She impulsively kissed him and then ran for the Beaton house. A couple of soldiers out walking stared at her as she hiked up her skirts so that she could run faster. When she reached the door of the Beaton house she glanced behind her and saw Matthew heading back toward the river with what looked to be a dozen armed men. That sight comforted her for it meant Matthew was not facing the danger alone.

Abigail opened the door and ran into the house only to nearly run down Mrs. Beaton. She stopped and fought to catch her breath as she said, "We have to go to the jail again. Now. They are coming in at the river."

"I begin to think we should just move there," said Mrs. Beaton even as she headed into the sitting room to order the women there to get moving.

As soon as she could breathe properly, Abigail hurried up the stairs, but when she rushed into her room she found Julia's bed empty. She was relieved to find the baby sleeping peacefully and picked him up, wrapping a second small blanket around him. Grabbing the bag she had begun to keep packed in case they needed to run again, she headed back down the stairs.

"Rose," she called, catching the woman just as she was headed out the door, "have you seen Julia?"

"Damn. No, I haven't. You think she has wandered off again?"

"I do and I know where she has gone. Could you take the baby and my bag?"

Rose quickly took both and Abigail said, "Go on now. I will get her to the jail."

"Be careful!" Rose called as she rushed out the door.

Abigail waved and headed for the back door. She paused a moment in the kitchen when she saw Mabel working on the evening meal. She supposed she ought not to be so shocked that no one had thought to tell the woman to flee or to where, or even that the enemy might be coming, but it did trouble her.

"Mabel, there is some trouble and the lieutenant has asked that we all shelter in the jail."

"Is it a lot of trouble?" Mabel asked as she set her work aside and hastily washed her hands.

"No idea. The lieutenant got some men and is facing them down by the river. It may end there, but he still told me to get us all to the jail. Says it is the strongest building in town. So get your family and get over there as fast as you can."

Mabel nodded and ran out. Abigail followed but headed straight for the graveyard. When she saw Julia at Robert's grave she was more angry than concerned, until she got closer. The woman was ghostly pale and slumped against the wooden cross that marked the grave. She hurried over and touched Julia's arm, finding it alarmingly chilled. Another quick check found the woman's heart still beat.

"Julia," she called and shook her gently. "We have to run to the jail."

"Again?" Julia asked, her voice whisper soft and a bit slurred.

"Yes, I fear so." Abigail helped Julia stand, not surprised at how much of the woman's weight she had to shoulder. "You are out here in your nightclothes again."

"No matter. No one to see."

The woman spoke as if she was drunk, and it worried Abigail. "Are you feeling well, Julia?"

"Just feel as if all my innards are falling out."

Since she had heard the complaint from other women after childbirth, Abigail was inclined to ignore it, but some instinct made her look Julia over as they staggered toward the jail. The back of her nightgown was soaked in blood and Abigail felt a stab of fear. She did her best to get Julia to the jail as quickly as possible. By the time she staggered through the door, she was almost carrying the woman.

Maude and Rose hurried over to help and Abigail released her grip on Julia. Betsy noticed the blood and quickly moved all the children to a different cell then busied herself with hanging up a sheet to block any view of Julia and what might happen. Maude handed Abigail some rags and she quickly replaced the ones Julia was wearing. She then bound them on as tightly as she could. Next, she tilted up Julia's hips and legs as best she could with folded blankets and a couple of cushions. Abigail saw no sign that any of what she did was helping.

"I am going to have to get the doctor," she said and dragged her hand through her hair, fleetingly wondering what had happened to the ribbon that she had tied it back with. "I've never dealt with bleeding this bad."

"Nor I," said Maude, and Rose shook her head in an echo of Maude's words. "She can't last long if it doesn't stop. Should we take her to him?"

"I'll bring him back. Moving her now could only add to the problem. I'll be back as soon as I can."

"Take your rifle," called Rose as Abigail ran to the door.

"I planned on that." She grabbed her rifle from where it leaned against the wall just inside the door and, after a careful survey of the street, bolted for the infirmary.

She had barely gotten inside the door of the infirmary when the doctor appeared at her side. He looked at her in shock, but she had no idea why nor the time or patience to find out. It was hard enough to ignore the sounds and smells of wounded men.

"Julia is bleeding too much," she blurted out.

"I thought you said the birth went well."

"It did or so I thought. She was bleeding but not badly, no worse than any other I have helped. Now it is just flowing out of her and I can't stop it."

"What have you done for her?"

"Tied her rags on as tightly as I could and raised up her hips and legs. It isn't really helping."

"I see. I'll look at her, but you need to finish up here for me." He put a threaded needle in her hand. "It is a long shallow cut low on the belly. Didn't go deep enough to open him up but still needs closing." He turned and pushed her gently toward the nearest bed.

"Matthew!" she cried out when she saw the man sprawled on that bed.

"It's not deep," the doctor said in a firm, steady voice. "He jumped back in time. Are you going to be able to do this?"

Abigail took a deep breath and, as she let it out slowly, she wrestled down her fear. "I can do it."

"Good. I'll go see if there is anything I can do for Julia."

"She is in the jail," she told him as he started to leave.

Forcing herself to think only of closing the wound, Abigail hurried to Matthew's side. His eyes were closed but, she was fairly sure he was not sleeping. Looking at what the doctor had on his table, she found something to clean off the wound area. The cut was a long ugly slice across his belly and he was extremely lucky that it had not been deeper.

What really troubled her was how difficult she found it to make that first stitch. She had stitched up a lot of wounds, yet the thought of running a needle through Matthew's flesh made her stomach churn. Scolding herself for cowardice and sternly reminding herself of how important it was to close his wound in order to stave off infection, she finally took that first stitch and proceeded to work with her usual speed.

Matthew grit his teeth against the pain. Forcing open one eye he realized it was Abbie stitching him up. He looked around for the doctor, did not see him anywhere, then looked back at Abbie who was busy working with her usual concentration and speed. When she tied off the stitching and sat back, the way she stared at his wound and covered her mouth gave him the distinct feeling that she was trying not to laugh. Since he saw nothing funny about a stomach wound, shallow or not, he frowned at her.

"Abbie," he called, and she looked at him in surprise. "Why are ye here?"

"The doctor had to go see if he can help Julia. I did not realize you were the one who needed stitching. I worked as fast as I could," she said as she carefully sat down on the edge of the bed. "Any other wounds?"

"The doctor already tended to them. Two." He appreciated the look of worry on her face as she hurriedly searched him for signs of the wounds. "One wee scrape on my arm and a through and through wound on my leg."

She reached for the sheet covering his wounded leg, but he snatched it out of her hands. "Nay. Best not."

"Is it that bad?"

He used his other hand to point to a pile of clothing on the floor. "Doc doesnae cut the clothes off or make any attempt to protect one's modesty."

"Too much trouble," said the doctor as he walked up to them.

"Julia?" Abigail asked warily, worried that he was back so soon, and felt the sting of tears in her eyes when he shook his head.

"I am sorry, Abbie. It happens sometimes. I examined her and she is badly torn up inside. Something must have just given out. She is desperate to speak to you, however." When Abbie frowned and looked at Matthew, he added, "I'll watch this fool."

"Fool?" Matthew grumbled, but they both ignored him.

"Go, Abbie. There is not much time left and she was very adamant about talking to you."

Abbie stood, lightly kissed Matthew, and then hurried away. She hated to leave him, wounded and bedridden as he was, but he was not dying. This time her friend truly did take precedence and she could be sure of the reason because the doctor had told her.

"The woman is dying?" asked Matthew.

The doctor nodded. "Bleeding to death. The strange thing is she talks to her dead husband."

"Abbie said that. She kept going out to his grave to talk with him."

"Which was probably enough to start her bleeding. Gave me a chill when she talked to him because she acted as if she could see him at her side."

"Weel, maybe she finds comfort in that wee dream."

"I find myself hoping that it is more than a dream."

He checked Abbie's stitching and then grinned. "This will leave an interesting scar."

"What does it look like? Abbie looked as if she was going to smile, too."

"You are going to have a big grin on your belly. It is placed very nicely beneath your belly button. Tattoo on a couple of eyes and you'd have a whole face there." He laughed.

"Ha. Funny mon. And what the hell is your name anyway?"

The doctor blinked. "Harvey Deacon Pettibone the Third."

Matthew shook his head. "Eastern nobility."

"And always a doctor. One in every generation. When are you going to marry that girl?"

"Abbie?" He blushed at the disgusted look the doctor gave him. "I dinnae ken."

"Coward."

"About that? Aye, straight down to the bone." He smiled faintly when the doctor laughed.

* * *

Abbie slowed her step as she approached Julia's bed in the cell. She had run all the way from the infirmary but her step had lagged once she reached the door of the jail. She had nursed a spark of hope all the way to the jail but it had begun to die as she neared the place. Now it completely died. The scent of death lingered over Julia and she was as pale as any still living person Abbie had ever seen.

"Thank you for getting the doctor to come," said Julia as she tried to hold out her child to Abbie. "Please, take him."

Taking the child, Abbie held him cradled in one arm and sat on the edge of the bed to clasp Julia's cold hand. "The doctor said you were anxious to talk to me."

"Yes. I know I am dying and there is something I have to settle before I go join my Robert." She shook her head when Abbie started to speak. "No, I know the truth, Abbie. The doctor was very kind, but he did not try to hide the truth from me. I want you to raise my boy. Take him. He will be an orphan soon. You will do that, won't you?"

Abbie did not know what to say. She was a young, unmarried woman. How could she raise a child? She did not even have a place to live.

"Abbie, promise me. Promise me you will care for my boy."

"As best I can, Julia," she finally said, prompted by the woman's growing agitation.

"Thank you. It makes it easier to let go. The address

for his family is in with my things so maybe you could send them word?"

"I will. Do not worry on that."

"Good. They lost their son and may be pleased to know he lives on in his boy." She struggled to reach out and was finally able to smooth her hand over her baby's head. "Be a good boy for Abbie."

Julia closed her eyes before Abbie could say anything more. It was a huge responsibility Julia was setting in her lap. Abigail had no idea how she was supposed to take care of a newborn. The woman's hand slipped off the child and when Abigail looked back at Julia's face, she sighed. There was no arguing the matter now. The woman was very close to dying. Abbie sat watch and a few minutes later she knew her friend was gone.

Getting up, she turned toward the women and saw them all watching her. "We best prepare her for burial now."

Maude walked over and looked at the baby. "How are you going to care for a child?"

"I have no idea, but it was what she wanted. Her dying wish, if you will, so how can I do anything but what she asked? Now is not the time to think on it though."

"No, it isn't." Maude looked back at the other women. "Come along, ladies. Let us get her ready. Never seen a woman so eager to join her husband."

Neither had Abigail. She could not help but wonder if that need to be with Robert had aided in Julia's death. The woman had not really had any great need to stay alive, had no fight in her. Not even her child had changed her mind as Abbie had hoped it would.

When it was finally safe again and time to take Julia

to the graveyard, Abbie briefly wished they had a minister, but the man had fled to save his own skin. Wrapping the child up warmly, she followed the women out to the graveyard, Maude and Rose carrying Julia's body. She gave a start when she saw two soldiers finishing the digging of a grave next to Robert's. They nodded at the women politely and quietly went to stand near the trees ringing the graveyard.

Mrs. Beaton set a large basket by Abbie's feet and she settled the baby in it. She then turned her attention to saying a final farewell to her friend. She wished they had a coffin, but there were none around and no one to make one. The man who did such work had been killed in the first attack on the town.

When Rose said a rather beautiful prayer then sang, Abigail had to swallow hard to keep from weeping. Then the men returned to bury her friend. She picked up the babe and found one standing right in front of her.

"How did you know to come and do this?"

"The doc sent us."

"That was good of him."

"We'll mark a wooden cross for her, ma'am," he said quietly.

"Thank you. I was just wondering how to get one put up. She was Robert's wife, a mother, and only twenty-three."

"A sad business this. You should ask the major if there is any money for a soldier's widow even if only Robert's pay that he didn't collect."

She nodded and made her way back to the house. It took some time to find a source of milk for the baby and a way to give it to him but fortunately Mrs. Beaton kept a few goats and one had just birthed a kid. By then the baby was sound asleep and Abbie felt it would be acceptable if she left for a little while to see how Matthew was doing.

A tickle of guilt struck her and she frowned. It was sad that she was able to go and see the man she loved but Julia never could have. Then she abruptly stopped and thought over what she had just accidentally confessed to herself. She loved Matthew MacEnroy. It was past time she stopped playing and do something about it.

But what could she do? she thought. It was not the woman's place to speak or push the man to speak. She certainly had no idea how to nudge him to speak or even if he felt the same way. It seemed the only thing she could do was just what she had been doing, even if it was breaking a lot of rules. She would continue to show him, in all ways she could, that she cared and hope he would finally speak of how he felt. Unsatisfactory as that solution was, it irritated and she marched into the infirmary.

Chapter Twelve

Matthew tried to shift his body into a more comfortable position. It was not easy when his stomach was sewn up. Every move he made seemed to tug on the stitches. He cursed softly as that pinching pain struck again when he shifted his hips.

"Such language. Tsk. Tsk," drawled James.

Matthew scowled up at his friend. "If not for that idiot with his knife I wouldn't be in this uncomfortable position."

"Better this than the gutting the man was trying to accomplish."

"True. Just dinnae feel inclined to admit it. Will have to remind myself of that more."

"It was a fierce skirmish. Good thing you saw them coming."

"Abbie did. One of the fools lost his cap and she saw it on the water. Gave it to me and I looked down the river for them but almost gave up too soon. They werenae even being quiet. That's why I finally spotted them. Voices carry well on the river."

"They were not soldiers. They were Night Riders or marauders or whatever the hell they call themselves now. Hell, they could even have just been some good old boys who thought they'd kill them some blue bellies. So, you and Abbie were down by the river, eh?"

Matthew sighed. "Why is everyone suddenly interested in my love life? The doc and now you."

"So, it is a love life, is it? Going to marry the girl?"

"That is my business and my business alone."

"You're no fun."

"Could be because I am in pain."

"Well, here's something to take your mind off that. They just buried Julia."

"Ah, hell."

"Yup. Doc sent some men over to the graveyard to dig a spot next to Robert. No coffin. We ran out of the ones we had and no one around to build another."

"I could have except for this hole in my leg."

"And shoulder and belly. They put her in a sheet. Abbie was tending to the baby, poor mite. Orphan now."

"I suspect there will be a lot of those when this war ends. Will certainly be a lot of bairns with no das."

"News is we are headed out."

"Where to?"

"South.

"We're already south."

"Obviously not the right part. They are already packing up things so think it must be true. Rumor is there is going to be a hard drive into the enemy's lands in an attempt to end all this. The army in Virginia needs more men. Thinking this is going to take a long time to end as there are a lot of places where there is fighting. This area will be slow to let it go. Still a lot of Reb soldiers in the area or Reb sympathizers."

"Already feels as if this war has gone on too long."

"Much too long," said the doctor as he walked up

and began to check Matthew's wounds, "and the hate and resentment will last even longer. Always does."

"That's cheerful news."

"Realistic news. I studied a lot of history. Fascinating subject." He glanced at Matthew. "Or are all you Scots close friends with the English?"

Matthew glared at James who just laughed. He then caught sight of Abbie pausing to talk to Boyd who still could not move his arm and helped out at the infirmary where he could. She looked a strange mixture of annoyed and deeply saddened.

"Ah, Julia was interred a little while ago."

"Interred? Listen to our doc with his fancy words," said James and laughed when the man glared at him.

"You should hit him for that. Hard. Set him straight," urged Matthew and then grinned. "Right in that big smile he is always flashing." He laughed along with the doctor but then winced as that also pulled at his stitches.

"Just thought you ought to be warned," the doctor said to Matthew.

"Ah, aye. I could read it on her face." He nodded toward where Abbie still talked with Boyd. "Since I am wounded and bed-bound"—he rubbed his forehead to try and chase away a throbbing headache—"I thought she would be gentle even if her mood was sour."

"Such naivete," the doctor murmured. "We're moving out soon. Day or two at the most."

"What about the people in the town?" asked James.

"I am afraid they will be left to fend for themselves or leave for someplace they believe will be safer. You"—the doctor pointed at Matthew—"will be and so will Boyd. No need to drag either of you to a new posting when you are both wounded as you are. So you can go home."

"That could prove a dangerous journey"—he rubbed his bandaged arm—"especially since I wouldnae be able to shoot nor would Boyd."

"Then I will speak to the major as soon as I can and he'll send one able-bodied soldier with you."

"I'll just meander over there with you, Harvey," said James.

"Hey, how did ye ken his name?" asked Matthew.

"I asked." James turned to smile at Abbie as she walked over. "How do, Miss Abbie. Sorry about your friend."

"Yes, it was a sad waste. Thank you."

She watched the doctor and James walk away and then sat down on the edge of Matthew's bed. "Why are you rubbing your head?"

"Headache, and it is getting worse, so let me apologize now if I get a wee bit snappish."

She grinned. "I think I can survive."

"I am sorry about Julia, Abbie." He took her hand in his and brushed his thumb over the back of it.

"She was the first friend I made in this place." She shook her head. "Since I left Pennsylvania, too."

"I think Rose and Maude like you well enough."

"Oh, they do, but they are a bit older, have lived more, and all that. Julia and I had a more common ground to work on. Perhaps that is why she chose me."

"Chose you? For what?"

"To care for her son." She smiled faintly at the way his eyes widened with shock. "She made me promise. So, I fear I am no longer a simple country lass"—she grinned—"to go for a stroll with. I am a mother now. Julia even made out a rough will, had it signed by some of the other women too, naming me the boy's guardian. I also promised to try and contact Robert's family."

"Ye think they might want the bairn?"

"They might, but Julia made no allowances for that, and if they take a long time to come around, I may not want to oblige them, either. Then I have to wonder why she didn't mention them or choose them for her baby. She gave me no warning about them. It is a puzzle I will have to solve when and if it arises." Abigail frowned when he let go of her hand to yank the blanket over himself. "Are you cold?"

"Just a wee bit chilly. Guess winter hasnae completely left us yet."

He closed his eyes and Abbie frowned, unable to hide her concern. When she saw the flush grow on his cheeks and beads of sweat form on his forehead, she knew her concern was warranted. Standing up and looking around, she spotted the doctor and waved him over. The man hesitated, glanced at another wounded man, and then hurried to her side.

"Ask quickly as I need to tend to a man with an infection forming," he said.

"I think Matthew is getting feverish." She tried to speak calmly but knew some of her growing fear must have leaked into her voice when the doctor patted her on the shoulder before checking on Matthew.

"Definitely a fever starting, but it might not get too high. It's not unusual for a wounded man to run a fever. After all, his body just took a severe battering. Get a bucket of cool water and some rags to wash him down. Check his wounds now and then for any hint of infection and he should recover from this. He was astonishingly healthy before he went down."

She watched as he hurried back to the other wounded man. Moving quickly she got a bucket of cool water and several rags. She was proud that the doctor trusted her to do what was needed but she dearly wished he could have stayed to supervise anyway, or simply help. It was not just any man she was going to work to heal, it was Matthew. She wanted all the skill and power the good doctor could bestow.

Dipping a rag into the water, she then wrung it out and gently bathed his face. By the time she had wiped his neck and shoulders the cloth was no longer cool. The increasing fever heat in his body had almost dried it out. She did it again with close to the same result. Next she wiped the cloth over his arms and chest twice before doing the same for his legs and feet.

As she wet the cloth again she thought over things she had read in her father's books, ones saved from when he had trained to be a doctor. Her mother had hated her looking through such books but her father had often sat with her explaining what she had read and the pictures. She knew all the places where a wound to them could prove fatal, because the person would bleed out. He had thought it good knowledge for her to have in case she was attacked when she had no gun.

She rested her fingers against the vein in his neck and felt the strong pulse there. Then she checked his wrists. Pausing to check his shoulder wound and seeing no hint of infection, she then checked his leg wound and decided it was also clean. As carefully as she could, she folded the sheet down to study the wound on his stomach. Then she ripped two rags into strips, wet them, and laid them over his neck, wrists, and ankles.

"What are you doing?"

Abigail screeched softly and spun around to stare at the doctor. "You walk mighty softly."

"You want me to stomp?" He smiled briefly at the cross look she gave him. "Now, answer the question, please."

She explained what she had learned from her father and his books. "I just thought it might work to stop the fever from rising."

"Seems to be working," he murmured after checking Matthew over. "You found no hint of infection at the wound sites?"

"No. All his wounds look as good as something like that can."

"Good. I best get back to my patient. It might be wise to do that only now and then."

She nodded, tempted to ask why, only to see that he had already gone back to his other patient. Abigail thought hard about his advice and decided to follow it even though he had given her no reason for it. She could think of several but did not have the medical knowledge to know if she was right. Using each rag to wash down a part of him, she removed the strips of cloth.

Tossing the cloths into the bucket of water, she checked Matthew for any sign of his fever. It was still there but had lessened considerably. Abigail doubted he was cured of his fever, but a respite from it could only help him heal. Then he opened his eyes and looked at her. In his eyes was a cloudiness that told her he was not yet free of the fever's effects even if his skin had cooled.

"Sorry, Abbie, I must have fallen into a wee nap." He winced and rubbed at his forehead. "I dinnae suppose ye have anything for the ache in my head."

"A cold cloth," she said, picking a rag out of the bucket, wringing it out, and slapping it on his forehead. "If it still troubles you after this, I can rub it. That sometimes helps."

"Anything to stop this throbbing."

Abigail sat at the head of the bed, gently settled his head in her lap, and waited a few moments before moving the damp rag and beginning to rub his temples. The lines of pain on his face began to smooth out and she knew he was falling asleep. She waited, continuing to rub his forehead but with lessening firmness, until she was sure he had fallen asleep. Then she grimaced as she tried to get off the bed without waking him. She was beginning to think she was stuck until he woke up again when she was grasped under the arms and neatly pulled out then set down on her feet. Looking over her shoulder, she found a grinning James standing behind her.

"Looked like you were stuck," he said.

"Thank you."

"No trouble, pigeon."

"Why do you call me that?"

"You are on the small side and you do wear gray a lot."

"My mother liked the color. She had a lot of gowns in that color. I stitched the gown to fit me." She glared at her chest. "Sometimes a lot." She ignored the soft snort of laughter James let slip.

"Is he going to sleep for a long time?"

"I hope so. He needs it. Not just for the wounds to heal but for the fever trying to settle on him. Why?"

"Well, I will keep a watch over him for a while."

"That is very kind of you, but there is no need."

"There is. You need to get ready to travel."

"Why?"

"Because you need to take a journey."

Abigail felt the twitch of a headache and rubbed at her forehead. "Again—why?"

James sighed. "He needs to go home," he said with a nod toward Matthew. "These soldiers are all heading out to join up with the main army. Grant is gathering all the men he can. God knows why. So our officer has decided we will all go. But Boyd and Matt will be sent to Matt's family to finish their healing."

"Why do I need to go?"

"You have to drive the wagon so I can keep a close watch over Matt and Boyd if there is trouble."

"Dan," she began.

"Nope. He wants to go with the major. Seems he has family in the same direction they are going and thinks he might get to see them for a bit."

"I hope they have gotten through this mess unharmed thus far."

"So do I. Go on. I will watch over him and you get done what you need to so we can be on the road first thing in the morning."

"I do hate the mornings," she muttered and almost smiled when he laughed.

Abigail slowly walked back to Mrs. Beaton's home. She was unsure about traveling to Matthew's home but knew someone was needed to drive the wagon. If she insisted Dan do it, she could well be forced to say a final farewell to Matthew, and that was something she did not want. If he wanted her gone he would have to be man enough to tell her to go. Nor did she want to deprive Dan of the chance to see his family. Considering what he was riding into, it could be the last meeting for all of them.

There was also a lot she had to get ready. Her chests were almost fully packed as she had kept them as the storage for her things. Unfortunately she had gained a few new things. There was a baby she had to get ready. Then there was the problem of how to carry the goat's milk so it did not spoil or, even more difficult, the goat itself.

Then she thought of Noah and winced. She had the strong feeling he would want to come with her but she was going to have to make him understand that he could not, that she would have to come back for him. She had no home and she had no husband. It was going to be difficult to make people understand the baby was not hers by blood and the fewer people who believed that, the greater the problems would be in settling somewhere.

She suddenly stopped and looked toward Mrs. Dunmore's house. There was one thing she could do to ease whatever trouble she would have with Noah. It was close to the time the woman had said she could have the puppy, she thought as she hurried toward the house, and knocked on the door.

"Hello, Miss Abigail," the woman said as she opened the door. "I was wondering when you would come or if you had changed your mind."

"No, I still want the puppy. You still have him?"

"Yes, yes, come on in."

Abbie stepped inside and followed the woman as she walked toward the back of the house. "Is he ready to leave his mother?"

"He is. There is just one thing. He is not going to get very big, I think."

"That would actually be nice."

"I hope the boy thinks so."

"I think he will not care."

She saw the puppy the moment they stepped into what looked to be the woman's laundry room. The quick glance around she took told her Mrs. Dunmore did the wash for the soldiers. Then her gaze went back to the puppy she had picked out for Noah. It was still small, a little black and white ball of fur sitting there watching his siblings wrestle.

Mrs. Dunmore picked the puppy up and walked back to Abigail. She held up one of the dog's paws and said, "See? The paw is small and he is still the smallest of the bunch. So thinking he is going to be small. Not a runt, but smaller than all the others."

"I think Noah will be very happy with that. Thank you."

"No, thank *you* for taking him. I was afraid I would have to put him down because no one would want him and I can't keep him. Have too many damn dogs now." She frowned as they started back toward the front door. "Are you sure Mrs. Beaton will be fine with you bringing the pup home?"

"Not at all." Abigail smiled when the woman laughed. "I haven't asked or told her and I am certain I will be made to pay for that, but it doesn't matter. For one thing I am leaving soon."

"Well, sorry to see you go and hope you have a safe journey."

Abigail thanked her and left the house. The puppy kept licking her face so the rest of her walk home was both slow and crooked. She was laughing when she stepped into the Beaton house only to come face-to-face with Mrs. Beaton. The woman stared at the puppy but not with the horror Abbie had expected. The woman stepped closer and patted the dog's head, much to Abbie's surprise.

"If it messes inside the house it will not be the puppy's face that gets rubbed in it."

"I understand."

"One of Mrs. Dunmore's?"

"Yes, the smallest one."

"Good choice. My little dog was one of hers too, also one of the smallest ones, but the Rebs shot it when they rode through town."

"I'm sorry. They killed Noah's puppy, too. And my cat. Makes no sense."

"Just meanness." She frowned faintly. "Noah's been wondering where you were. Is the lieutenant doing well?"

"I think so. He developed a fever but I think the fever isn't a dangerous one but we are taking him home tomorrow. And the army is leaving very soon after."

She nodded. "I am not surprised. We will be fine here. I have faced this before. I know how to hide what needs hiding, and how to keep from being shot because some fool is in the mood to shed blood."

Abigail started up the stairs and prayed Mrs. Beaton's confidence was not misplaced. She stepped into her room and found Noah sprawled on her bed looking at a book. He sat up and immediately saw the puppy. His eyes wide with surprise and hope, he slid off the bed and walked over cautiously. He patted the puppy who immediately bathed his face with enthusiasm, making the boy giggle.

"What are you going to name him?" she asked.

"I can name him?"

"Of course. I got him for you."

"He's mine?"

"He cannot make a mess in the house. Mrs. Beaton is very firm on that."

Noah took the puppy from her and hugged him to his chest. "He won't. I will make very sure of that. I was good with my puppy." He studied the little black and white dog wriggling in his arms. "This one doesn't look like my puppy at all. Mine was all brown. I think I will name him Wags."

"Wags?"

"Because he does a lot of that. See?" He held him out from his body for a minute and the whole animal shook from the force of the tail wagging he did.

"I guess he does." She patted the dog then moved to her chests, opening the one she used most often and beginning to toss things inside.

"What you doing?"

"Packing. I need to leave in the morning."

"I'll go pack, too."

Abigail sighed. "No, love, there is no need for you to pack."

Noah stopped heading out the door and walked back to her side. "Why?"

"Because you can't come with me now. It would be too dangerous."

"Then you should not go!"

"I have to. I have to drive the wagon." She reached out to take his hand in hers, but he stepped back and put the hand on the puppy. "I need to have a place to live before I take you with me. I have no home, no husband, and no idea when I will find either. When I gain at least a home to call my own, I will come back for you."

"You are taking the baby."

A direct hit, she thought, and scrambled to think of a way to explain that. "A baby needs an adult to care for it all the time. I promised Julia I would care for her child. Promises are meant to be kept, you know."

Noah nodded. "He needs to eat round the clock and he cannot even go to the bathroom by himself but needs his napkin changed, and he cannot run away from any trouble that finds him."

"I don't want you to leave me. I could help you with the baby."

"You probably could but there is still the problem that I have no place ready for us to live. After I find a house for us, I will come back for you, Noah. This isn't a forever type of leaving. I am just taking Matthew home because he is badly wounded. Once he is settled and has his family to care for him, I will look for a place to live where you can come and stay with me. Noah?" she called when he just turned around and walked out.

He kept on going and she heard him run to his room. For a moment, she thought about going after him then shook her head. She could not give him what he wanted. The tears shining in his eyes had cut her to the heart but she had to harden herself against them. She had a very good reason to make him wait. He would have to accept that.

Finishing her packing she fetched her gun from where it stood near the door downstairs and put it with the chests. She had saved so little she did not want to lose it now. Once done she went down the stairs and into the kitchen to help Mabel one last time. When the children trooped in to sit at the small table set aside for them, she was saddened by the fact that Noah did not come down with them. Each child sent her angry glares and she accepted that she was now the bad one.

"So you are leaving us," said Maude as the stew was passed around the table.

"Yes. Matthew is too injured to join the army when

it leaves to join with one of the bigger forces south of here."

"The soldiers are leaving, too?" asked Anne, her sultry voice a little high with shock.

"They are but I am not sure when. Fairly soon I think, as they were packing stuff up when I left the infirmary."

Rose frowned. "So, there will be no one here to protect the town."

"No soldiers, but with no soldiers here perhaps there will be no trouble."

"Ha!" Maude shook her head. "With men running about with guns and eager to shoot something, there is guaranteed to be trouble. We can handle it. We did before the soldiers settled in here."

"It would be better if they stayed," muttered Anne.

"Just because you can't make up your mind which one you want is not a good reason for one or more of them to desert," said Maude and she winked at Abigail.

Abigail hid her answering smile by eating a spoonful of stew. Anne went out walking a lot and with an impressive array of soldiers. The young woman's busy and varied social life was about to die out.

When the meal was over she asked Mary if they wanted a story and was politely told no. Abbie was not surprised, but Maude and Rose looked shocked. She shook her head at them, afraid they were about to say something.

"But why?" Maude asked the moment they were out of the room. "You read to them every night and they seemed to love it."

"I am not taking Noah with me."

"Oh. I gather he expected to go with you."

"He did and I had to say no. It is still not all that safe to travel. Worse, he pointed out that I was taking the baby." She nodded when Rose winced as they reached the main room. "I explained why the baby has to go and why he has to wait. I don't even have a house to live in. I need to get settled somewhere then I can take him. He doesn't like the waiting part and I think he is trying to think of a way to persuade me. He had that look."

"Oh dear," said Maude. "Don't worry about him. Me and Rose will keep an eye on him and remind him that it is only a wait."

"Thank you."

After getting ready for bed, Abigail crawled beneath the covers and tried very hard to put her concern for Noah aside. Since she was the cause of his unhappiness, it was not easy. She knew she was right. He had to wait for a while. She would work as hard as she could to get herself a place where they could live. A whisper in her mind reminded her that she also needed a husband, but she ignored it as she fell asleep.

Chapter Thirteen

She smoothed out the blankets she had put on the floor of the wagon between her two chests. It was not a proper bed but it would serve well enough. They would not be traveling for too long, she hoped. Matthew's fever had returned in force and she spent a great deal of time washing him down, desperately trying to erase the heat in him.

As she scrambled out of the wagon she watched as James and Dan carried Matthew out of the infirmary and set him down on the rough bed she had made. The moment they were out of the way she scrambled back into the wagon and covered him over with another blanket. She worried about taking him on a journey in such a condition, but soon the town would be unprotected and she could not make herself believe it would be safe for him. As she climbed onto the driver's bench she promised herself she would drive as carefully as she could while still moving along at a reasonably fast pace.

Looking at the Beaton house as the wagon rolled by it slowly, she worried about all the ones inside it as well. Maude and Rose stood at the windows and waved, and she waved back. They were smiling even as they wiped away tears, and Abigail decided that was a picture she would hold fast to. She did wish she could take them all but it was not her property they were traveling to. Then James signaled to her to pick up a little speed and Abigail did so. George was an excellent cart horse and she felt confident he would get them where they needed to go. She was just not sure he would get them there very fast.

As the wagon rolled out of town she glanced at Boyd who sat on the seat beside her. The doctor had told her he was beginning to think the young man was afraid to try and move his arm. Whether Boyd was afraid it would prove to be permanently weakened or he just did not wish to heal enough to be thrust back into the fighting, the doctor could not be certain. Abigail doubted even Boyd knew what he was doing and she began to wonder how one fixed such a problem if the doctor was right.

Then despite her best effort to think of something else, anything else, she thought of Noah. She could see him as clearly as if he was standing right in front of her, his puppy in his arms and his eyes shiny with tears. He had watched as she had packed her things and even as she had readied the baby for travel. Even his puppy had stared at her with sad, accusatory eyes. She had done her best to explain to him that she could not take him with her, that there could be a danger in the journey, that she had to settle somewhere first, and that she would come for him as quickly as she could, but he had just walked away. Having seen the thoughtful look that came over his face, the moment he left the room she had grabbed her things and hurried down to the evening meal. She could not shake the feeling, however, that Noah thought her the cruelest woman in the world. Abigail did not know how or when, but she would make it up to him.

"You are looking very sad," said Boyd. "Going to miss the other women?"

"Of course, but I was actually thinking of Noah. I don't think he believed me when I tried to tell him I would come back for him especially since I could not tell him exactly when I would do that."

"Ah, well, he is only five. You can't give a child some vague time in the future. He wants a day and a time if only so he can keep asking if it is here yet."

Abigail laughed but stopped quickly and frowned. "You are right, but I couldn't do that because I had no date or time to give him. It didn't help that I took the baby anyway. That probably made it seem as if I was lying."

"Not if you haven't lied to him before. Young children have to learn to mistrust a person, have a lot of promises broken before they understand not to trust a certain person. I'd wager you haven't done anything to make him mistrust you. You gave him a puppy."

"I did. I didn't tell him I was going to because, well, because puppies can too easily die on you. He is going to be a small dog."

"Probably not bad for a small boy. He'll be able to control it." He wrinkled his nose. "I think young Jeremiah—"

"Stinks."

Abigail looked back to find Matthew awake and frowning toward the small crate they had made into a bed for Jeremiah. "I'll pull up in a minute and take care of that."

James rode up on her side. "Pull into those bushes

just up ahead. They will hide the wagon and George. I think something is coming."

She nodded and headed for the bushes. As soon as she got the cart tucked behind, she unhitched George. Gently she then urged him down on the grass. It was something her father had taught the beast because there was no hiding a huge horse like George. Once he was settled and idly chewing on the grass, she fetched Jeremiah and the bag with his things.

Sitting on the grass, she flipped his blanket over it and then proceeded to clean up the child. She used one of the several buckets of water she had brought to clean up his soiled cloth and set it aside before putting a fresh one on him. Fetching a bottle of goat's milk from another bucket she proceeded to feed the baby, as much to keep him quiet as because it was about that time. She noticed that the goat she had finally decided to take with them had walked out from under the wagon and was feasting on a bush. Once the child was done she hastily rubbed his back to get the air out while trying to keep his mouth against her shoulder so, if he burped, the sound would be muffled.

Settling the baby back in his bed, she tended to Matthew's wounds as she struggled to keep herself below the sides of the wagon bed. Nothing had appeared yet, but James was keeping a very close watch on the road, his rifle at the ready. Even Boyd was watching, holding a pistol in his good hand.

"James has a knack. My mother would call it the sight. If he said something was coming, it is," said Matthew.

"A good skill if you are going into the army, I suppose," she whispered back then tensed as she heard hoof beats.

"It has certainly served us well."

She watched as the men she had heard rode into view. There were eight of them and they rode along silently. The way they kept such a close watch all around them made her nervous, but they did not appear to notice the wagon and George was behaving. She glanced down at the horse and realized he had decided to have a nice nap.

She then glanced toward the goat and tensed. It was too small to be seen but the bush it was chomping on was moving a lot and might be visible. She crept to the back edge of the wagon and grabbed the animal's tether then paused. If she pulled the animal away there was sure to be some loud protest.

Before she could decide if she would take that chance, it proved unnecessary. It was not the stubborn goat who alerted the men to where they were but the baby. Jeremiah suddenly let out a loud wail, demanding attention. He got it. All eight men on the road turned their way and raised their weapons. She suspected the only thing holding them back from shooting was the fact that it was a baby's cry.

James backed up and disappeared into the trees. As he passed her, he whispered he would be watching but for her to act like a distraught mother. Boyd faded away with him. Abigail covered Matthew with everything she could and set the crate Jeremiah was in on his chest, praying it would be disguise enough. Then she picked up the baby and rubbed at his back.

Cautiously two men came over to her. Abigail was terrified and found that made her mad. It was a curious reaction to fear but she held to it, needing the burst of strength it gave her. The goat moved to chew on the tall one's coat and he aimed his gun at it.

"Don't you dare shoot my child's source of food," she snapped.

"He's eating my damn coat!"

"You can just push him aside. He isn't even a big goat."

"What the hell are you doing out here?" asked the short stout one she felt sure was an officer.

"There is no need to be profane, sir," she said, trying to sound like Mrs. Beaton at her haughtiest. "I have stopped to feed my babe. I just changed him."

"Where are you going?" he asked, speaking slowly as if she was particularly stupid, and she frowned.

"I am going away from here, which obviously is a place filled with fools with guns," she said in the same tone of voice, and thought she may have been too sassy because he scowled at her and his knuckles whitened with the grip he had on his gun.

"Well, don't stay here for long. Get yourself someplace safe." He headed back to the road, and after shooting her a glare the other two men followed him.

Abigail did not breathe a sigh of relief until the men kicked their mounts into a trot and disappeared down the road. She then looked back and saw James and Boyd come out of the trees. Still clutching Jeremiah, she pulled away the things she had piled on top of Matthew. She met his dark frown with a shrug and a smile.

"Thought you were going to get yourself shot there for a moment," said James.

"So did I," she said, and patted her chest over her rapidly beating heart.

"Then why weren't you a bit more meek and conciliatory?"

"Because they didn't shoot me the minute they saw

me. I assumed they were the sort that had a problem shooting a woman and child."

"That was a gamble," muttered Matthew.

"Not a big one," said James as he helped Boyd get back into the seat. "When they aren't in the middle of a fight, the regular soldiers don't much try to kill women and kids." He bent down and eased George back up on his feet before leading him to the traces to put him back in harness. "That was a clever thing to get him to do."

"My da taught him," Abigail said, feeling an echo of pain. "He is such a big fellow, it is the only way to hide him if you have to." She put the baby back into his bed, patted George's neck as she passed him, and climbed back up in the seat to take the reins.

"Here's hoping those are the only ones we run into," James said as he mounted and nudged his horse into motion.

Abigail prayed his hope proved sound as she got the wagon back on the road and started to follow James. Soon she was going along smoothly enough that he dropped back behind them and took up watch again. Boyd watched the ground as she drove.

"What are you looking for?" she asked him.

"Just watching to see if they turn off anywhere along here."

"I hope they do, although I have no idea where they would turn off to. Do we turn off anywhere?"

"Not for quite a ways."

"Let me know when the turn is near."

"Why?"

"Because George hates turning off a road and requires a little coaxing." She heard Matthew laugh and wished she could reach back and smack him. "He'll walk this road pulling us for as long as we want, but a turn"—she shook her head—"no. He gets a bit stubborn."

"Your horse is an odd stick, Abbie," said Matthew.

"He has character."

"Ah, of course. The baby is humming. Badly."

She listened for a moment and smiled. "He'll go to sleep soon. I think he does that to comfort himself."

"Wish he would learn a real tune."

Abigail laughed. "Perhaps you could sing one until he learns it."

"I just might if he keeps this up for too long."

Matthew looked at the baby. He lay on his back with his fingers in his mouth droning away. His eyes were more shut than open and Matthew was certain he was fighting to keep them open as little as he did. He did not know that much about babies except that they could wake the dead with their cries, but he did think this one was particularly well behaved. Then again, it had been the baby who had let the riders know where they were. He was not a man who paid much attention to babies, either, but he did think this one was a fairly handsome little man.

And all that was probably a good thing as the child was now Abigail's. She may not have birthed him but her promise to a dying woman had created the bond. If he did finally get the courage or need up to ask her to stay with him, he would have to accept this child. And Noah, he thought and shook his head. He liked the little boy but he was going to have to be sure he was ready to be a father if he decided he wanted to be her only lover. Abigail would not give either up and he was sure of that, even though she had never spoken of it.

Since he had nothing better to do than think about things, he decided he needed to give the matter of him and Abigail some serious hard thought. He would not be just taking on a woman if he kept her; he would be taking on a small family. It was a serious business and he had to be sure he felt enough depth of emotion to do it right.

Emotions, he decided, were messy and confusing but he needed to stop dithering around. Abigail would not remain his lover for long. What he had to think about was whether that pang he got whenever he thought about that stemmed from a selfish disappointment over a loss of something pleasurable or something far deeper.

The sun was beginning its descent when James rode ahead for a while. He came back and told her they would pull off for the night just up ahead. Her shoulders ached and she was more than ready to stop driving the wagon. The moment they reached the place he had pointed out, she began to coax George into going there. She liked the fact that James had chosen a very nice grassy spot with some trees to shade it.

"I'll have a check for snakes," Boyd said as he got down.

"You didn't have to tell me," Abigail grumbled as she also got down and moved to unhitch George.

"What?"

"Well, I had not given a thought to snakes until you spoke up and stuck it in my head."

"Ah, I see." Boyd suddenly grinned. "I'll just have a check for bunnies."

Even as she thought it would be wrong to strike a wounded man, Abigail found herself appreciating his smile. He really was a handsome young man. She idly wondered if he was one Anne had walked out with.

"Did you ever walk out with Anne?" she asked suddenly and his bright red flush told her the answer was yes, but she decided she would not tease him about it because James was already doing a good job of that.

"That was mean, Abbie," said Matthew as he raised himself up on his arms and waited for someone to help him sit up properly.

"So was mentioning snakes."

"Only a fool doesn't check for them in these hills."

"Well, he could be a quiet, conscientious fellow."

Looking at George as she looped his reins around a tree branch, Matthew shook his head. "That is a damn big horse."

"I know. He is magnificent and he knows it." She rubbed the animal's nose before going to the wagon to check Matthew for any sign of fever.

"It appears to have passed," he said when she finally helped him sit up and piled a bunch of blankets at his back. "Can you send James to me?"

"Yes, but where did he go?" she asked as she looked around.

"He always walks a circle around any place we camp in. He should be coming in behind you before long."

Abigail turned to watch for some sign of the man. When he ambled back through the trees, she hurried over to him. "See any trouble?"

"Nope. No one's been in this area for some time, I'd guess."

"Good. Matthew would like to speak with you."

James went to Matthew and a moment later she saw him helping Matthew out of the wagon. She started over to ask what they thought they were doing when it occurred to her that Matthew might be in desperate need of a moment of privacy. The moment they came back she slipped away for one of her own. By the time she returned, all the men were seated on the ground and James was attempting to get a small fire burning. Matthew leaned against a tree looking as if the short walk had sucked all the energy out of him, but he did not look feverish so she said nothing, just sat down near him on a rough blanket spread on the ground.

"Just how much farther do we have to go?" she asked Matthew.

"If we have no trouble we should be there by the end of the day tomorrow," he answered, and she could hear a hint of eagerness in his tired voice.

"So close to where you were fighting. No wonder the major sent you home."

"That, and the fact that very soon I would have to sign papers to join up again. He didn't see the sense in that. The man is sick to death of this business and gives no one any argument if they are badly wounded or near time to leave anyway. The conscripts are not so lucky. Major doesn't like conscripts. Doesn't like how men who didn't want to fight are shoved into the war."

"How ever did he become an officer with such ideas?"

"Went to the right school. I hope he makes it out of this mess in one piece."

"So do I, for Maude's sake if nothing else."

He laughed. "Did notice her hanging around his office a lot."

"Yes, she was taken with him. Said he had seasoning." She smiled faintly.

For a while they talked about the soldiers and the

women they had mixed with. Abigail realized she had not been wrong about Anne. The woman had walked out with a lot of soldiers. The way Matthew occasionally smiled faintly when he mentioned her told Abigail she had been right to think Anne fit with Maude's teasing reference to the word *walking* when meaning something completely different. She had to wonder if Mrs. Beaton was aware of it.

Abigail finally got up to see what she might make for a meal for them all. She went to the basket Mrs. Beaton had pressed her to take and smiled when she opened it. It was hard to know if it was good manners or friendship that had caused the woman to pack such a vast amount of food, but Abigail did not care. A moment later she had James at her side looking it all over.

"Unless you had a wish to make us a meal, I can do just fine with this. She has packed a lot of things that work well for camp food. Maybe her husband was a soldier once."

"Feel free," she said, more than willing to hand over the chore as her arms and shoulders still ached.

She returned to Matthew's side and quietly asked, "James can cook?"

"Aye. He is skilled at meals in a pot over a campfire."

She crossed her arms over her chest, leaned back against the tree, and closed her eyes. "Good. Driving the wagon was more than enough work for me today."

"Even with a great cart horse like George?"

"Even then."

He just smiled and watched James. "Is the baby still sleeping?"

"He is, and who knows how long he will continue?"

She listened, heard gurgling, and sighed. "Not long, I guess."

A moment later a soft whine sounded and she got up to go to the wagon. Picking up the baby, she grabbed a new changing cloth and, laying him down on the wagon bed, quickly changed him into a dry one. Tossing the wet cloth into an empty bucket, she wished she knew where some water was. She got a bottle, saw that she would have to milk the goat, and went to sit down near Matthew again to feed the baby.

"He has lost that newly born look," he said and idly rubbed the baby's foot.

"Babies this young change every week. It is actually quite fascinating to watch. Well, if you are not the only caretaker. I suspect that can leave one too tired to get excited over little changes. Which is a bit of a shame."

"Aye, it is. He is a good-looking little fellow, but then his mother and father were fair to look at."

"I don't see either of them in him yet. Perhaps as he grows something will show." She sniffed the air. "Whatever James is doing it certainly smells good."

"Told you. We had to shoo off the other fellows in camp when he cooked. They would all come wandering in looking to help themselves to some."

She grinned. "And you proved to be very unwelcoming, I suspect."

"Verra. Then they tried to get James assigned to their group. Major didn't oblige." He glanced at Boyd. "Do ye think Boyd will ever get the use of that arm back?"

"No idea. The doctor told me he can find nothing truly wrong with it but there are a lot of reasons for Boyd to not want to test that."

"I was wondering about that. It will probably be a

surprise to him one day when he just uses it without thinking."

"That was exactly what I thought but can't think of anything that would work to tempt it."

James stepped over to hand them each a plate. Abbie hastily set the baby down on the blanket next to her. It was a thick stew of beef and some vegetables and Abigail had to admit it was surprisingly tasty. By the time she finished, she was full and feeling increasingly sleepy. It had been a very long day. She glanced at the baby, saw he was sound asleep, and wondered if the two of them should curl up in the wagon. She hoped the night did not grow too cold.

Picking up the baby, she stood up and walked back to the wagon. To her surprise, James brought Matthew back and settled him on his bed. As he walked away, she climbed into the back and put the baby's crate at the very head of the bed. Once she had swaddled the child in a warm blanket and put him in the bed, she placed another small blanket over him and then lay down on the other half of the bed Matthew had.

"Going to sleep here with me, are ye?"

"I am not sleeping on the hard ground if I don't have to."

Good." He slid his arm around her and tugged her close, ignoring the twinge it caused his healing wound. "This will be much warmer."

"Careful of your wounds."

"They are healing much better than I thought they would. Family has always been fast healers if we get the wound dressed fast."

"That is convenient." She covered her mouth as another yawn tore through her. "Sorry."

"Why? Ye are obviously tired out. Go to sleep,

Abbie. I am sure the wee lad will be waking ye up soon enough."

"He will," she murmured as she closed her eyes. "I am hoping he is quick to grow out of that."

Matthew pulled the blanket up until it covered them both and he watched her fall asleep. She cuddled closer with a sleepy sigh. He had to admit he was deeply curious about how she would be to sleep with. He did not mind the snuggling at all.

"Shall I move her?" asked James, and Matthew could hear the laughter in his voice.

"Nay, thank ye, but I believe I can stand it." He glanced back at James who had rested his arms on the side of the wagon. "Dinnae ye have anything to do?"

"Did it. How are your wounds? It looked like you were moving with more ease today. Still careful, but not wincing with each movement."

"They do pinch from time to time. Once the stitches can come out that will end."

"Are you gonna marry the girl or not?"

"I'm thinking on it."

"You do know you can overthink things."

"I ken it. I am just thinking on the many things that matter when a mon makes such a move. Like whether she snores or kicks like a mule in bed." He grinned when James laughed.

"It really doesn't need so much planning, you know."

"It needs some so one can be sure."

"Sure of what?"

"That when ye ask she willnae say nay."

James winced. "True. There is always that to consider. Want my opinion?"

"If I say nay, ye will still give it to me, willnae ye?"

"I will. I think you are worrying about something that will never happen."

"Ye cannae ken what her feelings are."

"Nope, but I can know she is not a woman who goes out *walking* with a man if she is not willing to marry him."

"What if willing is not all I am looking for."

"Figured that and don't think it is all you'd get." James straightened up. "Rest well, my friend. We will get to your home on the morrow."

Matthew thought about that as he watched James go and settle down on his rough bed near the fire and begin talking softly with Boyd. It had not actually been that long since he had been home, but too long for him. He had begun to pine for his home months ago. It almost made him laugh because he had spent most of the time fighting in these hills but still ached for home.

He knew what it was he ached for. He wanted his brothers. It embarrassed him in a small way since he was a grown man, but he had never actually spent any time away from his brothers and, annoying though they could be, he heartily missed them. There were too many times he would see or do or think of something and wish one of his brothers was there to share it with. He had always understood that they were a close family, but he had never realized just how close. He wondered if any of them suffered or had done in the same way but could not think of a time when any of them had been away for as long as he had.

Then he wondered what they would think of Abigail. The very fact that he wondered made him believe, yet again, that he had to stop being a coward and ask the question before she decided she was wasting her time and walked away. It made him think though, because he would be bringing her into the family, just as Iain had brought in Emily. He felt suddenly sure that Abigail would fold in neatly and calmly. The baby would disappear into the growing number of children around the place. As would Noah, he thought, knowing she would get the boy, and grinned as he nuzzled her hair and curled his body around hers.

Chapter Fourteen

Abigail yawned widely behind her hand as James secured George into the traces. It was still early but she suspected it was going to be a warm day. And a sunny one, she thought happily. It could prove a good day for travel, but she hoped it did not get too warm. She was especially pleased that the night had not grown too cold, however. She had bundled the baby up as well as she could but had not really needed to. Abbie prayed her good fortune would continue. Jeremiah was still too young to fight off the illnesses a chill could give him.

Matthew braced for some pain but experienced little as he sat up and rested up against the back of the driver's seat. He did wish his arm was not still a bit sore and useless. Abigail knew how to drive the wagon very well but he had seen all the signs yesterday of sore shoulders and arms. It was too much for a woman to do for any length of time, especially if it was not something they did regularly. If he tried to do the gentlemanly thing and take over for her he would no doubt pull out all his stitches, which would just make more work for her.

"We're set to go," said James after patting George's neck. "I'll take point."

"Ready," said Boyd as he climbed up into the wagon seat next to Abigail and placed the pistol he carried on his lap.

Abigail made sure her rifle was in reach, then checked her ammunition, and picked up the reins. Her shoulders protested a little at the start and she knew, at the end of this journey, they were going to be very painful, but she said nothing. James was the only able-bodied man and she could not call on him to give her a respite. They needed him scouting for trouble and able to deal with it. She only had to do the job today, she told herself.

By the time they halted for a midday meal, Abigail was no longer so happy about the sun. It was much too hot. Good weather for the baby to travel in, if properly shaded, but not so pleasant for someone stuck on a wagon seat with it beating down on her head and in her eyes. She searched through her chests and dug out an old sunbonnet her mother had liked. It would not only cover her head but shade her eyes and, she hoped, that would ease the pounding headache she was getting.

Eating a little food, which her stomach protested about, she then tended to Jeremiah and got him back to sleep. She settled him back in his bed under the shade of the canopy she had stretched over it and paused to take a few minutes for herself in the hope of getting rid of her headache. Lying down next to the baby's bed, she held a cool damp cloth to her forehead and closed her eyes.

* * *

"Our wagon is stuck," said James as he sat on a rock next to Matthew.

Matthew looked at the wagon and frowned. "Doesnae look stuck."

"It's stuck right where it is until the driver wakes up."

"Then wake her up."

"Nope. I have a rule. Never wake a woman."

"Stupid rule," Matthew muttered as he got up to walk over to the wagon, the other two men quickly following.

Matthew stood by the side of the wagon staring down at Abbie, his companions flanking him. He noticed she had put a canopy over the baby's bed to keep him shaded. The cloth spread over her forehead told him she had gotten a headache and he suspected that was also why she was sleeping. He felt an odd feeling in his chest and sighed. He was well and truly caught and, he had to admit, he had not fought it at all.

"Why won't ye wake a woman?" he quietly asked James.

"Because every time I would be sent to wake up my sister, Rebecca, she would punch me in the face."

"Ye probably deserved it."

"My sister Nell screamed and kicked," said Boyd. "I'd just give her a little shake and she'd scream as if I was killing her, then kick me. My mother always said she was probably having a nightmare."

"I complained to my father," said James, "and he said my mother punched too so he just gave her a poke with a stick, a long stick. So I started doing that, right up until she got married. My sister's husband doesn't have bruises so I have to wonder if he does the same. Pa might have warned him."

"My mother told me to just stare at her, that a

person can sense that and wake up. Just to be sure, I had my brothers and sisters come with me and we all stared at her. It worked," said Boyd, and nodded as if it had been the greatest hint of knowledge he had ever been given.

"How many brothers and sisters do ye have?" asked Matthew.

"Four brothers and three sisters," Boyd answered. "The girls were the worst at waking up. Boys just cursed you, rolled over, and tried to go back to sleep."

Matthew shook his head. "I just have brothers but, while they might not wake up cheerful, they do wake up without any trouble."

"Then you wake her up," said James.

"Why not just let the lass sleep for a bit?"

That sounded like a good idea, Abigail thought, but doubted she would be able to after hearing their ridiculous conversation. For grown, battle-hardened men, they could certainly talk a lot of nonsense. Then she wondered if they had these moments of silliness because of how ugly their lives had to be sometimes when caught up in a war. It was a sad thought and she quickly shook it away.

"What is that on her head?" asked Matthew.

"A sunbonnet," replied Boyd. "My mother always wore one."

"Looks like a coal scuttle."

Abigail decided that was more than any woman should have to endure and, fighting the urge to grin, she grabbed her rifle. She heard James curse and, when she rose up on her knees, she saw that all three men had ducked down, hiding by the side of the wagon. She put her rifle aside, moved to the side of the wagon, and peered over. It was nearly painful to hold back the urge to laugh.

"Why are you down there?" she asked.

"Checking on the goat," said Matthew as he awkwardly stood up.

"Is she all right?"

"Looks fine," said Boyd.

He brushed off his coat and frowned at her. "Where is your rifle?"

"Over there." She pointed to where it was always set, away from the baby but still within reach, and allowed herself a small grin since her face was turned away from them.

Matthew glared at James who just shrugged and grinned. "I panicked."

Ignoring them, Abbie checked to be sure Jeremiah was still safely shaded and asleep then climbed into the driver's seat. "I think we ought to put the goat into the wagon," she told Boyd when he climbed up beside her.

"Why? She really did look just fine. Only a bit dusty."

"Because I need her milk for Jeremiah and I don't think it is good for her to be trotting along under there. It is too hot and dusty. Even a goat has to be bothered by that."

"Ah, I suppose it is possible it could affect her enough for her milk to dry up."

He climbed into the back and used her chests to form a pen for the animal, pushing them to the sides and angling them to make a square with the wagon side. Abbie climbed into the back and stretched a blanket out to shade the area. She hoped the goat wouldn't eat it as she secured it to the wagon. She got down to drag the goat out and heft her into the wagon, placed her in her newly constructed pen, then tied her rope to the back of the seat.

As Abbie got back into her seat she decided she needed a new name for the animal. She could not understand what had possessed Mrs. Beaton to call the goat Delphinium. Perhaps the animal ate some of hers, she decided as she picked up the reins and they started on their way.

"Are ye going to wear that hat all the way?" Matthew asked as he rode up by her side.

"At least until the sun sets, the coal scuttle stays on."

Matthew winced, realizing she had been awake longer than he had suspected. Boyd hid a faint smile behind his hand but James was grinning widely and he knew the man was fighting not to laugh. Matthew tried to think of something to say, something that sounded like an apology, but he could not think of a thing. He did really hate that hat on her.

"Does the sun give ye freckles? I have heard women try to avoid those."

"No. It burns me. I don't get freckles but I get badly burned skin. So it does not even make me get darker in color, just peels horribly."

He decided he would try to forget about the hat for a while. It was more important for him to concentrate staying on his horse. It was proving far more difficult than he had thought it would be.

Matthew sighed and fought to ignore how his wounds felt. James was acting as their scout because he could not ride hard, but it was beginning to feel like he should not be riding at all. The doctor had warned him but he had not listened, had not wanted to. He could tolerate the ache in his arm and leg but the pinching pain and ache in his belly was a bit more than he could bear, especially since every movement of the horse caused it to ache or sting.

Abbie glanced at Matthew and suspected he should not be riding his horse so soon after being wounded. He was looking a little gray. She just hoped he had the sense to get in the wagon if he got too sore or weary. Out of the corner of her eye, she watched him cover his stomach and then she silently cursed. She had to bite her lip to keep herself from yelling at him to get in the wagon. Since she could see no sign of renewed bleeding she would just leave him to his misery for now.

"Has the goat left enough room for me?" Matthew asked a half hour later.

Abbie looked at him. "I believe so. Shall I halt the wagon?"

"Aye. It was too soon for this," he muttered.

"I thought it might be," she said quietly as she halted the wagon.

"What's wrong?" asked James as he rode up and then he looked at Matthew. "Ah. Giving up."

"Too soon," Matthew said as he dismounted with as much help as Boyd could give him. "Arm and leg are all right but the damned stomach wound isnae cooperating." He climbed into the wagon and leaned back against the wagon seat back. "It complains with every move."

"Harvey said it would," said James as he unsaddled Matthew's horse and tied it to the back of the wagon. "Maybe you ought to have listened to him."

"As ye would have, I suspicion."

James laughed. "Not at all. To my way of thinking, if it is sewn up and blood's not flowing, it's mended. Always been proved wrong and survived. Pa always said 'grin and bear it' and I took that to heart. Then again, Pa never went to a real doctor. Probably should remind myself of that from time to time." James re-mounted his horse. "Going to be riding around you for a while. Want to check the rear, your flanks, and be sure we don't ride right into something. Just have a feeling it would be best." He turned his horse and road off.

"He gets a lot of 'feelings,' doesn't he?" said Abbie as she started the wagon moving again.

"Aye, and we always heed them. My mother would have said James has the gift."

"Gift? What gift?"

"Gift of sight or some other thing. She had belief in all the old ways. James has some instinct that warns him of trouble, a kind nay everyone else is blessed with."

"Ah. My brother had something like that. It was one reason we were so stunned when we were caught by surprise by those men on the day they took him. It must have failed him because he was caught and taken."

"Or it didnae fail him at all. He might have kenned about the attack but thought he could save his kin."

Abbie sighed and shook her head. "That would be just like Reid. Trying to be the hero and instead running right into a trap. Do you want me to check your wounds?"

"Nay. They just ache. I cannae feel any hint of bleeding and that's good, aye? It is that stupid grin on my belly causing me pain but no bleeding there either."

"Good. So all you did was use them all too soon. You may be stitched up but the skin is still broken over the wounds, held together only by stitching—delicate, expert stitches done by a skilled and steady hand."

Matthew struggled to keep his chuckles smothered. He liked her bite but, at the moment, he was feeling too battered to show her just how much. Perhaps after he was home for a few days. The sound of someone approaching quickly yanked him out of the delightfully bawdy daydream he had been indulging in.

He turned to get a clear look behind them and cursed himself for letting pride make him ride the horse. That bit of vanity had weakened him at a time when he could be needed to fight.

"Why is James riding up so fast?" asked Abbie, glancing behind her and then tugging on the reins to slow them down. "I have a *feeling* right now and it is telling me that's not good."

"Keep going!" yelled James. "Don't slow down!"

"Go, Abbie," ordered Matthew as he picked up his gun. "What's coming?" he called back to James.

"About two dozen armed men. They are wearing a mix of regular clothes and Confederate uniforms."

"So, marauders or whatever name they want to use this month." Matthew carefully moved until he was poised to fire out the back of the wagon. "Why the hell didn't they choose to go south?"

"Because all the folk down there are Confederates and they are keen on slaughtering blue bellies?" He just laughed when Matthew gave him a rude gesture.

James rode up and untied his horse. Matthew waved his thanks and watched the road behind them. He glanced quickly over his shoulder and noticed Abbie had slumped in her seat enough to protect her back some. With a final look at the baby and the sleeping goat, he prayed no shots could reach them and turned his full attention to the men rounding the bend in the road, shifting enough so that his own body also provided some protection for the baby.

The wagon began to move faster but was still moving at a pace that could easily be caught by a man on a galloping horse. All it did was make steadying his rifle harder. All the men following them were pushing their mounts hard. His job was to kill anyone who got too close so he took aim and fired. He cursed at the pain using his rifle caused his injured arm but was pleased that he had hit a man.

Abbie secured the reins, confident that George would keep on the road, and then climbed into the back of the wagon. She grabbed her rifle, checked to be certain it was loaded, and took up a position next to Matthew. She could hear Boyd struggling to get into the back of the wagon himself, but could not lend him a hand. Abbie suspected he would be sorely embarrassed if she tried. Aiming carefully, she fired, and a man fell out of his saddle.

"The horse," Matthew said, glancing back at George who was staying steady on the road even though his pace was a lot slower than Matthew was comfortable with.

"George will stay straight on the road. It is what he is very good at. He really doesn't like turning off a road. Doesn't this lead to your home?"

"Aye, right to the gates. We're going by the Jones brothers' cabins now." He switched to his pistol and fired it, hitting a man who was getting too close to them.

James rode up beside them even as Boyd finally managed to get into the back of the wagon. He leapt from his horse onto the seat and the horses he left stayed close, running alongside George. He then picked up the reins to hold the animal steady.

"George wouldn't have veered off the road, James," Abbie said.

"George is a contrary beast, isn't he? I just thought he'd feel better knowing someone held the reins."

"Quite possibly. Thank you." She shot another man at the same time Boyd fired his pistol and a man screamed.

Abbie was just reloading when she heard shots sound from behind them, from behind the men chasing them, too. She frowned as the men pursuing them began to slow their pace and search behind them and to the sides. Puzzled, she was just about to ask Matthew what was happening when he whooped in glee.

"I was hoping they would come," Matthew said and grinned. "The sound of shooting must have brought them."

"Who would come?"

"The Jones brothers. Our shepherds."

"Shepherds?" said Boyd in what sounded very much like horror to Abbie.

"Sorry, lad, but our family raises sheep." Matthew laughed at the look of sheer disappointment on Boyd's face. "Makes a nice living."

Boyd just shook his head. "Is that them?" he asked and pointed to two men riding hard through the trees on the right. "How much help can two shepherds be?"

"Yup, that's them. And they are Welsh. Trust me, long history of fighting with the Welsh. Although I think those two have been practicing their shooting," he mumbled as two men fell out of their saddles. "Owen and David Jones."

The men chasing them hesitated only a moment before they finally noticed how many of them were dead. Helping up the ones wounded, they fled. Abbie had no liking for killing or wounding actual people so made no attempt to shoot at anyone trying to pick up the wounded, but she did wonder why they left. Even with the addition of the shepherds and accounting for the dead and wounded, the men were not yet outnumbered. She shrugged thinking that they had probably thought they had found an easy target only to have it turn out to be not so easy at all.

Then the wagon slowed to a halt and she scrambled over to pick up a now-screaming Jeremiah. It took her several moments to quiet the baby. He was sucking furiously on his fists so she knew the quiet wouldn't last long. Hunger might not have woken him up, but he would feel it now. The noise and the rough ride were proving to be upsetting for him. Yet she could do little about that. She just hoped they did not have that far left to go.

She got out the nursing jug and moved to the goat only to find one of the Jones brothers petting the animal. "I need to fill his nursing jug."

"I'll do that for you, miss."

He took the jug and easily milked the goat, talking softly to the animal in some language she did not recognize. "Which Jones brother are you?"

"Owen." He grinned. "The smart one. Ow!" He cast a glare at his brother who had slapped him on the back of the head. "This is David."

"Nice goat," said David. "What's her name?"

"I fear it is Delphinium."

"Oh, that'll never work. Got to call them by a name they might answer to, if they are in the right mood to listen." Owen handed her back the full nursing jug. "Didn't like all the shooting, did you?" he said to the goat, who nuzzled him and then grabbed his hat in her teeth.

As Owen fought to get his hat back from the stubborn goat, which caused his brother to laugh heartily, Abbie sat down and fed Jeremiah. The Jones boys were a handsome pair in a rough way. Thick, unruly black hair and striking blue eyes in a faintly rugged face made for a look any woman would appreciate. It was not a surprise that David's wife was trying to help get the other brother for her sister. Not only would the woman be getting her sister a very fine-looking man but it would keep them sisters.

She listened to the men talk as she fed the baby, Matthew and the brothers exchanging news about his family, and she began to feel nervous. There were so many of them. She always felt awkward meeting new people and it was beginning to sound as if there were a lot of them at Matthew's home. By the time she was patting Jeremiah's back, Matthew had moved to sit beside her. She noticed he was looking a bit flushed and had beads of sweat on his forehead. Both could be the result of heat and exertion, but she was worried.

"Ready to head out?" he asked.

"In a little bit. He was badly upset by all the gunfire but I think he will settle down well in a minute now that he is full."

"Settle him now," said James. "I'm getting the feeling those idiots have found friends or courage." James jumped on his horse.

"Another feeling?" she grumbled. "Am I going to have to make George run again? He really hates that."

"I fear so," James said, his voice full of laughter. "He's strange, but he is a big boy. He can handle it."

"We'll go and make certain the gates are opened for you, Matthew, and that they know you are running in," said Owen and hurried back to his horse, his brother following him. "Be back to lend you a hand in a bit so don't get shot."

"That was kind of him," she said and then sighed because Matthew was laughing. Abbie decided she would never understand the things men thought were funny.

She settled Jeremiah in his bed, prayed the baby would be allowed to sleep, petted the goat, and got back in the wagon seat. Abbie really hoped that this time James's feeling was wrong. She just wanted to settle somewhere for a little while before there was any more danger. She was not so naïve she believed there was any place on earth where there was not some danger, but she really wanted just a little while to enjoy quiet and safety.

"He really needs to stop having *feelings,*" she muttered as she picked up the reins.

"Until he does, we will listen to them," said Boyd as he sat down next to her. "Matthew and Dan say his feelings have saved their hides many times."

"Then let's head for these gates," she said, and urged George into a quick pace.

Boyd clutched at the seat. Abbie noticed that even the hand on his wounded arm was working to hold him in his seat but she said nothing. The young man was just too afraid to knowingly try it out but she suspected that would change soon. It would have to occur to him soon. She idly wondered if there was any trick she could use to make him notice it faster.

Her eyes widened with a touch of fear as she glanced back and saw more armed men running after them. Abbie wondered where they were coming from since she had heard that a lot of the army had left the area. She also wondered what they thought they could gain from them as there was nothing obvious that would tempt their greed.

Matthew and the others were doing a fine job of holding them back but she worried about them, especially when she saw that Matthew was back on his horse again. She was going to smack him when she got off the wagon. She understood his need to stand by his friend James but the fool was going to rip his stitches open.

She heard Boyd curse and looked at him but he was staring forward. Following his gaze she frowned as she saw the large stockade come into view. The Jones brothers stood on either side of the open gates and she urged George toward them even though she knew the animal was tiring. The moment she did so, the men ran to leap onto their horses and rush to aid Matthew and James.

"I didn't think we were going to a fort."

"This is his home," said Boyd. "He told me they had put up a fence."

"A fence." She shook her head. "He probably thinks that is funny. Are those men up on the walls?"

"I think so. Like coming to a castle, ain't it, only this one is made of wood."

"Right now what it looks like to me is safety."

Chapter Fifteen

Abbie sped through the gates and quickly drew the wagon to a halt. People came running out of the house. She leapt down and rushed to take George out of his harness. She was just freeing him when a tall, dark-haired man rushed up with straw to rub him down. Abbie abruptly stopped murmuring soothing words to George and stared at the man, trying to find something that would tell her he was one of Matthew's brothers.

"Fine sturdy cart horse, lass. Havenae seen one like this for a while. I am Iain, Matthew's older brother."

"Hello, Iain. I am Abigail Jenson." She then heard gunfire and quickly looked around. "I thought we had run into a fort."

"Lots of folk think that. Just the MacEnroy place."

"Oh, Jeremiah," Abbie cried when a wail came from the back of the wagon, and she hurried over, getting back in the wagon, to collect the baby.

Matthew, James, and the Jones brothers rode in just as she picked up the child. When she began to get out of the wagon several men shut the gates then ran up ladders to a walkway at the top of the wall. She had to wonder what kind of life the MacEnroys lived that made them believe they needed such protection. The moment she was back on the ground a small, blond woman hurried over to her.

"I am Emily, Iain's wife. Do you want me to hold the babe as you get your goat down?"

"If you would, please." She gently handed over Jeremiah who still fussed but quickly grew quiet. "It has just been too much noise and fast, rough travel for the child." She kissed Jeremiah's cheek then went to fetch the goat.

When Abbie brought Delphinium down, she stood and stared at the goat for a moment. "You need a new name. We are going to be stuck with each other for a while and I cannot keep calling you Delphinium."

"Delphinium? Who would name the poor beast that?"

"The woman I was staying with. I wondered if the goat ate her flowers so she stuck it with a name, but it could be she just thought it was an elegant word. She kept her goats in her cellar whenever there was trouble and at night. She used to have over a dozen of them but only had five left. I needed the milk though and traded her one of my mother's quilts for him."

"He seems to be doing well on the goat's milk."

"It does appear to agree with him. Jeremiah is an orphan. The Rebs killed his da and his mother died soon after he was born."

"So you took him . . ."

"I am not that good. There was an older boy I was thinking of taking, another orphan. I knew babies were a great deal of work and there would be hundreds of other problems to be faced with, but she made me promise to care for him. She was dying." Abbie shook her head and sighed as she took Jeremiah back into her arms. "The poor boy is stuck with me."

"Babes don't require all that much to feel secure. Food, warmth, hugs, and getting their cloths changed regularly. Older children can be much more work," she added softly as a young boy walked over to her and glared at the baby.

Abbie studied the boy and immediately missed Noah. He had a mass of black curls on his head and lovely brown eyes. "He looks just like a boy I know," she said. "Well, not just like as the boy I know has red hair but those eyes look very familiar."

"Where is he?" asked the boy.

"I had to leave him behind for now as I knew it would be a risky journey. I hope it won't be for too long though."

"How old is he?"

"Five." She smiled faintly, wondering if Noah was five yet and knowing he'd be pleased to hear himself called it.

"Oh, so he is still little. I am Ned."

"Hello, Ned."

"My nephew, my late sister's child," said Emily and she ruffled the boy's hair. "Look, Ned. I was just meeting Jeremiah."

"Is that the baby? Is he going to scream a lot, too?"

One look at Emily's face told Abbie she best swallow the laugh that tickled her throat. Ned obviously had a problem with babies and she recalled some mention of Emily having borne two. So a little jealousy, she guessed.

"Ned, babies cry. They cannot speak like you or I can so it is the only way they have of getting our attention. Now be nice. You know what manners are. Use them."

"Jeremiah is a very, very young baby, too. He cannot even sit up or hold things." She smiled softly. "I fear he is so young, he does it in the middle of the night, too."

"Oh. Just like your two do. Or did. Nuala is pretty big now and quiet. Maybe I should move in with the O'Neals," he grumbled, and stomped off.

Emily stared after her nephew, and by the time she turned back Abbie was laughing. "How can you laugh?" Emily said even though her lips twitched as if she wanted to join in. "That was horribly rude."

"I know. Such a boy thing to say. For a moment I feared he was going to say Nuala was at least human now." Emily started to laugh and Abbie grinned. "Think he will actually attempt to move in with the O'Neals?"

"Who knows? They only live in a small cottage out the back so it is not like he is running away very far. I fear he may be a bit jealous."

"A bit?" Abbie shook her head. "Just be glad he is not one to brood on it."

"I suppose. I fear I know little about boys."

"I had a brother. Rather hoping I still do. One of those lawless groups of men attacked our home and took him off to fight with them. They beat my da near to death and attacked my mother."

"And you?" Emily asked in a voice softened by horror.

"I was hiding. I know nothing that happened was my fault, but it is hard to break free of that thought when you know you were hiding away while all the bad happened."

"You just would have been killed or attacked like your mother and left behind broken."

"And that is just what she was: broken. She died

when Matthew, James, and Boyd helped me fight off another attack. She would not duck, kept trying to protect my senseless and dying father. Eventually a shot took them both down. Then a fire took my home. I left what little word I could for my brother in case he ever returns."

"It has been a very sad, bloody few years up in these hills."

"What troubles me is all the innocents. There is no gain there."

Abbie looked around, spotted Matthew standing between James and Boyd. They talked to three other men she suspected were more of Matthew's brothers. She narrowed her eyes when she noticed how Matthew kept shifting his stance as if he was having difficulty holding it. The color was stronger on his cheeks again.

"Emily? Could you hold Jeremiah for me again?"

"Certainly." She took the baby into her arms. "Is something wrong?"

"Might be. I begin to think Matthew is about to fall on his face. It also looks like his fever is back."

Abbie did not wait for any reply from Emily but walked straight to Matthew and slipped her arm through his. "Matthew, I think it would be best if we go inside."

"Probably would be. Not feeling too right."

James moved up to put his arm around Matthew's waist and one of the young men in front of her started toward the house, waving her to follow him. "Damn, Matt, you should have said something."

"Just need to lie down for a while."

Matthew then began to sink down and Abbie stumbled trying to hold him up. Two of the young men moved nearer, each one grabbing one of Matthew's legs. James took more of his weight and the four of them carried him up the stairs.

"Just be careful with his legs. He has a bad wound on one of them," said Abigail.

"Where?" asked the one in front of her.

"Top, left leg."

They got him into a room and onto a bed. As Abbie searched out some cool water and a few rags with Mrs. O'Neal's help from the moment she rushed into the room, the men stripped Matthew and pulled the covers over him. Abbie stepped over and began to wash him down with cool water.

"Where was he hurt?" asked Mrs. O'Neal.

"That arm. A through shot, this leg, a bit of meat lost. And his belly." Abbie heard the woman suck in her breath. "It was shallow." She cautiously moved the covering and showed her the wound. "Someone was trying to gut him, but he turned. That is why it is shaped oddly."

"Doctor said that it only needs a pair of eyes," said James, and the three young men snickered but Mrs. O'Neal slapped him on the back of the head.

"Ow! It was just a joke the doc was making."

"You don't go making jokes about such things."

"Sorry, ma'am. Fellow tends to forget how to talk around the ladies after a time spent in the military."

"No, no. I'm sorry. This cursed war has made me forget my manners and sense of humor." She looked at Abbie. "You do this stitching, child?"

"Yes, ma'am."

"Abbie even impressed our doc, and him Harvard educated and all. Even better than how neatly she does the stitching is the fact that she can do it fast," said James and patted Abbie on the head then ducked her swing at him.

"Fast?"

"Less pain," said Abbie. "I practiced until I could do it faster than my da who was a doctor in Pennsylvania."

"What's wrong with Matthew?" demanded Iain as he stormed into the room with Emily hurrying behind him.

"Aside from the fact that he is an idiot male who doesn't know when to rest? Nothing. He has a fever," Abbie said as she wiped down his arms, "but it is not too high. A few days resting and he should be fine."

Iain came to stand by the bed and look his brother over. He stared down at Matthew's stomach wound for a long time and Abbie watched his expression change slowly from worry to puzzlement. He tugged the sheet up over Matthew's belly and looked at James.

"Why is his belly smiling at me?" Iain asked.

James said very quietly, "He turned as the knife started to go in and so the cut was lighter and across instead of deep."

"But it should heal well?"

"Doctor said it would. Of course he also told him to stay off horses and Matthew didn't obey that well at all. Then there was the fighting as we traveled here. It brought his fever back. Stitches held though."

"So bed rest and getting the fever down."

"That's it."

"He's nay going to like that."

"He'll learn."

Iain grinned. "Suspect he might. Nigel, Duncan, Lachlan? Time to feed the stock." All three young men hurried out the door. "Thank you, Abbie. And you, Mrs. O'Neal."

Emily hurried over and gave Jeremiah back to Abbie then followed her husband out of the room. Abbie tossed the damp cloth back into the bucket and, with her free hand, felt Matthew's forehead and cheeks. He was noticeably cooler and she breathed a sigh of relief.

"Better?" James asked.

"Very much so. Cooler and, by the looks of it, sleeping peacefully."

"I've got to ride back."

"Back to where?"

"The town. Meeting up with the doc and then it is off to fight in the far South."

"Oh, I see. Didn't you sign up only for a while?"

"I did and I'm pretty sure that time is rapidly coming to a close. Plan to wave them all fare-thee-well when it does but have to heed orders now."

She impulsively hugged him, holding the baby to the side. "Take care. Sorry he's not awake to see you off."

"Yeah, but I know he will wake up and that will do for now. You watch yourself, pigeon."

She watched him leave, even walking over to the window to see him mount his horse and ride away. Abigail really hoped he continued to have good luck. After putting Jeremiah to bed in the nursery, she also hoped he would find a good companion to watch his back as he had so skillfully watched theirs. Abigail then went to Matthew's room.

"Well, Matthew, you missed James's farewell. So best you get better soon or there may be others." She pulled a chair over to the bed and sat down then looked at Mrs. O'Neal. "Where can I find a book?"

"Is it all right to leave him?"

"I think so, but we won't be gone that long, will we?"

"No, just heading down to the library. I am just not sure the boys will have anything that will suit you."

After some looking through a lot of books, Abigail found one that looked good. She did wonder how the MacEnroys got so many books on how to do so many different things. The book she picked had probably been added by Emily. As she walked back into the bedroom where Matthew was she caught him sliding one leg out of bed.

"Get back in that bed." She would have laughed at how fast he did so except she was too angry. "Are you crazy? How many times do you have to nearly fall on your face before you accept that you need to rest?" she asked as she marched up to the side of the bed.

"Did I fall on my face?"

"No, because I was there, and so were James and several of your brothers."

"Did I open up any stitches?"

"They are all fine and there appears to be no infection in any of the wounds. The fever comes from doing things too early and doing too much. So now you will have to play the invalid for a while. In fact, you should probably do that until the stitches can be taken out."

"Where is James?"

"James has returned to the town and the army."

"Oh hell. He can leave it soon, so why rush back into it? I had thought to keep him here somehow until it was done."

"The time he signed up for or the war?"

"Both. But now he is in the middle of it without any of us to watch his back."

"I suspect he knows how to cover himself if he has to. After all, he is the one who never got wounded."

Abigail made herself comfortable on the side of the

bed and opened her book. She was only a few pages in when a heavy sigh came from Matthew. He was clearly not a good reading companion. She turned on her side to look at him and absently pondered the possibility of smacking him with her book.

"Do you want me to get you a book?"

"Nay. I want someone to give me a hand so I can take care of some private business."

"Okay." She stood up and left the room.

Matthew hoped she was just going to get someone. He knew he had nearly fallen on his face outside, but he did not think he needed the added humiliation of wetting the bed, which he would do soon if he did not get some help. He swore he would rest as instructed until he could do such things on his own without risking his stitches. He had missed James's leaving because he did not have the patience to heal himself properly, and that was a hard lesson. Just as he was prepared to yell for Abbie, Iain walked into the room.

"Come on then. Did she say how many days she is thinking of when she says rest?" He put an arm around Matthew's waist and nearly carried him to the washroom.

"No, but I suspect she has some idea."

Once done, Matthew allowed himself to be nearly carried back to the bed. "I am not a complete invalid, ye ken."

"I find that the easiest way to do this. Much easier than just holding ye up while we both stumble along." After setting Matthew on the bed, Iain sprawled on his back at his brother's side.

"I suppose. I am angry because I missed James's leave-taking."

"I barely had a chance to wish him good luck. He thanked us and rode off."

"He probably just wanted to get it done. I just hope his luck holds for whatever time he has left."

"Did he sign up the same time ye did?"

"I think he might have."

"Then he has ten days."

"How do ye ken that?"

"Because we marked it down and it is now on the day list for this month. We actually talked about your coming home the other day."

"Huh, so me, James, Dan, and Boyd are all pretty much done with this mess." He nudged his brother. "I haven't seen your new son."

"I'll bring him in for a visit when he wakes. Lad is sleeping now, and when he sleeps Emily does, too."

"Then that must be Jeremiah singing," said Matthew as a baby's cry echoed through the house.

"Yup, and that Abbie is fast at hushing him," Iain said as the noise went away. "That's a blessing as Emily didnae get much sleep last night because the bairn is getting a few teeth."

"Hope that misery doesnae last long, for Emily's and the bairn's sake."

"So this lass, Abigail? Are ye gonna wed her or just borrow her for a wee bit longer?"

Matthew grimaced. "I dinnae ken. I keep going round and round then recall it is for life and am back to I just dinnae ken."

"I am thinking ye best get your wee head on straight about it and soon."

"Why? She say something about leaving?"

"Nay, and probably wouldnae say it to me. But I tell ye plain, there is only so long a lass will wait around before she decides the mon doesnae want marriage and there are better places to be." Iain stood up and stretched then looked down at Matthew. "Make up your mind, fool."

Watching Iain leave the room, Matthew grumbled a vast array of insults toward the man's back.

Family was supposed to give one support, he thought, and shook his head. Since Iain said pretty much the same thing everyone else did, he guessed he better accept that as the best advice possible. It was a shame it was useless to him.

Abigail walked in still holding her book.

She stood by the side of the bed and stared down at Matthew, her head cocked slightly to one side. "You look better." She placed her hand on his forehead. "Definitely cooler still. So might be that you don't have to linger in bed for weeks. Just a couple of days."

"That's good, as I would go crazy."

"That's what they all say."

He reached out, grabbed her round the waist, and pulled her down onto the bed. "But if I had something to keep me pleasantly busy, I might be able to endure it." He kissed her throat as she laughed.

"Such pleasantries can do harm to your stitches." She dragged her fingers across his belly, along the line of the stitches.

"Not if one takes it easy."

"Afraid no one is sure just what stress can break the stitches." She rested her cheek against his chest. "Best to err on the side of caution."

"Then we will indulge in cautious play."

"Not with the door wide open." She hopped off the bed and went to shut the door, then hurried back across the room to crawl into bed beside him.

"Isn't it a bit early in the day to be indulging in such things?"

"Never too early and never too late." He unbuttoned the bodice of her gown.

The feel of his hand gently petting her breasts had Abigail shivering. Then she thought of where she would like to touch him. As he brushed warm kisses over the swell of her breasts, she undid his shirt and gently tugged it off him. For a moment she studied his broad chest lightly sprinkled with hair. Red hair, she thought as she studied it.

"Why do you have red hair here?" she asked as she idly smoothed it down only to watch it spring back up.

"I dinnae have red hair anywhere."

She sat back a little and frowned at him as he hurriedly redid his shirt. "That hair is red."

"It was just the light that made it look a bit red."

"No, it was red. Really red. Cannot hide it away red." She undid his shirt again, slapping away his hands when he tried to stop her. "There. Brilliant red." She began to look very carefully at the hair on his head. "I wager in the right light I could see some red here, too."

"Nay," he began to say and a growing familiar wail went through the house. "Damnation, Abbie," he said as she jumped off the bed, buttoning her bodice all the way to the door.

"Playing will have to wait. Can't let him wake up the whole house," she said as she opened the door and sped down the hall to the small nursery.

Matthew fell back into the bed and cursed. Then scolded himself for being a selfish man. It would have been nice playing with Abigail but she could not ignore the scream of a hungry bairn, and he should never expect her to. Play would have to wait.

Then again, he did not think she was aware of where her place to sleep was. He hurriedly smoothed out the sheets and made sure the blanket was in place and tucked in. Matthew shed his pants and shirt before he settled on his back and waited for her to realize. Forgetting how long feeding a child, cleaning him up, and settling him down to sleep again could take, Matthew slipped quietly into sleep.

It was late when Abbie came back to the room. She sighed because she could tell he had gone to sleep. Not that she blamed him. He was still sick even if he chose to ignore it. Jeremiah had not been cooperative. He had wanted to take his time then wanted to be held again. She had almost fallen asleep in the nursery. It was then that she realized she had not been shown to a room for her. If she was going to sleep in a bed for the night she had to go back to Matthew's room.

Slipping off her shoes, she rubbed her feet a little so they were not cold. She carefully removed her gown and laid it on the chair near the bed. Then she eased beneath the blankets. Once her body warmed up she rolled close to Matthew. He mumbled something and pulled her close. Abbie smiled, snuggled even closer to his warmth, and closed her eyes.

Chapter Sixteen

Matthew yawned and opened his eyes. There was something soft and warm in his bed. He could not believe he had gone to sleep then decided his injuries and recurrent bouts of fever had taken their toll as everyone had warned him they would. He glanced down and realized the soft warmth he was clutching close was Abigail. He grinned. The night may have been lost but the new day had only just begun, he mused.

He pulled her close and kissed her throat. She was warm and sweet. To his delight she had shed her gown before crawling into bed with him. She wore her drawers, stockings, and chemise. He unlaced her chemise and kissed her soft rounded breasts. A soft murmur escaped her and she cuddled up closer.

Abbie slowly woke up and snuggled into the warmth. Drowsy, she murmured in pleasure when a damp warmth played over her breasts. Slowly she realized that Matthew was wide-awake now and taking full advantage. She wondered if she should get angry but found no inclination to do so and smiled as he ran his hands over her back.

She slipped her hands over his chest and realized he was in as great a state of undress as she was. Then he kissed her and she realized he sensed she was awake. She wrapped her arms around his neck and returned his kiss with a sleepy passion.

Matthew knew Abbie was awake but she was also still caught in the last hold of sleep, her kiss slow and delicious but her every move equally slow. She acted as if she was in some strange waking dream.

Even as his own body grew more demanding, he wondered if he should stop this until she was fully herself. He turned so that she was on her back and he sprawled on top of her. She wrapped her legs around his hips and held him close.

"Abbie, are ye really awake?"

"Of course I am." She kissed the hollow at the base of his throat. "Do you think I could even move if I wasn't?"

"No idea. Have never really slept with ye." She rubbed herself against his groin and his eyes crossed. "I just wanted to be sure."

"Are you always so talkative in the morning?"

"Ah, nay."

"Thank God."

His laughter was cut off by her mouth. Her kiss was hungry, even greedy, and he held her tightly as he returned that hunger. Whatever was making Abbie so willing, even subtly demanding, he would have to figure it out later. He was reaching the sharp edge of his ability to play, his body demanding the satisfaction her kisses promised. He tried to hold fast as he wanted slow and easy, felt they had both earned it, but with each moment that ticked by he knew that this would not be the time.

When his mouth closed over the tip of her breast,

Abbie's body bowed upward. She knew he was taking off her drawers but did not care, simply lifted her hips to make it easier. He eased into her so slowly she was tempted to pound her fists on his back so that he would move. She slid her hands down his back and clutched at his bottom, which prompted the movement she was seeking. As she settled into the rhythm he set, meeting his every thrust, she told herself she should remember that.

Matthew pushed himself up on his forearms and watched the way their bodies moved together. He looked at her breasts, neither too large nor too small, with their hard red nipples, and had to have a taste. He tasted the other and by then his body was tightening, the sharp need for release building with every thrust. He bent his head and kissed her as she tightened her grip on his hips.

When he felt her begin to tense, her grip on him tighten, he rubbed at her breasts. She was making very soft little sounds of pleasure that were music to his ears. Then he felt her reach her release, felt her whole body clench on his, and slammed home to join her. As soon as his body was done emptying into hers, he slumped down, twisting a little to the side so that his whole weight did not rest on her. They both panted for a short time while they got their breathing back under control.

"Good morning," Abbie said in as prim a voice as she could muster and felt Matthew grin against her shoulder.

"Good morning to ye as weel."

"Do we have to move anytime soon?"

"Nay. I am a sick mon, recall."

"Oh no! I can't believe I didn't even think of that."

Abbie patted his chest, looked at his wounds, and

sat up enough to give him a delightful look at her breasts. He crossed his arms beneath his head and just smiled as he enjoyed her frantic checking to make sure she had not hurt him. Then she spoiled his pleasure by yanking on the hair on his chest.

"I am all concerned and you are just lying there grinning like a buffoon."

"A *lusty* buffoon. And I wasnae just lying here, I was enjoying the scenery. I was watching your lovely breasts bounce a bit as ye checked my poor used body for signs of injury caused by your voracious hunger."

Abbie really wanted to laugh but she also did not want to encourage him. She could not quite form an offended expression so she just shook her head and hid her expression by turning to pick up her clothes. She was finding it a little difficult to believe what had just happened. She had been having a nice dream, a romantic one, as she had slowly roused herself from a good, deep sleep and somehow that dream had turned into a rather lusty reality. A few times she had caught her mother laughing and blushing at some strange comment her father had made about mornings and she was suddenly sure she knew what the joke had been.

The moment she got her chemise done up and her drawers back on she stood up to put on her dress. The man had left her stockings on but she decided not to mention that and ask why, as she was afraid of what he would say. It appeared she was a thoroughly naughty woman and should probably do what several people had advised and just do the proposing herself.

Unfortunately, he could just say no, and the thought alone broke her heart. She would never be able to stand it. So she would go and try to have something to eat and some coffee before Jeremiah woke and started to demand food, a change, and some affection.

"I need food and coffee," she said and started for the door.

"Going to bring me some?"

He sounded so annoyingly cheerful, she thought as she turned to stare at him, pausing as if in thought. There was the look of a sweet hopeful puppy on his face and she had to wonder how a grown man could do that. She tapped her finger against her chin a couple of times, took a deep breath, and said "No." With her back straight she walked out of the room and quietly shut the door behind her.

The moment the door shut, Matthew buried his face in his pillow and howled with laughter. As he caught his breath, he then wondered if he had offended her with his teasing but could not feel that he had. Getting out of bed he washed up, cleaned his teeth, and started to get dressed. He had no idea what he should or should not do now that a new day was here and hoped someone would have some project or job he could help with. He needed something to do, something useful yet not enough to strain his wounds. He suspected Iain would have some simple but needed chores he could dole out to him.

Abigail followed the scent of food and coffee into the kitchen. "Morning, Emily. Hope you had a good and quiet night."

"Actually I did. Young Niall's teeth have broken through and I had nearly a full night of sleep. Sadly I then woke up to a man."

"Oh yes, waking up to a man can be a sore trial."

Abbie poured herself some coffee and set it on the table then looked for something to eat.

"I know. I was in a good, playful mood and now it has flown."

"As was I, and it is also gone, because they will then spoil that mood by talking."

"Exactly. Or even worse, attempt to make a joke, at that time of the day."

"The sheer effrontery of it leaves one speechless."

Abbie heard a giggle by the stove and peeked behind her to see Mrs. O'Neal making eggs and chortling away to herself. "Perhaps it flew to her."

"Well, then, she will have a very, very good day."

"I should say so."

Mrs. O'Neal ran out of the kitchen and stood on the back porch laughing heartily. Emily and Abbie just smiled at each other and began to help themselves to oatmeal and some fruit. Abbie stood up to deal with the eggs and Emily got some cream to put on the fruit. By the time they sat back down to eat Mrs. O'Neal was back at the stove cooking bacon.

"I thought I might wander into town today," said Emily.

"I thought it was nearly deserted because of all the troubles?"

"No. People have been carefully slipping back and trying to have normal lives for a year or so now. The general store has reopened. It is next to the saloon, which was utterly ruined last year. I thought it would be enjoyable to go see what they are carrying, if anything. I was rather hoping some of the trading routes had opened up again. Do you wish to come along? You too, Mrs. O'Neal?"

"Very nice of you to ask, Emily, but I have several things I need to bake and store, others to just store.

Just picked a lot of the first berries of the spring and need to make them into jam."

"Perhaps we should stay and help," said Abbie.

"No. I don't need help so badly you two cannot go do a little shopping. You can lend a hand before you go and after you come back if you want. I have been doing these things for so many years, it is barely work at all."

"I doubt we will be in town all that long anyway. Even if a store is open it must be having a difficult time getting supplies or stock to sell. I just like to go in every now and then so I can see what is changing, what is coming back, and what is truly gone."

"That is a very good idea. We need to know that to know if where we go now is still the best choice or if we may soon have a proper place to get our supplies closer at hand. Just be careful. There are still a lot of rough men about who seem to be eager to kill anyone and steal anything."

"I will take my rifle with us," said Abbie.

"Can you shoot it well?" asked Mrs. O'Neal.

"Better than me," said Matthew as he walked into the kitchen, a yawning Iain right behind him.

"Who's getting shot?" asked Iain as he sat down next to Emily and swiftly kissed her cheek.

"I was just talking about Abbie's skill with a rifle." Matthew poured himself some coffee and took a seat next to her. "Her da said she had a good eye."

"Huh."

"Why huh?" asked Emily.

"Because it is not often a skill a woman has. They can use the gun, maybe wound something, but a good eye and a good shot is just not something you often find in a woman." He narrowed his eyes at his wife.

"And ye will let me keep rambling until I say something ye can start a fight about, aye?"

"Aye," Emily said cheerfully then finished her coffee. "You were doing very well. It would have been a fine argument if you had not caught on and shut your mouth." She winked at Matthew who was having a quiet laugh. "We are planning a trip to town."

"If ye take your rifle and plenty of ammunition and dinnae stay too long, it should be all right," said Matthew "After all, they have hit the town so often it emptied out and a lot of the Confederates are running after the battles, which means heading down Virginia way. I would say we could take a ride round the town to do a wee bit of scouting but I am nay allowed to ride until my wounds close."

"Weel, there are seven of us, we ought to be able to find enough to do that without risking your delicate health."

"Thank ye, dear brother, your kindness is boundless."

"Shall we go then?" asked Abbie.

"We'll just collect up what we need and what we must."

Emily stood and headed out of the kitchen and Abbie quickly followed her. Matthew frowned but could not see any true danger to what they planned. Charlotte and George still lived in the town and several others had begun to return to the place. The men that had chased him and the others as they traveled here had not come from the direction of the town but from the direction of the troublesome border with Missouri.

"Are ye sure Abbie can protect them if it is needed?" asked Iain.

"Aye. She is nearly a crack shot. Steady arm and keen eye."

"And she has no trouble shooting men?"

"I don't think so. Only showed a hint once and that was when the man turned and faced her and he was not that far away. But otherwise, I think she soothes her mind and heart about it somehow."

"I truly cannot believe they let us go. With both the babies!" Emily shook her head as she drove the cart along the road to the town. "We better not get injured or endangered in any way or I will be bound to the house until I am old and gray."

"I *can* shoot, you know," said Abbie.

"I'm sure you can, but it has been rather dangerous around here for several years now and Iain is good at worrying. To be fair, I know why, I have all his children with me, Nuala, his son, and Ned. How did you learn to shoot so well?"

"My da had a rifle and I think he was just playing about when he handed it to me one day and pointed out a pinecone he wanted me to shoot. He showed me how to hold the gun, aim it, and fire it. Then I did. Hit the pinecone. He said I had the gift, that some people just can and others can practice all they want and can't. For a while he took bets on what I could shoot and made a nice little pile of money."

"You can make money off shooting?"

"Lots of men are more than ready to take a bet on what some little woman can or cannot shoot. They are so sure they can beat her."

"I would like to be able to shoot but all I manage to do is accidentally kill some poor bird flying by. The minute I try to fire the rifle up, it goes and I get rained on by feathers." As she waited for Abbie to stop laughing, she looked at the shawl Abbie was carrying Jeremiah in. "How do you tie those on and keep the babe safe inside?"

"I will show you when we get back to the house. It is surprisingly easy. I was taught by a pretty farmgirl down the road from us in Pennsylvania. She traded the knowledge and a pretty scarf for hints on how to shoot her gun as she was fed up with the teasing of her brothers when they went hunting."

Abbie looked all around her as they drove. It was a nice piece of woodland but she did not trust tree coverage. It was a favorite place for the outlaws to hide and attack. She hoped the men were successful in their circular scouting party because she really was fed up with the attacks she had been under lately.

When Emily drew up in front of what had undoubtedly been a saloon, Abbie was shocked by how much had been destroyed. All the glass had been cleaned up off the walk in front of it but none of the smashed windows had been fixed.

"The store is the attached building. It has all its windows." Emily got down and then lifted her basket. Abbie got a quick view of waving little arms before Emily covered them with a blanket.

Adjusting Jeremiah against her chest, Abbie followed. There were people outside the store and a decent amount of people inside. The store may have lagged in its selection but its prices were edging swiftly up into the highway robbery range. She suspected most general stores were the same. Just out of curiosity's sake she would have to think of someone back East she could write to and ask.

While Ned and Nuala looked over the candy, she

walked toward a small collection of children's books and sighed. These would have been useful to her a month ago. Carefully going through the pile she decided she would have to give it some thought because once she collected Noah and Wags, storybooks were definitely going to be needed.

"You need some books?"

Looking at Emily, Abbie nodded. "Where I was staying they had very few and, unless you wanted to steal from some person's house, you just had to make up a story for the children."

"And you are thinking it might be a wise thing to get for young Noah when he joins you."

"Exactly." Abbie frowned. "Unless he is so angry with me he has tossed out the idea of living with me."

"Do you think she will be mad at me for coming?"

"You have asked that a hundred times. No, I don't believe so. If she really said you were to join her, then you will join her, just earlier than she had planned. So why not go back and wait?"

"No, I will give her that chance."

Reid looked over his shoulder. "That is truly noble of you, son."

"I know you are just being scratchy, but this is serious."

"Scratchy?"

"Yup. You know, saying something just to poke at a people." He made a strange noise and twisted his fingers.

"Do you mean rub it in?"

"That's it! Abbie might be a little mad with me to

start, but then she'll be all happy to see me. I bet even the lieutenant will be."

"If you believe it. I will like meeting this man traveling around with my sister." Reid felt a nudge at his side and looked down to see a red curly head peering around his arm, big brown eyes narrowed as the boy tried to detect a lie or insult.

"You know you really shouldn't have made me take you along with me."

"Why? You're going to find Abbie and I know where she was going and I want to see her, too."

"Logic from a four-year-old. What is the world coming to?"

"I'm five."

"So old."

"It is my birthday today."

"Happy birthday." He pulled a stick of beef jerky out of his coat and handed it over his shoulder to the child. "Here you go. A treat."

"It's brown. Treats aren't s'posed to be brown. 'Less it's chocolate."

"This one is brown."

There was peace and quiet for a moment or two and Reid smiled. He suspected the boy was struggling to eat it but he paid no attention. He had little to do with children but he did not think they were supposed to talk so much. He had to wonder if he was being lied to, but the child had been so determined, following him for a long way with his bag and his puppy, that he had finally given up trying to make him go away. It did not help that he could not make himself desert the boy.

He thought of Abbie and smiled. She may not have promised she would take him in but he doubted she would send the child away either. She had a soft heart.

He rather thought the two of them would make a great pair. He hoped she was still all right.

Thinking of her made him think of his parents but he forced the sadness that brought aside. There had been nothing he could have done about it except grieve, and he had done enough of that lately. All he had to worry about now was that he was not found by the Confederate Army, for they could well charge him with being a deserter. The fate of such men was not one he wished to meet.

Abbie looked around when they stepped back out onto the street. They had each bought a few small things and enough material to make something for the babies. The cloth was the most expensive, and she suspected it would be costly for quite a while. Matthew said they had yarn made from the wool so she might be able to get some of that to make something.

She stroked Jeremiah's back as she walked, noticing that, although there were not many people, at least the town was not completely deserted. She did not think it would come back to what it appeared to have been though. There were some messages and grim notices hanging on a few of the houses. Notes to whatever relative might come by to tell them where the family was or a death notice, probably put up so the person searching would know there was no more point in doing so. She thought of the message she had left for her brother and hoped he would see it. He would at least find out that she still lived.

"I rather think this town is going to die, don't you?"

"I do. I was just reading a few of these papers tacked up on some of the houses. They are not hopeful. Not a single one saying, 'Wait here. I will come back.'

New directions or death notices. Mostly for young men. That is one of the saddest things about wars. I have read a lot about wars, from the ancient wars to the English wars, to the Greek wars, and they all share one thing. War devours the young and strong."

"It does, doesn't it? It is as if someone decides we are getting too many and starts one of these to cut down the numbers."

"I really hope that is not the case. It is darker and holds less hope than what I said. My dark remark was just a cold fact whereas yours is almost a prophecy."

"I'm English."

"Yes, I noticed. What does that have to do with it?"

"We are a naturally dour people."

"I thought it was the Scots who were dour."

"Huh, I think you may be right. Well, the English are definitely gloomy. Our weather is terrible and it is all we ever talk about." Emily smiled when Abbie giggled.

"I think it is nearing the middle of the day," Emily said a short while later as she glanced up at the sky.

"The sun certainly feels like it."

"Then let us go home and have some lunch. At least we don't have to buy food."

"And that is a true blessing."

Looking behind them Abbie saw a couple of rough-looking men ambling along as if they were not following them, but they were not walking toward anything either, and that made her wonder. They were the first lone men she had seen in the town. Abbie hoped they were not as bad as they looked, but she took Emily by the arm and gently urged her toward the wagon.

"Is something wrong?" Emily asked quietly.

"I don't think so, or rather have no proof. It is just

that two men are walking along behind us, but what are they walking toward? There is nothing down here to interest them."

"Another reason to head home."

Emily hurried the children into the wagon, settled the babies in their little boxes then climbed in and picked up the reins. Abbie got up beside her and pulled out her rifle, holding it openly across her arms. As Emily started the wagon rolling, Abbie checked the ammunition in her rifle. She had known it was loaded but this action let the men know it was loaded as well. They did not run off but they did suddenly find something of interest in the opposite direction.

"I do hope the rough ones brought out by the war disappear soon," Abbie said.

"They'll head west like many others. Everyone thinks they can make their fortune out there in the mines and so on."

"Only if they discover the mine."

"That is what I said to a friend of mine once when she talked of her fiancé going out there. Well, he went, ending up working some horrible mine for a year, and then got blown up in some silly mine accident. You would have thought I had personally cursed the fool. Fortunately, we moved from that place in a very short while so being treated as an evil witch was short-lived."

"I didn't know anyone believed in witches any longer."

"In some areas they do, enough so one tale can grow and grow until it sounds absurd to anyone not from the area."

"Sometimes not being from the area is enough."

"True, and unfortunately I cannot hide the fact that I am English."

"Get Iain to teach you how to talk like he does."

Emily laughed. "Tempting, but I am what I am." Emily looked at Abbie for a while and asked, "Are you in love with Matthew?"

Abigail sighed. "I rather think I am. Why?"

"Just wondering. I think he is in love with you."

"And why do you think that?"

"Just the way he acts. And talks. And made sure the chests with your things in them were put in his room. Mrs. O'Neal started to lecture him, just as she lectured Iain once upon a time, and he just looked at her and said, 'Don't,' and she didn't."

"And what does that prove?"

"That he wouldn't let the woman say anything that might make you sound less of a lady. She wouldn't mean that you were, but her lecture can get a bit colorful. He also had no intention no matter what she said of having you be separate from him."

Abbie frowned. "I suspect those could be good signs, but I want words."

"Doesn't every girl?"

"I know, deep inside, the man would never speak the words unless he meant them."

"I had to hear the words, too." Emily sighed. "Some of it was because I believed they should be said and some because I can be a silly romantic but, under it all, is just what you said. I knew if he said the words they were true, they were meant, and I could trust in them. So, are you going to make him say it first or will you marry him if asked and hope for them after?"

"He will say them before or I will punch him right in the nose."

Emily laughed so hard she woke her son and had to spend the remainder of the ride home calming him down.

Chapter Seventeen

Matthew went to the door to answer the knock. He peered out the small window at the side, saw the Jones brothers, and relaxed. He opened the door then gave a start when he saw the tall, bone-thin man standing with them. Under the man's long dark coat was the hint of gray and Matthew tensed.

"Who have ye brought us, boys?" he asked the Jones brothers, pleased to see that both men were armed.

"Man is looking for your woman. Says he is her kinsman, her brother," answered Owen.

Looking at the man again, Matthew could see no similarities, no hint of Abbie in his face or eyes. The man's hair was a deep brown and his eyes were blue. He had looked at Abigail's parents so little that he could not even tell if this man looked like one of them. His thinness and the scar on his cheek also made seeing any similarities difficult.

"What is your name?" he asked the man.

"Reid Aaron Jenson. I found the cabin burned and the bones of my parents." His deep voice broke a little as he said those words. "Also saw the stone for Ab's damn cat and that George and the wagon were gone.

Found her scrawled message in George's stall. So I then started tracking you, too. Wasn't easy, got even less so when the war began to draw to an end."

"So how did ye track me down?" Matthew opened the door wider.

"Found your officer, Major Cummings. He was still in the hospital and this woman was with him." Reid stepped inside when the Jones brothers nudged him.

"How badly was he hurt?"

"Dr. Pettibone said he would heal and I don't think that Maude lady will let your major prove the man wrong."

Matthew nodded, unable to hide his relief. "Good. Pleased to hear it. He is a good man. As for Maude, a very strong-willed woman. Come on in. We'll go into the kitchen."

"Mrs. O'Neal been cooking?" asked David as he started walking toward the kitchen.

"Always thinking with your stomach," said Owen as he followed him.

Matthew finally noticed that there was something or someone behind the man. "Who is with you?" he asked and sighed when an all-too-familiar small face peered around Reid. "Noah."

"Hello, Lieutenant. I came with Abbie's brother."

"I can see that." He looked at Reid who was smiling a little. "What I cannae understand is how is it he let ye tag along?"

"He would not turn back," said Reid, not hiding his exasperation. "Only thing I did not try was shooting him. Stuck like a burr. Claims my sister forgot him."

Looking at the boy who was staring at one of Iain's paintings and trying to appear innocent, Matthew attempted to look stern. "Ye told him that Abbie forgot ye? Ye ken that isnae true."

Noah glanced at him and stuck his bottom lip out. "She didn't give me time to talk to her."

Crouching down, Matthew said, "Laddie, she didnae want to leave, but she has no house to live in, no husband to help her raise ye. It is verra difficult for a lone woman to raise a child and she already has one because of a promise she made to a dying woman."

The child's mouth quivered and his eyes filled with tears. Matthew felt like the meanest man alive and that annoyed him. It also roused some guilt for it was his fault, his own cowardice, that kept Abbie from having a solution to her problem. It made Abigail think she had no future that would allow her to keep Noah. He was going to have to get some backbone when he next had the woman alone.

"I don't care. I just want Abbie. I brought my puppy and a bag with my things." He held up the bag, then held the dog out and Matthew scratched the little animal's ears. "I just want Abbie."

Matthew stood up and ran his hand through his hair. "I ken it. Weel, she will be back soon and ye can talk to her then."

"Okay. Where is Jeremiah?"

"With her. She went to get him a few clothes."

Noah nodded. "Women like to buy clothes for itty bitty babies. Or make some."

Shaking his head, Matthew led Noah and Reid into the kitchen. Mrs. O'Neal was busy setting food on the table and a glance at Noah showed him the boy was stunned by what he saw. The boy looked at him and Matthew nudged him over to one of the benches.

"Sit down, lad," Matthew said as he took his own seat.

"And who is this?" asked Mrs. O'Neal.

"I am Noah. Abbie forgot me so I came here with her brother." She placed a plate in front of each of them and set the rest around the table for the others who would soon arrive.

"And how old are you, Noah?" asked Mrs. O'Neal.

"Five. I had my birthday four days ago." He sighed. "I got no cake or sweet."

"Hey!" Reid carried over a large tureen filled with stew. "I gave you some of my beef jerky."

"Yes, you did. It was very kind of you." Noah turned his head and made a face that clearly showed what he truly thought of that kindness. Then he looked sweetly innocent again and Matthew coughed as he choked on a laugh. Mrs. O'Neal hid a smile behind her hand as his brothers and her children came in.

"Ah, I believe I hear the ladies returning," Mrs. O'Neal said, wiped her hands, and left the kitchen to meet them.

Abbie smiled at Mrs. O'Neal as she took Jeremiah from her arms after the woman had held him while she had shed her coat. "Are we late for lunch?"

"No." Mrs. O'Neal said hello to Ned as the boy hurried into the kitchen. She turned to put her arm around Iain's daughter and smiled at Emily. "Food is on the table."

"Then we best hurry," said Emily.

They followed Mrs. O'Neal into the kitchen. Abbie smiled at everyone and then froze in midstep toward her seat. She stared hard at the man seated on Matthew's left.

"Hello, Ab," Reid said quietly and smiled at her.

Abbie burst into tears and ran over to him. He caught her easily and she slumped against him, pressing her face into his shirt. She heard herself rambling on and on, but even she was not sure of what she was saying.

"Ab, if you want answers to those questions, you have to calm down."

She sat up and wiped her face with the handkerchief he handed her. "What questions?" She scowled at Matthew who laughed, but quickly returned her full attention to Reid. "You get wounded anywhere else?" she asked as she lightly stroked his scarred cheek.

"No. Now, I will answer those other questions as soon as someone stops punching me." He turned his head and glared down at the boy by his side.

"You made her cry!" Noah punched his arm again.

"Noah? Noah!" Abbie sat up and stared at the child. "What are you doing here?"

"I came with him. You forgot me."

"I did not forget you. I explained why I couldn't take you. I thought you understood."

Noah shook his head. "I needed to think of how to say why you were wrong but when I was ready, you were already gone."

"And just how were you going to explain that I was wrong?"

"Well, how could you pick out the right house without me to help you?"

"I could pick out one. It just needs enough rooms and to be weather tight."

Noah shook his head and sat down next to Reid. "And you were going to put two boys in it. I'm a boy and you needed one to tell you all the other things you needed to look for."

"Such as what?" Abbie asked as she went and sat down across from Reid.

"A yard. Windows you can latch tight so bad boys don't climb out and run around the yard at night." His eyes widened and Abbie knew they were about to take a journey into Noah's far too vivid imagination. "And secret passages."

Abbie stared at the smiling boy for a brief moment then crossed her arms on the table, lowered her head to them, and laughed. She tried to muffle the sound but the laughter of others at the table was too much to ignore. There was no solution to her problem yet, but she already knew that she would not be sending the boy back to Mrs. Beaton.

"I think she is laughing at what you said, boy," said Reid and gave a chuckling Mrs. O'Neal a big smile when she filled his bowl with stew and set it in front of him.

"She does that a lot when I try to have a talk with her. When she is done, then I can tell her more." Noah stared wide-eyed at the full bowl Mrs. O'Neal set in front of him and picked up his spoon, then barely mumbled out a thank you before he dug in.

The idea that Noah had even more to lecture her about only made Abbie laugh harder. Forcing herself to calm down, she wiped her eyes and sat up just as Mrs. O'Neal bent close to set her bowl in front of her.

"The lad will settle in very nicely, miss," she said softly. "He could go sit with the others if he isn't scared."

Abigail glanced at another table set near the window where Mrs. O'Neal's older children and young Ned sat. There was an empty seat next to Ned so she slowly coaxed Noah over there. She returned to her seat but kept an eye on him until she was certain he was again relaxed and settling in well. As she began eating again she glanced at her brother, still a bit stunned that he was there.

"How did he end up with you?" she asked.

"I tracked you to the Beaton house and he was suddenly there. He had already heard Mrs. Beaton and the others tell me about your stay and where you were headed. He even had that puppy and a little bag and politely told me he would go with me. I said no and he never said a word. Just walked away. Then I was leaving and just happened to look behind me to see him following."

"Oh dear."

"'Oh dear' is right. As I told Matthew, I did everything short of shooting him to make him go back, but he kept on coming."

"He can be stubborn."

"Bullheaded."

Abbie laughed and nodded. "So you gave in."

"Not much choice. He was company too, and I had little of that in the last few years. He even got me telling him stories at night because I was told you did it."

"Ah. So, of course you had to." She shook her head. "He is going to be a challenge to raise."

"What he is is smart and a survivor."

"He is only five years old."

"He is smart and he is a survivor," he repeated. "Never forget that about him."

"It is a good thing, miss," said Mrs. O'Neal from beside her. "Doesn't often show so young, but bet the war drew it out. And your brother is right. It is a good thing to keep in mind about the boy. It is what he is deep at his core. Like our Iain," she added softly.

Abbie thought about it for a while but soon got caught up in the men's talk. They included her brother without pause and she could see he appreciated it. She started to wonder how he had gotten out of the service he had been forced into.

"How did you get out of the Confederate hold?"

"It was Night Riders who took me, or so they liked to call themselves. Butchering ba"—he blushed and continued—"pigs." He dragged a hand through his hair and grimaced. "Fortunately, it seems they just wanted someone to do all the work they hated. I mucked up after their horses, cared for the beasts, which I didn't much mind as they treated them poorly, and even had to cook a lot. Then one of them caught me trying to free a young woman they had grabbed. I killed him, freed her, and then ran for my life. Knew they'd find the man, so had to get as far away as I could. Stole one of their horses I was particularly fond of and just rode."

"Where did the woman go?"

"She headed straight for the town not far from our camp. Told her it might not be the safest place but she was determined. Figured she knew someone there she felt would protect her."

"So you aren't a deserter?"

"Don't think so. Never signed or swore to anything but that won't necessarily stop someone from trying to try me for it."

"I feared they would have made you fight in the war for them."

"They didn't do much fighting in the war," he said, disgust thick in his voice. "They attacked innocents, stole money and anything else they could get their hands on, and raped the women they found. They were outlaws wearing the shield of war."

"There were a lot of those, especially up this way," said Matthew.

"Some of them were even disowned by the army they supported," Reid said and shrugged.

"Sad, but I think a lot of them will just go into straight outlawry once the war ends."

Reid shrugged again. "They are little better than that now."

"At least you are free of all that now."

"I just wish I could have been there when they came to burn the house."

"I had a lot of help." Abbie briefly smiled at Matthew then looked back at her brother. "I am sorry about what you had to find but we couldn't stay long enough to put out the fire and have a proper burial."

"I know that. I buried them. In the orchard near the child they lost."

"Thank you."

"Ye have an orchard?" asked Matthew's brother Robbie. "What sort?"

"Apples. Two kinds," Reid replied.

Robbie limped down the table to sit next to Reid. To Abbie's surprise the two men were soon deep into discussion. She eavesdropped for only a few moments and then decided they knew what they were discussing, but they had lost her early on in the discussion. All she knew was that it had something to do with cider. What mattered to her was that Reid looked interested, even eager.

Seeing that Mrs. O'Neal was getting up, Abbie moved to help clear off the table. They put out the stewed fruit and cream plus small bowls. Abbie dished out some for Ned and Noah then returned to a seat near Matthew to have some of her own.

"What are they talking so seriously about?" asked Matthew with a nod toward Robbie and Reid.

"I am not sure. I believe it has to do with the apple orchard my father planted and cider."

"Ah. Robbie has been eager to try his hand at cider making but the apples are not always easy to come by. A steady supply was needed."

"Well, we have that, but that is about all there is on the old land. Oh, there is the barn too, I think. Or the fire could have reached that."

"It didn't because your brother found your message on George's stall. So, I have to assume the building was still standing. Care to go for a walk this afternoon?"

"That would be nice if I can impose on someone to watch the boys."

After lunch was done, Abbie discovered it was not difficult at all to get someone to watch out for the boys. She wandered off to go to the barn and milk the goat and wondered why Mrs. O'Neal and Emily had not even hesitated to consider what they had to do but said yes and wished her a good afternoon. She told herself to not try and read some conspiracy in it all and greeted the goat.

She was just stepping out of the barn when Reid walked up to her and took the pail of milk she held. "So how close are you and Matthew?"

Abigail blinked and frantically wondered why he asked, if she and Matthew had given themselves away in some way. "What do you mean?"

"What I mean is how close are you? Friends or more?"

"Well, I believe we are friends. If we are more he hasn't said so. Why are you interested?"

"I might have a chance to turn the old place into a new and profitable one with some care and help. Robbie wants to try his hand at making cider. We have an orchard. Perfect match. Well, if I can prove I own the land."

"You can. I have the papers."

He laughed and shook his head. "Did not expect it to be so easy. See, Robbie has been searching his brain for something he might make a living at since he got hurt. He can't do his weaving anymore because he can't stand at the loom for long and, at the moment, the fingers on one hand are not as nimble as they used to be."

"What happened to him?"

"Sort of what happened to me except they didn't take him. Tried, but he fought and they beat him senseless before his brothers could get to him." He shook his head. "Broke his leg in so many places he is lucky he just limps, and they stomped on his hands. He says that made him feel they knew enough about him to know what he did and they went for his hands on purpose. So I thought I'd give his idea a chance."

"Of course, you should do that. I will get the papers."

He followed her as they left the bucket of milk with Mrs. O'Neal and then as she went up the stairs to the room she had been given. She blushed deeply when she saw Matthew's shirt draped at the end of the bed. Reid walked over, picked it up, and looked at her with one eyebrow raised.

"I think you and he are more than friends."

She snatched the shirt out of his hands and hung it on a bedpost. "What we are is none of your business." She went to the chest that held the box with all the papers.

"Why don't you just ask him to marry you?"

"A woman doesn't do the asking."

"No, maybe not, but I rather think she can lead a

man into doing it especially when he should," he said, stressing the last three words.

"I am not having this discussion with you." She took out the box that held all their papers and held it out to him. "I think what you seek is in there."

He shook his head as he opened the box and began to look over all the papers. "As your sole male relative I should do something about all this. Maybe I will just go down and punch him a few times."

"You will do no such thing."

He opened up one set of papers and carefully read them. "This is what I need." He looked at her. "It is what any brother would do."

"But not one who is so bright and understanding."

Reid laughed heartily but it stopped abruptly when he spotted the blue quilt in the chest. "I recall when Mother finished that. She was so pleased until she realized it did not match anything else she had in the room."

"Do you want it? I managed to save several and have only had to give away one, in trade for Rosie."

He knelt down and smoothed his hand over the quilt. "Who is Rosie?"

"The goat. That is her new name."

"Good one. Easy, and one she might learn to answer to, although with a goat you can never be sure."

"Do you want it?" she asked quietly as she watched how he almost petted the quilt.

"Yeh, I believe I do. You sure you still have one for yourself?"

"I do." She moved to the other chest and glanced at his feet. "Doubt these will fit any longer," she said as she pulled out his old boots, "but I saved them. And this." She held up his mouth organ. "I fear most everything else burned."

"I know. Except for the things I kept hidden in the barn."

"Why would you hide stuff in the barn?"

"You know how Mother hated Da's old books?" When Abbie nodded, he continued. "Well, I hid some in the barn. Thought she would get over her hate and he would welcome them back. I think our mother was very upset when we left Pennsylvania and that anger never really left her. She was never really happy at the cabin."

"She never spoke of it."

"Of course she wouldn't because it was Da who caused it and she would never criticize him, except about the books that reminded her of the life they used to have."

"Oh. I never thought of that reason for her hatred of the books."

"Because you were too fascinated with them all. He loved that you were interested and the two of you would spend hours going over some of the stuff."

"Were you jealous of that?"

"No. just didn't understand that. Never much liked the idea of becoming a doctor even though I knew Da would have been pleased. Unfortunately, women rarely get near doctoring. There are a few but they have a real struggle and mostly care for women and children. You have Da's gift, that keen understanding of people and their ailments."

"I have got some practice in since this war began." She closed the chest and stood up.

With his papers and quilt in one arm, he took Abbie by the hand with the other. "So am I going to have to call Noah *nephew*?"

"I fear so," she said, and laughed at his sigh.

"That puppy of his is never going to be a big dog, you know."

"I know. I hope he is not too disappointed. When do you and Robbie plan to go out and look at the orchard?"

"In a few days. Want to come?"

"I am not sure. I will see how I feel about it when you are ready to go. It is not too far from here, I think. I just don't know if I am ready to see the remains or the graves. It was all so sad. Mother did nothing to save herself. She made sure she died with Da."

Reid shook his head as they went down the stairs. "She was far too attached to Da, as if he was her reason for living. You aren't that much younger than me but maybe too young to have noticed. It is hard to admit, but if given a choice between either of us or Da she would have chosen Da without hesitation. I think she was actually a bit jealous of how you and Da shared an interest. I know the men hurt her, as they boasted of it, and I suspect that made her cling to Da even more. It was why I made sure to bury them together."

"I planted flowers on the baby's grave."

"I thought it might have been Da, but it was a good thing to do. I think what you planted is spreading over the grave for it was all ablaze with color."

"There ye are, Abbie," said Matthew when she and Reid reached the bottom of the stairs. "Ready for a walk?" When she nodded he trotted up the stairs.

Reid looked up and called, "Shirt is hanging on the bedpost." He grinned when the man's steps faltered briefly before he continued up the stairs. "Ow." He rubbed his arm where Abbie had just punched him.

"That was rude," she said primly. "You are a guest in his home."

"He deserved it. Still think it is my duty to punch him."

"Punch who?" asked Robbie as he stepped into the hall.

"Your brother Matthew."

"Ah, probably deserved." He stepped closer and looked at the quilt Reid held then looked at Abbie. "Your work?"

"No, our mother's. The only thing I can do is embroider and stitch up people."

"So it was you who put the snake on Matthew's coat."

"It hides the mend I had to do to the sleeve."

Robbie grinned. "Very nicely done. Like James's dragon; better though. Hope you don't try to hide the mend when you stitch up people."

Abbie laughed. "No, that would make them suffer for too long, and I would have to take it apart when the wound healed."

"Shame. Do you plan to make use of George and the wagon in the next few days?"

"Have no plans to do so," she replied.

"Good." He looked at Reid. "We have something to carry a few things over there that would make the decisions needed easier to make."

Reid walked off with Robbie, both men talking seriously and quietly. They were really going to give Robbie's idea a try. She wished them both luck. It would be good if the land continued to be worked by a Jenson. Her father would be happy, she thought, and wiped aside a stray tear. Reid now had a plan and she knew her brother liked that. She suspected it would do Robbie a lot of good as well.

Matthew came to stand beside her and kissed her cheek. "What's wrong?"

"Nothing is wrong. I just thought my father would be happy to think Reid was going to work the land, and had a touch of sadness. It is gone now."

"Good, we are going to take our walk now."

"It is not too late?"

"Nay, we have several hours of light left," he said as he led her out, picking up a small basket from off a table on the way out the door. "Mrs. O'Neal put together some food and drink for us."

"Does she do everything around here?"

"Seems so some days, except when it is time for a heavy cleaning. Then she drags us all in and gives orders."

"Abbie!"

Hearing her brother's yell from the barn, Abbie hurried out the gate, dragging Matthew with her. "I think Reid just saw the wagon."

Matthew just laughed as they ran down the road.

Chapter Eighteen

Matthew glanced down at the woman by his side. She was rather delicate, even in her coat, and he was embarrassed by the fear he had over speaking a few words to her. He reminded himself that she was a soft-hearted, caring woman, had revealed that many times over. She would do her best to be kind and gentle even if she felt she had to push him aside.

"There is our flock," he said as they reached the top of the hill overlooking the grazing fields.

Abbie looked at all the white, black-faced sheep and smiled faintly. "They look nice from up here. I recall a boy I used to know who proudly took me to see the herd of cows he and his da were raising. The smell was horrible."

"Weel, bigger animals, bigger stink. Although I think sheep can get pretty stinky. Different sort of stink. People who dinnae like the beasts are particularly sensitive to it." He smiled. "Owen has gotten into a few fights over it. He doesnae always change his coat before heading into town. Tell the truth, I think he does that on purpose at times. It was cattlemen who cut his face."

"Idiots. What is the use in fighting over what kind of animals you raise? But, then we have just spent four years killing each other. Whose house is that?" she pointed at the small cabin in the distance, painted green.

"That one is Owen's." He pointed to another one a few yards farther on. "The one painted red is David's. He lives there with his wife. She is trying to interest Owen into marrying her sister."

Abbie laughed. "Is it working?"

"Hard to tell with Owen, but he did once say he thought Amberlee was adorable when she got angry."

"Amberlee?"

"Mother stuck her with it. She does have amber-colored eyes."

"But why does Owen's comment about her make you think he might be weakening?"

"It shows he is amused by the game. If all he is is amused, nay angry, then he just might be a bit interested."

Abbie thought about that for a moment and then shrugged. "I just hope he isn't mean to this sister."

"Owen would never be mean or even rude to a lass, especially not a young lass with long shining black hair and huge amber eyes." He took her by the hand and turned to head back to the house as she laughed.

"Oh, she sounds lovely."

"She is."

"I have to keep Noah," she said abruptly but in a soft voice as if confessing some sin.

"Ye dinnae *have* to do anything."

"Oh, but I do. I couldn't possibly send him away. It was hard enough to leave him behind even though it was only for a while."

He suddenly turned off the path to home and led

her down another trail, helping her over the rocks and rough spots until they were on a flat grassy spot. Matthew spread his coat on the grass, sat on it, and tugged her down beside him. He wondered if he had the courage to speak out now.

"Explain this. Ye left the lad behind, but now that he has found ye, ye cannae send him back?"

"Yes, that is it precisely. I suppose you need to have a reason for what looks like a dramatic change of mind."

"Aye, I do. Ye told the lad ye couldnae take him because ye had no home and no husband."

"I know, and it was a very sensible decision."

"I ken ye thought so. I am still of a mind to believe ye could easily turn aside gossip, just reminding people there was a war, which leaves orphans and widows."

Abbie sighed. "I know it and, as far as Noah goes, I suspect he would tell them all about how he ended up alone."

Matthew laughed. "With great embellishment."

"Exactly. The boy talks well for his age. It is as if the first time he said a word he liked it so much he has tried to learn as much as he can. He listens to everything that is said. He is one of those children you have to be very careful around and watch what you say because he will absorb it and use it later, probably when you would really rather he didn't. There is a part of me that is very sorry that I didn't stay long enough to hear him try to convince me I was wrong."

Matthew bit his tongue but quietly said, "Maybe ye were a little wrong."

"Of course I wasn't. Leaving him was wrong, certainly felt wrong, but the why I told him was *not* wrong."

"Except that ye thought ye could choose a house without his help."

Abbie laughed and flopped down onto her back, still laughing. "Little wretch." She sighed and rubbed her hands over her face. "I can't send him back though. I just can't. It was hard enough to leave him behind to wait."

He rolled until he was settled comfortably on top of her and brushed a kiss over her mouth. "I ken it. Ye didnae have to. I told ye that ye were coming to my house."

"It isn't just yours though, is it? I could not impose upon all the others. And I was already toting one baby."

"Weel, Jeremiah was easily accepted. Ye saw that."

"Exactly. I saw it, but accepting a baby is a lot different than accepting a boy, one who loves to talk, explore, and ask questions. Lots and lots of questions, some rather impolite at times. I shouldn't have left them with Emily."

"Why not? She has two close to their ages and Noah appeared to like Ned weel enough."

"He did, didn't he? He wasn't close to the other boys at Mrs. Beaton's house."

"Nay, but I think that was because they came together, and he came later. They were already a pair." She looked around. "Where are we?"

"At the riverside. This is a nice grassy spot overlooking the river. I thought ye would like sitting here watching the river pass by as ye struggled with your thoughts. Ye liked the other one we sat by until the Rebs came and spoiled it."

"That would be lovely, but I don't see the river. I can hear it but not see it."

"Ye have to get closer." He stood up and grabbed

her hand, pulling her up beside him, and walked toward the edge.

Abigail was not quite so sure about it when he led her to the edge and she realized exactly where she was. The grassy spot was a ledge on a steep hill that went down to the river. She clung to Matthew's arm as she looked over the edge. It was a long way down to the water and it was steep.

"I think this is a lot more dangerous than the other one."

He started to tug her back to the ridge of land they had climbed down. "It isnae dangerous over here. Ye dinnae need to fear falling. Solid rock under our feet. We willnae go romp at the edge of the drop."

Matthew sat down and tugged her back down by his side. He wrapped an arm around her shoulders and held her close. This was a good time and place to speak of the future, but he suddenly could not think of a single word to say.

"I was wondering if it would be possible to take over one of the empty houses in town," Abbie said. "I just wondered how that could work if the people came back."

"It wouldnae be as safe as where ye are now. Ye would be a woman alone with two bairns."

"But the war is over. Is that not what your brother said?"

"He *thinks* it is over. And even if it was over, these hills still hold more of the men who didnae seem to belong to either side or didnae claim loyalty to one or the other, just like to kill, rape, steal, and destroy."

"Oh."

She sighed and thought over the problem. Taking over one of the deserted homes would solve where she lived but it would not solve the problem of having two children and no husband. People's thoughts always wandered down the wrong path, not the one that reminded them there had just been a horrible war that had left a lot of orphans who needed care. She knew she should not fret so over how such people judged her but also knew it would not be just her who suffered under their suspicions. Now Matthew was forcing her to see that not all the dangers would go away when the war ended.

"I have to find a place to live. Maybe I could go with Reid and Robbie. The barn is still whole and they are sure to be building a shelter of some kind."

"Nay, ye will stay here with Jeremiah and Noah."

"I cannot impose . . ."

"It is not imposing." He pulled her into his arms. "Ye will be staying with me."

"It is not just your home, is it?"

"We all own it so it is my home."

"But . . ."

"We can take over one of the houses in the town if you are really bothered by sharing a house. Place is nearly deserted now. And several have notices that speak of the ones who died or where the people who were there went. Suppose one could contact one of them and make a deal."

"I noticed that, too."

Abigail snuggled into his embrace, savoring the heat and strength of him. He would probably think she was mad if she told him she even liked the smell of him. Clean skin and clean clothes. There was also that sense of being safe. She did not fully understand why as they were outside in an area that was overrun with marauders. They both had their guns, but she knew they could easily be outnumbered. So it was simply him; he made her feel safe.

She felt him spreading soft heated kisses over her face and sighed. They really needed to talk and when they started this they never got around to having any serious talk. It appeared it would be her who finally put her heart out there and prayed for the best. She had at least come to the conclusion that she did not *need* a husband, she *wanted* one, and this man was the one she wanted.

Then he grasped her chin, turned her face up to his, and kissed her. Abigail lost herself in the heat of the kiss and made no protest as he pushed her down onto the coat serving as their seat. She murmured her eager acceptance as he settled his body on top of hers. It was not until he tossed aside his shirt and undid the buttons of her bodice that she recalled they were outdoors.

"Someone could come by and see us," she said, and even to her it sounded like a weak protest.

"No one will see us. I left my hat up there hanging on a bush."

"And that matters how?"

"It tells any of the people going by that someone is down here and it stays private. The only ones who pass by here are my brothers and the Jones brothers. They ken what it means."

"I see. So you have more or less announced to anyone we know that we are behaving badly down here so please don't look?"

He frowned and looked thoughtful for a moment then nodded. "That's about it."

Abigail did not know whether she wanted to laugh or punch him so she just gave in to another kiss. She threaded her fingers into his hair to hold his mouth to hers. Only a small part of her was truly aware that he was neatly undressing her as they kissed. It was not until he shifted position to remove his pants and a cool breeze blew over her legs that she became aware of the fact that she was now completely naked.

Opening her eyes in shock, she was about to protest when she realized he was nearly naked himself. Her own embarrassment fled as she looked over his body while he yanked off his boots and socks. The man was all taut skin stretched over lean muscle. His scars did not detract from it at all. Then her gaze dropped to his groin. Unable to resist, she reached out to take him in her hand. A soft groan escaped him and he just sat there with his eyes closed as she stroked him.

He pulled her hand away and tugged her up onto his lap. Then, cupping her face in his hands he drew her face closer to his and kissed her. Abigail tightened her arms around his neck as she fervently returned his kiss. He smoothed his hands down her body until he grasped her by the hips and lifted her up. She groaned when he carefully slid her body onto his, driving deep inside her.

For a moment Abigail remained still, savoring the sensation of their joined bodies but then Matthew moved her, thrusting at the same time. It took her only a minute to gain the pace he set and she was soon riding him without assistance. He cupped her breasts in his hands, kneading them gently as she moved. When her release came, it swept over her so strongly she clung to him to steady herself. Then he began to thrust harder until he held her tightly against him as he emptied himself inside of her.

Clinging to him as she fought to catch her breath, Abigail allowed him to settle her back onto his coat. He then carefully pulled away and fell onto his back at her side. She was silently proud that she regained her breath faster than he did and sat up to dress herself.

Just as she was doing up her chemise he sat up to pull on his shoes and socks then his pants.

As she pulled her dress on and began to button it she realized he had left her stockings on again. "You always leave my stockings on."

He laughed. "Aye. I like how it looks." He shrugged on his shirt and began to do it up. "Ye have bonnie little legs but they do look even more bonnie with those high white stockings with the ribbon garters."

"If you say so."

"I do." He turned to find her dressed and looking around for her shoes so he pulled her into his arms. "We will get a house. The more I think on it the more I like us having a place of our own but near everyone else. Might even pick a place around here and build one. There is one condition."

"And what is that?" she asked with a touch of suspicion.

"Ye have to marry me." He looked away. "I cannae be sharing a house with a single lady."

Abigail was willing to swear that the man was trying to blush, and she nearly laughed. Then she sobered and took a deep steadying breath. She knew this was her chance to take a gamble and she prayed everyone was right.

"And I cannot wed a man who has no love for me."

The way he whipped his head back around and stared at her gave her a tiny hint of hope. He did not look shocked or horrified, but surprised. Then he frowned and she wondered if she was giving away something with a look in her eyes.

"Why would ye think he doesnae?"

"Perhaps because he has never said so."

"He did. Several times."

"Really? Was I perhaps asleep at the time?"

He grimaced but then said, "Ye might have been. I didnae make certain I was heard."

"I am awake now."

"Ah, so ye are." He pulled her into his arms and lightly kissed her. "I love ye, Abigail Jenson. And I also seem to have fallen in love with Noah and Jeremiah, though I think my love for the bairn needs a little nursing, will perhaps get stronger when he grows past the age of screaming in the middle of the night."

Abigail laughed then kissed him. "I love you, Matthew MacEnroy. And how can anyone not love Noah? And we can live as close to your family as you wish. I am rather fond of the whole lot. But, a warning, with Noah comes that puppy, and I am really looking fondly at a certain kitten in your barn."

"A cat? Ye do ask a lot of a poor mon. Fine. Maybe the dog will eat it." He laughed when she swatted his arm. "I dinnae mind cats."

She shivered and frowned up at the slowly darkening sky. "I think we best discuss this back at home." She wondered why he grinned. "I believe there is rain coming."

"I think ye are right."

He stood up and pulled her up beside him. It proved a lot easier to climb back up the hill than it was to go down, and a few minutes later he boosted her up into the saddle and then mounted his horse. They both ran fast for his home but the raindrops started to fall slowly by the time they got inside the gates, then they ran for the house.

Once inside, Matthew debated the best way to announce that he and Abigail were getting married. He had never said a word to anyone about even considering asking her today so tried to think of a way to lead into the news slowly. Then he realized he should have a ring to put on her finger. He followed her into the kitchen where everyone was already gathering for the evening meal. Taking his seat, he tugged her down to sit beside him.

"Did ye ask her then?" Iain asked calmly as he put a few slices of beef on his plate.

"Why would ye ask me that?"

"Because ye went to that place. It is where Emily caught me. Ow." He grinned and rubbed his arm where his wife hit him.

"No need to make it sound as if I set some huge bear trap for you," Emily grumbled then blushed when he whispered something in her ear.

"How do ye ken I went there?"

"Jones brothers stopped by and mentioned the placement of the hat."

Matthew looked at a blushing Abigail and shook his head. "Maybe we won't put a house real close to these people."

"Ye want your own house?" asked Nigel.

"Weel, there are already four of us," Matthew said.

"So ye asked and did she have the wisdom to say nay?" asked Lachlan.

Abigail started to laugh. "Sorry, I said yes."

Emily nodded. "So we will arrange the preacher and plan a wedding."

"Oh, I don't need any big celebration."

"It will be big even if we only have the family, so don't worry. Mrs. O'Neal loves arranging such things."

"I really do and these past few years have provided only the rare chance."

Before everyone could start to talk about the celebration, Abigail said, "I have something to ask before we all get caught up in planning. Can anyone draw well enough to make a drawing of Jeremiah? I need to write to Robert's parents and thought that, if I could get some likeness of the baby, it would be a good thing to send them."

"Ye still going to do that?" asked Matthew.

"I have to. I promised Julia I would. I told you, I have papers from her naming me guardian if there is some trouble, but I just cannot feel there will be."

"I can do it," said Iain. "Didnae used to be able to but practiced by doing some of our bairns. It willnae be done quickly as a bairn is a difficult subject but it willnae take too long."

"Thank you. I will work on a letter as I think it may be more difficult to write than I anticipated."

With that settled, Abigail let them toss around ideas of how to celebrate her coming marriage to Matthew. She had not yet gotten used to the fact that he loved her let alone that he meant to marry her. That was going to take a while. There was such a bubble of happiness inside of her, she was afraid she would break into a song or dance around the room if she did not keep herself in tight control.

Noah slipped up beside her and squeezed onto the seat next to her. He looked a little fretful and she tried to see this news from his viewpoint. She knew she always had to remember that he was a boy who had lost his entire family. That had left a few scars on his heart. She brushed his hair off his face and looked at him.

"What is the matter, Noah?"

"Are you leaving this house?"

"Oh, not for a while, darling. It is just something we thought would be good because we are already a family of four. Me, Matthew, you, and Jeremiah. And your puppy. And my cat," she added in a whisper, and heard Emily giggle.

"I will still stay with you?"

"Yes, me and Matthew."

She could almost see the tension in his small body leech away. He smiled at Matthew who nodded back then hopped down and rejoined the other children. She heard him tell the others that he was sure the new house would have a secret passage. She glanced at Matthew and he was staring at his plate as his shoulders shook with laughter.

"I'm sorry," she said, laughter tinting her voice. "I will have a little talk with him."

"Nay, dinnae bother. I think we will try to put one in." He glanced at Iain who grinned and nodded.

She jumped a little when arms surrounded her from behind then glanced up at her brother's grinning face. "Come to wish me congratulations or to punch him in the face?"

"Just wondering how I should feel that you are marrying a blue belly."

"Oh. I didn't realize that you might have become a true Rebel."

He laughed. "Not by a long shot. The men who took me weren't either. Not to worry, although you are stealing my traveling companion."

"You can't go riding about with a four-year-old."

"I am five!"

"Five-year-old."

"With big ears. Good luck, sis. Pleased to see you settled. Da would have liked him." He glanced around the table. "All of them."

"What are you going to do?"

"Robbie and I will leave soon after the wedding and start setting up to see what the chance is of having a cider mill." He sat down beside her. "We have nearly all that is needed back on the land. The orchard, and the water."

"Is this what you truly want to do?"

"I think it is, but we'll see how it goes. Have to take a chance. It will work or it will fail. That's life. And that is what I am really looking for. A life. This may well be it."

"I will hope that it does and that it makes you happy."

"No more than I do, darling." He kissed her cheek and went back to his seat.

Matthew leaned nearer to her. "I think there is a plan already to build them a good shelter. Need to have something they can at least get cover in for when the weather turns harsher. Finishing might take longer."

"It is a lot of work."

"So was this. So was Mrs. O'Neal's home. And the cabins for the Jones brothers. We have become quite quick and learned some shortcuts. And dinnae forget, when it isnae shearing time there are seven to twelve of us."

"That is a good-sized crew."

"It is, and a skilled one. There used to be a few men from town who'd lend a hand now and then too, kenning that we would return the favor if they needed it. Might not get ours until next year."

"That is fine." She lowered her voice. "I think Reid is more in need of a place."

"Aye," he answered in an equally low voice. "One

thing most soldiers ache for while away is home. Ye have yours now." He kissed her cheek.

"I do, don't I?" She glanced toward the children's table. "Noah! That puppy does not belong on the table."

"I was just showing them how he can dance," Noah answered and put the puppy down on the floor.

"I am sure they can see that just as well out on the back porch."

"Okay."

She looked at Matthew who was battling to hide a grin. "My family."

"Aye, one with a dancing puppy. Cannae beat that."

She laughed and shook her head. As they shared some freshly baked pie, she joined in on the planning for her wedding. It was still a bit difficult for her to believe, and she found herself doing more agreeing to someone else's idea than making any of her own. By the time she sought her bed she was tired and, for reasons she did not understand, nervous and a little afraid. Abigail was in her nightgown and ready to crawl into bed when Emily knocked.

"I just wanted to talk alone for a moment," she said as she stepped in. "Doubt Matthew will allow much more than that although I told Iain to keep him busy for a while. Are you sure about marrying Matthew?"

"Why would I not be?"

"I am married to one of these fellows, remember, and it can be a heady thing. And when one becomes intimate with a fellow it can make it even harder to know one's own mind. I just wondered because you said so little when we talked about the wedding."

"I didn't really have any ideas. It is not something I

have done and I have attended very few of them as well."

"Neither had I, and I also rather let them run with it. Mrs. O'Neal is very good. I am not quite sure why I am wondering if you want this but there was something that troubled me."

"It was a bit of a surprise to me. Perhaps that is what you sensed."

"Ah. Shock."

Abigail laughed. "Something like that. I had not expected it. He was talking about where we could all live then said he had a condition. I had to marry him."

"Oh, and save his reputation. Poor boy."

"So for some reason I decided to take a gamble and, believe me, I never do. I said I had a policy too, to never marry a man who did not love me."

"And he said it?"

"He did and he claimed he already had, a few times. Naturally I scoffed."

"I should hope so. As if any woman would miss that or not recall it."

"I know. Told him he must have said it while I was still asleep. Then he looked a bit embarrassed because that was exactly when he said it. He even demonstrated how he mumbled it. So I made him say it clearly while I was wide-awake and he did. I am glad he doesn't have the reputation of a tomcat but I got what I needed. I just never expected it and I think I keep worrying that somehow it will disappear."

Emily hugged her. "I know just how you feel. Once done it passes."

"Are you certain?"

"Oh yes. Because it is done. You are tied. It is forever, starting that day."

"I guess that is it. Do you think they feel the same or is it just women who overthink the whole thing?"

"Well, don't know if they feel the same thing. Some might. Some might just want to get the ceremony over. Men can be odd creatures."

"Matthew might have a good reason to be nervous. He marries me and he becomes a father to Noah and Jeremiah. No idea what Jeremiah will be like, but we all have had a good peek at Noah and what he might be."

"Noah is lovely. He will keep everything lively. An adorable boy."

There was a knock on the bedroom door and a moment later Matthew entered. "Had your chat, Emily?" Matthew asked her.

"All done," she said cheerfully and hugged him. "Good wishes for the future, Matthew." She walked out and shut the door behind her.

"What's this?" he asked, plucking at her nightgown.

"It is what one wears to bed."

He stepped closer and then yanked it off her over her head and tossed it aside. "Maybe in the winter. When it is verra cold and ye want a little extra."

Abigail tried to cover herself and hopped into bed, pulling the covers over herself. "So if the house catches on fire I can just run out naked?"

"At least ye wouldnae have to worry about flapping cloth catching fire," he said as he shed his clothes and climbed into bed. "Was Jeremiah all right?"

"Just wanted to eat and be changed. The usual demands." She squeaked in surprise when he pulled her into his arms then looked up to find him grinning at her.

"What are you looking so pleased about?"

"This. Soon it will be like this every night."

"Even in the winter?"

"Depends on how bad the winter is, and you have those quilts. More blankets will help."

She laughed and kissed him. That quickly led to more and Abbie willingly followed where he led. She decided there were many more advantages to getting married than she had considered.

Chapter Nineteen

Sealing the envelope, Abigail sighed and fought the urge to open it again and write a new letter. Iain had drawn a beautiful picture of the baby and was working on one of Robert and Julia on the day of their marriage when they had paid for a proper picture to be taken. She believed it would be something Jeremiah would like.

Glancing at the framed photograph on the edge of the desk she sat at, she sighed. They had been so young and had looked so hopeful and happy. It made her sad to think of how the life they had wanted together had been cut short. The dress Julia had worn had easily disguised her pregnancy so there was a sweet innocence to the picture.

Shaking her head, she pushed the thoughts of her dead friend aside. There were too many who had lost their chance at a future in this war, on both sides. She could not sink herself in misery over such things.

"Are ye finished?" asked Matthew as he walked into the small room Iain kept as an office so they could keep a good record of how much money they gained from all the things his family did.

"I am. I was just looking at the picture of Robert and Julia and feeling sad, especially since we will soon start the future they were denied."

He stepped up behind her and kissed the top of her head as he massaged her shoulders. "It is sad, but ye have given that to her son."

"*We* have," she said. "This needs to be posted. And now I need to see if the others need me." She shook her head. "I am not sure why they are doing so much work."

"They want to." He took the envelope from her. "I will post this and get out of everyone's way."

"Coward."

"Thoroughly and nay afraid to admit it."

Abigail laughed as he strode away then went to the kitchen where the women were busy making food for the ceremony tomorrow. "That is a lot of food. Are you sure we need so much?"

"We do," said Mrs. O'Neal. "We will have all this crowd, the Joneses, the preacher's family, and a few people who stayed in town, plus what few we have whom we can call neighbors."

"Why?"

"There has been little to celebrate round here, dear. It has become almost custom to invite everyone to any kind of celebration. This one? A marriage? It is something that speaks to a lot of people, of happiness, love, and a future." She shrugged. "It will be good for them. A happy time amidst all this killing."

"I suppose. What can I do to help?"

"You finished that letter to the Collinses?" asked Emily.

"Yes. I forced myself not to pull it out of the envelope and try yet again. I had already tried writing it more times than I care to count and told myself that was enough. Jeremiah would be headed to school before I finished it if I didn't stop." She smiled faintly when David Jones's wife, Sarah, laughed.

"Well? What shall I do?" Abbie asked again.

"Nothing. You are the guest of honor and need to rest."

"But . . ."

"No."

"There are a lot of nos for a guest of honor. No cooking, no laying out the tables . . ."

"No Matthew," said Emily, and all the women laughed when Abigail scowled.

"That makes the least sense of all."

"Makes the most sense," said Mrs. O'Neal. "Makes the night special."

"Or desperate," muttered Abigail and grinned when Emily and Sarah laughed.

"Go on with you."

She walked out, disappointed she would not be working with the others. There would be other times, she told herself. There were still four brothers left to get wives, plus her brother. There were also birthdays to celebrate and future christenings or births. The more she thought on it the better she felt. She saw Boyd talking with her brother and smiled. The MacEnroys welcomed people and Boyd was looking stronger. She prayed he would soon use that arm.

It was annoying that, only a day after she and Matthew had announced they were getting married, he had been forced out of her room. She hoped he was suffering as much as she was. Considering how they had behaved before then, she was not completely sure it was necessary, even to make the wedding night special, but Mrs. O'Neal had insisted and Abigail had quickly seen that the woman had become the matriarch of the family.

At least she had been able to make her gown, Abigail thought as she walked into the bedroom that would soon be hers and Matthew's. She took her wedding gown out of the armoire and laid it on the bed. It was too early to go to bed so she thought she would look at it, see if there was some way to make it a little bit fancier, a touch more personal. Pulling out her sewing box, she sat down and looked through her threads. She picked out a deep red, dark blue, and some dark green before staring thoughtfully at her gown. Smiling slowly, she threaded her needle and began to make her gown just a bit more her own.

Matthew tugged at the collar of his shirt and Iain smacked his hand off it. "You are wrinkling it."

"Where is she?"

"She is upstairs getting dressed."

"Why is it taking so long? It is just a dress."

"Matthew," Iain said and shook his head. "I sometimes wonder how ye convinced that lass to marry ye. It is *never* just a dress." Iain cocked his head to the side and murmured, "Ah, I hear the women. Come on, we will wait for them out back with the preacher and the others."

Following his brother out to the back porch, Matthew looked at all the well-dressed people milling around when an arm was suddenly wrapped around his neck and he was pulled up against a tall, muscular body. Twisting his head around as much as he could, he looked into Reid's face. The man had not come around much since he and Abbie had told him they were getting married. Seeing the hard look in Reid's eyes, Matthew rather wished he had stayed away.

"If ye objected to the marriage, ye should have said something before now," Matthew said.

"It is what she wants and I aren' here to object," he said. "Just warn."

"I'm marrying a woman who can shoot better than I can. What need is there to warn me?"

A smiled twitched into view on Reid's mouth, but he steadied it and scowled down at Matthew. "Don't hurt her, don't lie to her, and don't break her heart."

"Have no intention of doing so."

Reid let go of him. "Good."

Watching his soon-to-be brother-in-law walk away, Matthew rubbed at his throat, and shook his head. "If he thinks I would treat her badly, why did he nay protest the marriage?"

Iain shrugged. "Thinking on it. I expect the same thing to happen to me when Nuala gets of an age."

Matthew laughed. "Whatever lad goes for her will have to be a damn brave one, since she has one father and six uncles, and a growing assortment of honorary uncles, who will all be watching him."

Iain laughed and looked at Ned who was walking up to Noah. "And three cousins. So far. The bride will be walking in soon." Iain watched his wife signal the preacher.

Matthew watched and then Reid led his sister in. Abigail had her hair down; long waves of silken brown hair fell down her back and rippled over the front of her simple white gown. His eyes narrowed as he spotted signs of color on the gown that had not been there before when he had snuck a peek at it in the armoire. Until he got closer to her he could not know what she had done so he studied her face.

She was a little pale, he decided. The way her fingers twisted on the stems of the flowers she held, it was clear she was a bit nervous as well. Flanking her were Mrs. O'Neal and her daughter Maeve. Behind her walked Emily. Little Nuala walked in front, or skipped, he thought. Her little hand kept up a steady rhythm of picking flower petals out of the basket and scattering them across the floor under Abbie's feet.

Abbie finally reached the steps to the porch and Matthew stepped down to take her hand in his. He brushed a kiss over her knuckles. Around the wrist of the sleeves were bees, embroidered with the same precision she sewed the stitches into people's skin. On each she had done one bee that looked as if it was crawling out of her sleeve to follow his brethren. Around the modest neckline of the gown was a collection of butterflies. He smiled at her.

"Ye just couldnae bear all that blank canvas, could ye? Iain is the same."

Having Matthew compare what she did to the beautiful artistic work Iain did made her blush. "I just wanted to make it more personal to me."

"It is lovely, but I suspect I think so because of who is wearing it." He kissed her cheek.

"Thank you," she whispered and then looked at Reid who stepped up by her side. "You are looking well rested."

"I am. Feeling better in many ways. Good food and working can do wonders for the soul."

She nodded and looked down at little Nuala who was shaking the last few flower petals out of her basket. "Thank you, Nuala. You did a very good job," she said and smoothed her hand over the child's curls before stepping next to Matthew when Reid answered the preacher's question about who gives her to Matthew.

When it came time to exchange the rings, Noah stepped forward so slowly, holding out the rings that she began to think they could be standing there for an hour or more. She could feel Matthew smothering a laugh at her side. Even the preacher had to bite his lip to hide a grin. Finally, Matthew slid the ring on her finger, repeating the words the preacher gave him, and she felt tears sting her eyes as she slid a ring on his finger and repeated the words.

Matthew kissed her, a soft, gentle kiss, and she was hard put not to return a more passionate one. When she stepped back, their family and friends crowded around them hugging her and slapping Matthew on the back. Everyone offered wishes of good luck and she hoped they did not need so much. Then Reid took her by the shoulders and kissed each of her cheeks.

"Keep a tight hand on the reins, Ab," he murmured and grinned.

"What does that mean?" she asked, but he just stepped away.

"He was just being sassy," said Mrs. O'Neal and gave her a hug. "I love what you did with the gown. You are very good with a needle. Why is it you find it so hard to sew?"

"Mostly it is the cutting of the material I have trouble with. Mending a hole or embroidering seems simple to me. Thank you so much for taking over. I'd be getting wed in my chemise and drawers if you hadn't helped to make it."

"You just need some practice. I nearly burst out laughing at Noah," she confided softly. "Adorable little man so afraid of dropping those rings."

Matthew put his arm around her waist and tugged

her up against his side. Abbie was then swept up in meeting and talking to everyone who had come. There were only a few she had not met before. The number of people living in the hills had lessened a great deal. She hoped some would come back, but the war had gone on for a long time and the anger was deep on both sides.

By the time she had been through the meal and toasts, she was feeling done with it all. She wanted to be out of the gown and somewhere quiet. Abbie understood everyone's need for a happy time, a friendly get-together, but she just wanted to be alone with Matthew. She breathed a sigh of relief when he started their leave-taking although she did wonder where he thought they would go.

When they began to walk down the road, she frowned in confusion. "Where are we going?"

"Emily set us up a place to retreat to," Matthew said. "She said I would know it when I saw it and she laughed." Frowning, he added, "Not sure I trust that laugh."

"Not sure I do either."

They were almost to the cliffside when she saw it and started to laugh. It was a tent, one very like what the soldiers set up. It was in a small clearing opposite the cliff and river. When Matthew opened the tent flaps, they saw a large bed all ready and sprinkled with flower petals. When she sat on the bed she realized it was theirs, that somehow someone had lugged it all the way out here right after they got dressed and ready for the wedding.

"I dinnae even want to ask which of my brothers carried this all the way out here," said Matthew as he sat beside her.

"I'm sure they will do their best to tell you."

He laughed, put his arms around her, and fell back, taking her with him. "They will."

Matthew kissed her and Abigail sank into his arms, returning his kiss with all the need she felt for him. He was really hers now. In her heart, she knew he was a man who would do his best to honor all the vows he had just taken. It surprised her that she took such comfort in the fact, that being married to him eased a lot of concerns she had not even understood she had held.

It was not until she pulled back from the kiss to sit by his side that she realized he had undone all the buttons on the back of her gown. Shocked, she clutched at the sagging bodice and frowned at his grin. He was becoming very nimble with buttons.

Then Matthew stood up and began to take off his clothes. The man had no modesty, she thought, unable to avert her eyes. He was so nicely put together, she decided, and sucked her breath when he shed the last of his clothes revealing that he was ready for her.

"I understood what they were trying to do when they made me leave your room," he said as he began to strip off her clothes, "but I did not like it. Not one bit. Even if we are mad at each other over something we do not sleep apart from now on."

"Yes, sir." She giggled when he frowned at her then yanked her chemise off over her head.

By the time he got all her clothes off, except for her stockings again, Abigail was giggling like some little girl. He picked her up, yanked back the covers, and then tossed her down on the bed. Her laughter stopped when he sprawled on top of her, all his warm strength turning her mood from amused to amorous in a heartbeat.

Matthew kissed her and Abigail wrapped her arms around his neck to hold him to her. As they kissed she ran her hands up and down his strong back, finally settling them on his buttocks. Each time she stroked, he pushed against her. Then he kissed his way down to her breasts and the moment he closed it around the hard tip of one breast she stopped thinking.

She was so caught up in the pleasure of his kisses she did not notice the direction he was taking until she felt him kiss her on the inside of each thigh and then between. Abbie reached for his head but ended up threading her fingers in his hair as he began to use his tongue. Passion built in her with each intimate stroke and she tightened her grip on his hair to pull him away, pull him back up into her arms because she wanted him inside her.

Her release shuddered through her and she called out his name but he ignored her. He kept tormenting her until the passion began to build again. This time she called to him and he slowly returned to her arms. The cry that escaped her when he joined their bodies was one of grateful welcome. She held him tightly as he thrust inside her and she tried to meet every one with an equal strength. When her release again swept through her body he moved fast and hard several times and joined her.

After holding his forehead against hers for a moment, he rolled to the side with a soft groan. Abigail remained sprawled on her back but did tug up the covers to put over herself. She felt a strange mix of being drained of all strength and pleasantly sleepy. It was scandalous what he did, but she was sure he was not a man who did strange, uncommon things so didn't worry on it too much. She then began to wonder if she was supposed to do the same to him. When the thought did not disgust her she decided she probably should make an effort when she regained her strength. Then he turned and, putting an arm around her waist, pulled her up against him, and she stopped wondering.

"Missed ye in the bed," he murmured against her neck.

"And I missed you, but Mrs. O'Neal insisted."

"I ken it and she wields a mean wooden spoon," he said, and absently rubbed the back of his head.

Abbie laughed. "I think I might have heard that confrontation but was too tired to be certain."

"Ye probably did as she caught me just outside the door."

"Bad boy." She patted his thigh. "I simply got the look and did what she said."

"Been with the woman too long for the look to work weel on me."

Realizing she was rubbing his thigh, she started to take her hand away only to have him hold it there. "Our first night together as man and wife."

"Not night yet," he mumbled, and she realized he was going to sleep.

She felt his body grow heavy and smiled as she closed her eyes. A nap sounded like a good idea to her, too. Closing her eyes, she realized she was content, satisfied to the bone with him and with life. It was a good feeling.

Abbie slowly opened her eyes and realized it was night. The light in the tent came from the moon, streaming through a small opening between the tent flaps. She saw a basket set near the side of the tent and suspected it held food, but she was not feeling very hungry at the moment.

She lightly reached down and touched herself then shook her head. At some point Matthew must have woken up and cleaned them both off. It was something he did regularly and she had never gotten up the nerve to ask why. She hoped marriage would dim that kind of reticence because she knew this aspect of marriage was important to a man and she did not wish to fail in it.

For several moments, she lay there still and breathing softly so as not to wake him. When he murmured and briefly tightened his hold on her, she waited to make sure he was not awake. Then she slid beneath the covers and down until she found him. She was not sure if she could do much when he was soft but, to her surprise, he was not.

Certain she had a few moments before he would wake and, perhaps, push her away, she took the time to explore this part of him with her fingers. His body showed its appreciation of her touch and that encouraged her. She leaned forward and kissed him. He groaned and she tensed, but then his hand slipped beneath the covers and he wound his fingers in her hair to hold her in place. Deciding that was approval, she continued until he hoarsely asked her to put her mouth on him. Cautiously she did what he asked and his reaction was all she could have wished for.

Matthew could not believe his little bride was being so daring, but he intended to take full advantage of it. He threw the covers back to look at her pleasuring him. Her hair was spread out so far there was little he could see, but he liked the feel of its silkiness brushing against his thighs. Closing his eyes, he arched up as she grew more creative and then knew he could not play this game, pleasurable as it was, for too much longer.

When Matthew grabbed her under the arms and began to pull her up, Abbie released him. He sat her on top of him and she dared to settle herself onto him. She slid down very slowly until his eyes narrowed and he grabbed her by the hips to push her into place. He slowly sat up, still holding her in place, and then kissed her. After that, Abbie did not know who took control, only that they both reached the peak they sought at the same time. When he fell back taking her with him, Abbie curled up against him and he lazily separated them.

"There is food here," she murmured. "Over by the wall."

Moving Abbie off of him, he walked over to pick up the basket. "Heavy."

He sat down and started to take out two plates and two of everything else. Clutching the sheet to herself, Abbie sat up as he poured them each some cider. There were fat sandwiches and fried chicken and they both began to eat as if they were starved.

"We are being a bit piggy," said Abbie as she picked up a napkin and wiped her mouth.

"Need the fuel for what lies ahead."

"What do you mean?"

"It is now our wedding night and we have time to make up for."

"I thought we'd just done that. Twice."

"Nope. I figure we can stop and sleep at about dawn."

She stared at him for a moment. "I think you will be on your own for the last few hours of that." A grin tugged at her mouth when he laughed. "I actually could go to sleep now."

"Satisfaction followed by food. Always makes one sleepy. But I will wake ye up, for a while."

He did, and she was well satisfied with his efforts. Abbie could not stay awake any longer though and curled up beside him to go to sleep. They had years to play such games although she suspected they would enjoy them more now while still young and in good shape. She smiled as she slipped into sleep.

Matthew looked at Abbie asleep in his arms. He wrapped both arms around her and gave her a gentle hug. This was what he wanted, and he wondered why it had taken him so long to make up his mind. He had just feared the idea of marriage as he figured many men did.

No more overthinking it, he decided as he closed his eyes. This was where he wanted to be, who he wanted to be with. He already cared for the children she brought with her as well. It would be interesting to see what they produced together. He idly decided he should probably find out how she felt about having children but decided it could wait until he got a bit of rest.

After a few days they called their honeymoon, Abigail and Matthew started back. She was just about to say something when they both heard a horse coming up behind them. Matthew turned, shoving her behind him at the same time, but then he grinned.

"James! What are ye doing here?"

"You didn't invite me to the wedding?" James attempted to look offended, but his obvious delight in finding Matthew spoiled it.

"Didnae ken where ye were."

"Weel, we were helping them push their way through the South. It was brutal. Doc took a hit but he'll be fine."

"Heard that from Abbie's brother."

"Wondered if he got here. So, the major had the doctor sign these papers. We are all out of it. He isn't sure we even need these but decided we should have something official in case someone demands it and thinks to pull us back in."

"I heard it was all as good as over."

"I think it is. But you can never be sure what some officer might get into his head, and suspect the penalties for desertion and other such things will be handed out for a while. We have been officially released. Got one for Boyd, and Dan got his. Ran right home, he did."

"What are ye going to do?"

"No idea yet. Just meandering."

"Weel, come meander up to my home."

James dismounted, took his reins in hand, and walked beside Matthew. Abigail smiled faintly as the man fished for all the information he could on the area. The man might not recognize it but he was searching for a home. She recognized the signs for she had been doing the same. She had found hers.

Chapter Twenty

Abigail patted the dirt down carefully around the small rose bush she had planted. Maude had sent her two, called them beach roses, and swore they were hardy. Now she had one planted on each side of the front door. As she stood up and brushed the dirt off, she hoped the blooms would be the same color. She looked around trying to decide where to plant the lavender seeds Maude had also sent her.

She looked at the colorful red door on her home and smiled. It had taken two years but they finally had a home of their own a short walk down the road from the big MacEnroy house. In fact, they had put it in the spot where they had spent their wedding night. She always liked to pinch at Matthew by calling it the box. It was square and two stories high with a long front porch, a matching one running by the back door. It had none of the often elaborate decorative touches of the houses she had grown up seeing in Pennsylvania, but she loved it. With Robbie directing her when he could, she was even learning how to weave. She was no match for his artistic touch in the skill, but she had made a number of pretty carpets for her home and had even sold a few things, making enough so that they had the joy and comfort of indoor plumbing.

The sound of Matthew working on the fencing-in of the backyard made her think she should bestir herself to offer him a drink of either their brothers' cider or some lemonade. She was just moving toward the back to speak to him when she spotted a wagon approaching. As it drew closer she saw that it was being driven by an older man. An older woman sat near him while a small boy sat securely between them. In the back of the wagon was a younger woman, three girls who had to be in their late teens, and another young boy. Then she saw the little package the woman held, recognized it as the one she had mailed out to Robert's parents two years ago, and a chill went down her spine.

"Matthew!" she called as the wagon was pulling to a halt in front of the house and picked up Lily, her cat, because she knew the still-small Wags would follow Noah, who would follow Matthew when he answered her call. So would Jeremiah, she thought, and wished she had not called to her husband. She had the sudden strong urge to grab the boy and hide him away.

The older woman stepped down from the wagon seat and walked to the start of the path to the front door. "Mrs. MacEnroy?"

"Which one?" she asked, and cursed herself for a coward.

"Mrs. Abigail MacEnroy?"

"Yes."

Noah skipped up to her, and his dog, not much bigger than the puppy he had been two years ago, began hopping around Abigail, trying to reach Lily who watched him calmly from her spot on her shoulders.

Walking up the path the woman stopped in front of her and Abigail noticed that Jeremiah's eyes came from his grandmother. "You sent me this picture of Robert's child. Did the baby survive?"

"Oh yes." Forcing a stubborn reluctance aside, Abbie reached behind her and dragged Jeremiah to her side, pinning him in place with an arm around his thin shoulders.

The woman stared at Jeremiah and held her hand out behind her. "John." The man with her stepped up quickly, grabbed her hand, and stood beside her. "This child is Jeremiah?"

"He is," replied Abby. "Jeremiah Robert Collins. Jeremiah, this is your grandmother."

Even as she looked down on the child, Abbie kept a watch on the others who began to climb out of the wagon and slowly walk closer. They were all studying Jeremiah, and the boy pressed even closer to Abigail.

"I had three sons," the woman said quietly, her voice thick with unshed tears. "The war took them all. They all marched off to join the Union and not one marched back. The older boys left behind something. John, Jr. left his wife Miriam"—the woman with the children curtsied—"and his three children." Two of the girls and one of the boys stood with Miriam. "And the other left a daughter and a son. Then came your letter and the picture and I could see that even Robert, my golden boy, had left a piece of himself behind. He died before he could see him, didn't he?"

"I fear so," Abigail replied as Matthew stepped up beside her to introduce himself. "But he knew a child was coming, if that is any comfort."

"It is, or will be." The woman knelt down and looked

Jeremiah in the eye. "You do have the look of your papa, Jeremiah. Can you say hello?"

"'Lo. That is my brover, Noah," he said and pointed at Noah who had edged up nearer to Abigail. "That is my da," he said, pointing at Matthew and he grabbed hold of Abbie's skirts. "She is my ma."

"I see. You do have other family though. This is Miriam, your aunt. This is Beth and this is Alice," she said, pulling the girls over to stand in front of her. She waved the others forward. This is Gavin." She ruffled the hair of the one who had sat beside her. "This boy"—she tugged the one who had sat in the back of the wagon closer—"is Henry. They are all your cousins, as is Lillian here."

"I have a lot of cousins."

"Ye do, lad," said Matthew.

"You have to make cousins for Noah."

"I will tell my brothers to get busy on that." He looked down at the ground to hide his grin when the boy nodded.

"Come in and have a drink," invited Abigail. "We have cider and lemonade."

"I will tend to your horses," said Matthew, and started to walk toward the wagon.

Abigail led them all into the house and, with Miriam's aid, gathered enough seats to have them all settled by the table. She gave each one a tall drink of their choice then poured a tankard of cider for Matthew. He obviously saw the slight tremor in her hands because he smiled softly and kissed her cheek then stood behind her when she took her seat. Then he brought over a plate of the cookies and muffins she had baked that morning and set them out with a few plates for people to use.

"I did write to say we would come but I suspect it

will show up months from now. We have been trying to leave New York for quite a while. Then the land and house finally sold and we were on our way, and I prayed the whole way here that the child still lived."

"He is a very healthy little fellow," said Abigail. "Why did you sell everything to come here?"

"So that we could live near the child."

"Oh." At least it did not sound as if they expected the boy to be handed over to them immediately. Mrs. Collins reached across the table to pat Abigail's clenched hands. "We just want to be close at hand. The girl named you his guardian and we respect that. But we are his family and we should be close."

The knots in her stomach started to unravel and Abigail relaxed. They were not here to take Jeremiah or fight to take him. Glancing at all the others, she decided the woman had a large enough family as it was then scolded herself for the thought.

She had tried not to get too attached to the child but her heart had its own plans and now it would be as if someone wanted to take her own flesh and blood. It was the same with Noah. She had the sudden pang over the fact that she had not yet quickened with Matthew's child but shoved it aside.

"Do you know where you are going to be staying?" she asked.

"We do." She smiled at her husband. "Tell them, John."

"Well, we found an empty saloon. And the woman in the general store connected to it told us how to make an offer to the man who used to own it. We now do. He just wanted the place gone so the bargaining did not take long. I have no urge to run a drinking establishment but we figure we can make something of it and it has rooms for all of us."

"Which will be thoroughly scrubbed," muttered Mrs. Collins.

"So what do you think you will do with it?"

"Not really sure yet, but Molly and me did wonder about making it a place to gather but without the liquor. Not against a man having a drink, but don't want to deal with all the trouble that often comes with a saloon," said John.

"It could get rowdy," agreed Matthew.

"All we want to do is to be part of his life," said Mrs. Collins. "Get to know him and let him come to know us. It seems the children are all I have left of my sons. They are dead. Gavin's wife died. We have Miriam and the children and we mean to stick together." Miriam nodded as did the children.

Abigail listened to them talk about all the ideas they had for what used to be the saloon and bawdy house. She knew it would all depend on what sort of traffic there was through these hills now that the war was over. It would be good if a little life came back to the area.

"There is that lake a short walk away," said Matthew. "And fishing is good in the rivers and lakes. Maybe some folk would like that."

"It's a thought. Not to worry. We will think of something."

Matthew nodded and they all talked of what was in the area, what grew, what the weather was like, and other ordinary things. Abigail excused herself and walked up the stairs until she came to the small table in the hall. There was the picture of Robert and Julia. The little painting had gone to the Collinses but she now feared they might not have gotten it.

"Oh, she was very pretty. I can see what caught my Robert's eye."

Startled by the woman's approach, Abigail had to take a deep breath before turning to face Mrs. Collins. "I had the same man who did the picture of the babe do one of this but I guess you never got it."

"Or it came after we left. I will send a word to my neighbor and tell her to keep a watch for it. May I?" She nodded toward the picture.

"Of course."

"I think John would like to see it. We talked often after we got your letter but could never decide what sort of girl the boy would have married."

Abigail followed the woman back down the stairs and paused when the woman suddenly stopped at the bottom and turned to her. "We really have not come to take the child away from you. His mother chose you and we honor that. But I can see my Robert in him and I just want to be a part of his life."

"Of course. I can understand that. He is too young to grasp what this all means but he is growing fast."

"They always do."

By the time the Collins family left, Abigail was exhausted. She knew it was mostly from fighting the fear that they would decide to argue over the boy. Meeting such a pleasant woman and knowing she had lost all her sons had been hard as well. There was a part of Abigail that thought she ought to let them have the child but she ignored it with an ease that bothered her.

"They were a very pleasant family," said Matthew when they got ready for bed that night.

"They were but, oh, Matthew, she lost all her sons."

"I ken it." He crawled into bed and took her into his arms. "I dinnae want to even try and ken how that must feel, but it is something so many have suffered so many times over the centuries."

She sighed and rested her cheek on his chest. "I know, but that doesn't really make it any less sad."

"They are not going to demand the baby, are they?"

"No. She said I was the mother's choice and they honor that but want to be known to the child. I found myself wishing Jeremiah was older, a little more aware of who and what they were. I can understand why they are all together. Such a loss would be enough to pull them together."

"We were verra lucky."

"I think we were and so was your family."

"Weel, some think poorly of us because we didnae want to choose sides, didnae want anything to do with it."

"Smart."

"But nay verra wise. But it is done so things should calm down."

"I hope so." She covered her mouth when she yawned. "Tired, and I didn't even get to plant the lavender seeds."

"Tomorrow. Get some sleep. It has been a hard day."

"It made me think."

"Mmmm. Of what?"

"Of the importance of making sure you have made it clear what you want done with your children if something happens to you."

"We can sort that out in the morning."

She could tell he was close to going to sleep. "Unless we die in our sleep." She felt him jerk with surprise then squeaked when he slapped her on the backside. "Wretch."

In the morning, Abigail woke with a need to rush into the washroom. She was heartily sick. By the time she cleaned up and went downstairs, the kitchen showed signs that Matthew had already fed the boys. It puzzled her that she was so tired, but she had been a lot lately.

Once she had eaten some toasted bread and had a cup of coffee she was feeling better so went out to plant her lavender seeds. When they grew, she would be sure to send Maude a picture even if she had to draw it herself. She stood up then staggered to the house and braced herself against it until the spinning in her head went away.

Once her head cleared she thought over the morning and tensed. Carefully she tried to recall when she had had her last woman's time and felt her heart beat faster. She grabbed the bonnet Matthew still frowned at and started walking toward the big house, as they had begun to call it. She was almost certain she was with child but wanted to hear another woman give her opinion.

Finding Matthew and the boys there made it a little awkward to have a moment or two alone with the women, but she finally got Emily and Mrs. O'Neal cornered in the kitchen. They both stared at her expectantly as they sat around the table. Abigail suddenly had no idea how to start the conversation.

"Spit it out, child," said Mrs. O'Neal.

"I think I might be with child."

"All the signs are there?"

"Yes, no bleeding times, sick this morning, had to eat plain toasted bread this morning, and nearly fainted in the garden."

"Certainly sounds like it. Have you told Matthew?"

"No, I needed to be sure. I know he wanted a child but he never, well, pestered for one."

"Well, tell him carefully. Even men who really want

a child can get a little crazy when their woman says one is on its way."

Abigail kept that in mind as she went back home, linked arm in arm with Matthew as the two boys skipped along beside them. The puppy flopped on the grass the moment they reached the front yard of the house. Abbie felt sick as she realized how warm she was. She let go of Matthew and raced for the washroom.

Matthew quietly went in and held her hair back as she was wretchedly ill. He then handed her a cloth wet with cool water and waited as she washed her face and rinsed out her mouth. She glanced at him and he wondered why she looked a bit guilty. She had to know he would be delighted.

"I guess it will be no surprise when I tell you I am with child."

"Nay, but I do wonder why ye suddenly realized it. I have suspected it for two months."

"How?"

"I sleep with ye. I ken the time every month that ye dinnae really appreciate any attention."

"Oh. Are you happy?"

He laughed. "How can ye even ask? Of course I am." He pulled her into his arms. "I just need to ken that ye are all right."

"I am. It was the vomiting that clued me in and I nearly swooned in the garden."

"Ye will have to be careful then. It is only going to get hotter."

Abigail sighed. "I know. I guess gardening will be kept to a minimum."

"There is always next year."

"True."

"I love ye, Abbie."

She hugged him. "I love you, too. I cannot believe I had to be hanging my head over the basin before I knew."

"I didnae think women liked a mon to ask about their woman's time."

"Ah, no." She pulled away. "Thank you for holding my hair out of the way. I have lost my ribbon again." She laughed when he pulled it out of his pocket and handed it to her. "Thank you again." She tied back her hair. "I had best get the dinner started."

"Ye sure ye ought to do that?"

"I can do anything I did before. Just have to recognize when the sickness hits."

"We'll be fine, Abbie, and I ken we will be verra pleased with what we have made."

"Oh, we will be." She grinned at him over her shoulder. "I think this family will be the better for another girl." She laughed when he groaned and hurried down the stairs still laughing when he followed her complaining about having to fight off rowdy young gents.

"Why cannae I go in there?"

Emily stood between Matthew and the door to his wife's room. "If she wants you, she will ask. Having a baby is not a very tidy business and a lot of women would rather their husband didn't see it all."

He heard Abigail cry out. "But she is in pain!"

"Of course she is. She is having a damn baby!" Emily looked at her husband as he came up behind Matthew. "Oh, good. Do something with him, will you please?"

Matthew stared at the door as Emily went back into the room and slammed it in his face. Then Iain grabbed him by the arm and marched him downstairs.

When they reached the kitchen and he was shoved into a chair, Matthew sighed. He did not understand why he could not be with Abigail. It was a husband's place.

Iain sat down across from him. "Some women really don't want their mon in there watching them do this. All dignity is gone and it is messy. I had a hard time keeping my food down when Emily was birthing. Thought I understood because I'd been with animals when they birthed, but an animal isnae your woman who is in pain."

"But . . ."

"It is appallingly messy, Matthew. There is the blood to consider, too. It can look to a mon as if she is going to bleed to death, there is so much. Or what looks to be too much."

"Weel, the blood would trouble me because it would be Abbie's. I'll admit that."

"Good. I dinnae think it will be long, but be ready because there might be a screech or two." He grabbed Matthew by the arm when it looked as if he was about to race back up the stairs. "It is a lot to get out and it hurts. But, and this never ceases to amaze me, they seem to forget about it all once they have the bairn."

"Good thing or we would have all died out by now, I think."

Iain laughed. "True."

It was two long hours before a hot and exhausted Emily came down to get him. Matthew ran up into the room, barely missing knocking over Mrs. O'Neal. She also looked exhausted and hot but she kissed him on the cheek and walked out. No one had told him which he now had, a son or a daughter.

He cautiously approached the bed. Abigail looked exhausted as well but she was breathing and that was all he cared about. He sat down on the side of the bed and brushed her hair back from her face. Her eyes fluttered open and she smiled at him. His fears eased even more.

"How are ye?"

"Tired, hot, and sore," she replied. "The baby is fine."

She pointed toward the cradle near the wall and he moved to go look. New babies did not look like much, he decided. He just took note of the fact that the child slept, and looked whole and healthy. He looked back at her but her eyes were closed again so he knelt down and unwrapped the child. A heavy sigh escaped him as he wrapped the baby back up and returned to the bed.

Abigail felt him sit down near her again and looked at him. He was frowning at her and she grew a little worried. "She is still all right?"

"Aye, she is. Ye couldnae have just told me I had a daughter? Even Mrs. O'Neal wouldnae say which when I came in."

"You have a daughter, Matthew."

"I noticed. Noah will be disappointed." He smiled when she laughed.

"So will Jeremiah. Are you?"

"Nay, lass. It is only that we have so many lads one just expects it but, nay, I love the little lass. I suspect ye will have to yell at me from time to time so I dinnae spoil her."

"I can do that."

"I love ye."

"I love you, too. I was a little concerned when we were married two years and no child, but that was silly."

"Aye, it was. We may nay get what we expect all

the time but MacEnroys have never had a problem getting a child." He brushed a kiss across her mouth. "So what are we going to name her?"

"I have no idea. We didn't try out girls' names for all I teased you about it."

He nudged her to the side a little and settled down on the bed with her. "Caitlin."

"Oh, okay. I rather like that. Was it someone in your family?"

"A cousin. She was a rowdy girl and ended up wed to a magistrate. Had a good heart and seven bairns."

"Oh." She yawned. "I am not sure I want seven."

He laughed and kissed her. "We will be fine, lass. Sleep. Ye need it."

Matthew stayed with her until she fell asleep then slipped off the bed and went to look at his daughter. It was going to be interesting to watch her grow, and he was certain there would be many challenges for him, but he was not terribly concerned. They had Nuala so she would have a girl to look up to as she grew as well as her mother and Emily. Mrs. O'Neal and her daughters as well. He nodded. They would do very well indeed. He headed downstairs to accept his congratulations.

New York Times bestselling author Hannah Howell sweeps readers away with the passion-filled adventures of the MacEnroy brothers, seven daring Scotsmen who take on America in her most turbulent days—and capture the hearts of the ladies each is destined to wed . . .

With danger closing in from all sides, Abigail Jenson works tirelessly to protect her small Missouri farm. She doesn't require saving—but a handsome officer appears on horseback just as ruthless marauders set her cabin ablaze. With nowhere else to turn, Abigail allows the soldier with the seductive Highlander's gaze to escort her to shelter in a nearby town.

Matthew MacEnroy was reluctant to join his adopted nation's conflict—until an enemy attack wounded two of his brothers. Bravely doing battle has its price when a proud, independent beauty comes under his watch—no military man can risk the powerful emotions their attraction has unleashed. But when Matthew himself is caught in the crossfire, Abigail leads their long journey home to MacEnroy valley . . . and her caring touch sparks the promise of a bold future together.

ISBN-13: 978-1-4201-4305-8
ISBN-10: 1-4201-4305-0
50799
EAN
9 781420 143058
S

ZEBRA
U.S. $7.99
CAN $8.99
PRINTED IN U.S.A.